ALSO BY LIZA GYLLENHAAL

So Near
Local Knowledge

A Place for Us

LIZA GYLLENHAAL

NAL Accent
Published by New American Library,
a division of Penguin Group (USA) Inc.,
375 Hudson Street, New York, New York 10014, USA
Penguin Group (Canada), 90 Eglinton Avenue East, Suite 700, Toronto,
Ontario M4P 2Y3, Canada (a division of Pearson Penguin Canada Inc.)
Penguin Books Ltd., 80 Strand, London WC2R 0RL, England
Penguin Ireland, 25 St. Stephen's Green, Dublin 2,
Ireland (a division of Penguin Books Ltd.)
Penguin Group (Australia), 707 Collins Street, Melbourne,
Victoria 3008, Australia (a division of Pearson Australia Group Pty. Ltd.)
Penguin Books India Pvt. Ltd., 11 Community Centre,
Panchsheel Park, New Delhi–110 017, India
Penguin Group (NZ), 67 Apollo Drive, Rosedale, Auckland 0632,
New Zealand (a division of Pearson New Zealand Ltd.)
Penguin Books, Rosebank Office Park, 181 Jan Smuts Avenue,
Parktown North 2193, South Africa
Penguin China, B7 Jiaming Center, 27 East Third Ring Road North,
Chaoyang District, Beijing 100020, China

Penguin Books Ltd., Registered Offices:
80 Strand, London WC2R 0RL, England

First published by NAL Accent, an imprint of New American Library,
a division of Penguin Group (USA) Inc.

First Printing, March 2013
1 3 5 7 9 10 8 6 4 2

NAL
ACCENT   REGISTERED TRADEMARK—MARCA REGISTRADA

LIBRARY OF CONGRESS CATALOGING-IN-PUBLICATION DATA:

Gyllenhaal, Liza.
A place for us/Liza Gyllenhaal.
p. cm.
ISBN 978-0-451-23923-5
1. Families—Massachusetts—Fiction. 2. Rich people—Fiction. 3. Life change events—Fiction.
4. Domestic fiction. 5. Psychological fiction. I. Title.
PS3607.Y53P58 2013
813'.6—dc23   2012036845

Set in Sabon • Designed by Elke Sigal

Printed in the United States of America

PUBLISHER'S NOTE
This is a work of fiction. Names, characters, places, and incidents either are the product of the
author's imagination or are used fictitiously, and any resemblance to actual persons, living or
dead, business establishments, events, or locales is entirely coincidental.
The publisher does not have any control over and does not assume any responsibility for
author or third-party Web sites or their content.

For W.E.B., as always

A Place for Us

Part One

1

❧

*A*fter all this time it shouldn't have made a damned bit of difference, Brook Bostock told herself. She and Michael had been married for fifteen years, for heaven's sake! Happy years, she told herself, as she stood there staring blankly out the kitchen window. She barely noticed the morning snow sifting like confectioners' sugar over the lightly browned back lawn. Or the way the sun, luminous behind the clouds, glazed the distant hills an icy pink. Her world had gone suddenly gray. She'd ended her call to Alice, but still held the phone in her hands, cradled against her chest. It always took her a while to register pain. Her first reaction to bad news was usually: *It's fine. I'll be fine.* Even on that horrible Tuesday when she'd watched the collapsing World Trade Center towers from their sixth-floor loft on Warren Street. She remembered pulling Tilly into her arms and whispering aloud to the darkening morning: *It's fine. We're fine. We're all going to be just fine.*

She sighed now, trying not to cry. It hurt! Oh, how it hurt. And it was so ridiculous! After all these years. All their wonderful times together. Michael. Liam. Tilly. The whole life they had built as a family in Barnsbury, Massachusetts. And all it had taken was a couple of words from her business partner and best friend for everything to be cast into doubt. They'd been talking about David, Alice's soon-to-be third husband and perhaps tenth great, undying love, and the engagement–cum– holiday party that Brook was throwing in their honor that night at Alice's weekend place in Rhinebeck.

"I just really, really need for it to work this time," Alice had told her. "And I'm picking up these weird vibes. Like the fairy dust is starting to wear off—and David's beginning to see the real me."

"Which is okay," Brook had replied. "Which is great. Because the real you is such a wonderful person."

How many times had they had this conversation over the course of their friendship? It was all part of what Brook saw as Alice's self-fulfilling roller coaster of romantic failure: the initial ridiculously high hopes, followed by the exhilarating sexual twists and turns, giving way to the ups and downs of everyday life and the gradual leveling off to boredom, leading up to a clickety-clack of suspicion and distrust, ending with a teeth-rattling descent into screaming recriminations and the screeching of brakes. Ride over. And it worried Brook that Alice was already starting to foresee the relationship's demise, before most of their friends had even had a chance to get to know David and Alice as a couple.

"Yeah, well, your own fairy dust probably won't ever wear off. Money doesn't get stretch marks."

"Alice!" Brook said, shocked. Though they were able to kid occasionally about the vast differences in their social and financial standing, for the most part they avoided talking about

Brook's trust fund. It had bankrolled their business in the beginning and helped keep them afloat during the lean months after 9/11. But R.S.V.P. was firmly on its own financial feet now, and Brook was so proud of the event-planning business she and Alice had started together a few years out of college. It was a bad sign—one of desperation on Alice's part, really—that she would drag such a sensitive issue into her own marital worries.

"Sorry. I'm a nervous wreck. Pay no attention to me. You know Michael's always loved you for yourself alone, and not your golden hair—or whatever."

"Yellow hair," Brook told her, "if you mean the Yeats poem. 'Only God, my dear, could love you for yourself alone, and not your yellow hair.'" She and Alice had first met in a European literature course at Vassar. It had always been a minor bone of contention between them that Brook could quote long passages of poetry by heart and that Alice had the memory of a sieve. But why had Brook felt the need to flaunt that right then? If only she'd been more sensitive. Maybe if she'd been less harried, she would have taken a more supportive tone. But she had a hundred things to do before she and Michael could leave for Rhinebeck that afternoon. And Christmas was only three days away! She had lists and yellow stickies all over her workroom off the kitchen.

The truth was, she should never have volunteered to put on this party for Alice right before the holidays. It occurred to her that it had been her way of helping to prop up Alice's sagging confidence in David. That she, too, really, really needed Alice's third marriage to work. She was mulling this over and at the same time mentally ticking through her immediate to-dos—sheets for Liam's bedroom, cash for Phoebe, Tilly's supper—so she only half heard what Alice said next. It took her a second or two to register it fully.

". . . when I told him that night what it meant to be a Pendleton and he just kind of cocked his head and smiled."

"What? You told him *that* night?" And she'd felt her jaw tighten and her whole body stiffen as if bracing for a blow. Because there had been only one *that* night for Brook and Michael. The first night. The night they saw each other across a crowded benefit auction R.S.V.P. was handling and sensed instantly they were meant to be together. Before either knew anything at all about the other. It had just been some kind of kismet, they both agreed later. Something cosmic and beyond their control.

"Oh, please, don't sound that way."

"I don't think I'm sounding any particular way. It's just that you know perfectly well I thought that he didn't know anything about my background. And for a month you listened to me go on and on about how wonderful it was—*finally*—not to have my family play any kind of a role in—"

"Yes, I heard you go on and on. Because you've always been a total nutcase on the subject. And, yes, I let you think what you wanted, because it was pretty clear to me how you felt about the guy. Plus, I could tell Michael was totally into you, too. And he still is. It's disgusting how happy the two of you still are! So what's the big deal?"

Of course, Alice was right. This was not a big deal. Unless Brook allowed herself to buy into Alice's unhappiness. Because that's all this was about, really: Alice being nervous and self-doubting and needing to have everyone around her share in her angst. In fact, she might very well be working herself up into the kind of highly volatile state that Brook had seen many times before. During these episodes, Alice tended to suck in—

and then spit out—anything that got in her way. Well, Brook, for one, intended to stay well clear of Alice's destructive path.

She put the receiver back onto its base and took another deep breath. The pain seemed to be easing a little. How stupid, she told herself. Silly to get so worked up. After all these wonderful years.

❦

"You're late," Tilly said as she climbed into the backseat of the Volvo wagon. Brook's ten-year-old daughter dropped her ice skates into the cargo area and pulled off the bright red wool hat that made her look a little like Pippi Longstocking. Her fine light brown hair floated around her face. Brook reached over the seat back to tuck a loose strand behind her daughter's left ear and—zap!—an electrical charge snapped at her fingertips.

"Ouch!" Tilly said, pulling back. "What's the matter? Do I look weird?" She had Michael's dark brown, luminous eyes.

"No," Brook said, facing forward again. She had to keep reminding herself that Tilly didn't much like being touched these days. Though her daughter was naturally kind and tolerant, Brook could feel the way Tilly froze when she hugged her in front of her friends, or even when she kissed her good night in front of no one. It was about growing up, Brook knew. Claiming her independence. It was surely a good sign, a testament to Tilly's maturity, but Brook couldn't help that it made her feel sad. Especially today, when she needed someone to hold—or, perhaps more truthfully, someone to hold her.

"I have to swing around to the bank," Brook said. "Should we stop at Louie's and pick up one of those frozen pizzas you like? Or I have turkey burgers ready if you and Phoebe would prefer those."

"Oh, that's right!" Tilly said. "We're having a sleepover!"

Though Phoebe Lansing was, technically, Tilly's babysitter, Brook had long since stopped referring to her in that way. Not only would Tilly consider the term grossly inaccurate, but Phoebe's role in the Bostock household was larger and more amorphous than that. The Bostocks had a regular cleaning lady, but Brook enjoyed working with Phoebe on special household projects, such as repapering the shelves in the linen closet or reorganizing the butler's pantry. When Brook entertained on a large scale, Phoebe would help out in the kitchen. And she filled in occasionally when Brook needed extra hands for R.S.V.P. events in the area.

A local Barnsbury girl who had been one of Liam's classmates in elementary school, Phoebe always seemed to be there when Brook needed her. And, though she'd never really dwelled on the subject, Brook sensed that Phoebe looked up to her. Or, perhaps more accurately, looked *to* her for guidance in certain areas. Phoebe's parents were divorced and, an only child, she lived in a clapboarded Cape Cod cottage in town with her mother, an administrative assistant at the local high school. Wanda Lansing was perfectly nice, Brook felt, but there was something a little beaten-down and unhappy about her. Yet Phoebe was such an energetic and positive person! She was like Brook in that way; optimism seemed to be Phoebe's default setting.

"Phoebe will just be staying until Liam gets home—so it won't actually be a *sleepover*."

"When's he getting back?" Tilly asked as Brook turned right onto Route 31 out of the Deer Mountain school complex.

"Late tonight. Carey's brother is driving them up. Liam said they'd stop somewhere for dinner along the way, so they won't get here until eleven or so, I guess. I've made up the third-floor guest room for them." Just thinking about her son's return automatically made Brook feel better. She knew she probably worried about Liam too much for her own good—not to mention his. But she had reason to worry more than even Michael realized. And she couldn't help but feel that Liam was truly safe only when she had him within shouting distance.

"Oh, great," Tilly said. Brook glanced in the rearview mirror and caught her daughter's unhappy expression.

"What?"

"Nothing."

"Tell me."

"It's just—" Tilly hesitated, looking out the window at the fading afternoon. Though the air was frigid, the earlier flurries had left only a dusting of snow on the ground. "Carey's cool. But Brandon—I don't know. . . . I think he's kind of a jerk."

Brook was surprised that Tilly had formulated such strong opinions about Liam's roommate and his older brother. They'd both met the brothers on only two prior occasions: when the family had first dropped Liam off at Moorehouse, the prep school the boys attended in Connecticut, and then again on Columbus Day weekend. Then the two brothers had stayed the night, too, on their way home to Syracuse. If anything, tall, terse, acned Carey had struck Brook as far more of a jerk than his athletic and actually rather charming older brother. Brook wondered if Tilly's strong feelings didn't mask an unrecognized attraction. She wasn't too young to develop a crush, after all.

"Well, I'm sorry you feel that way," Brook said. "But it's a great help to have Brandon drive Liam home. It's only for one night, sweetie. And you'll be in bed by the time they get here anyway."

Brook and Tilly got cash for Phoebe at the drive-through, then frozen pizzas and the makings for ice cream sundaes. Back at the house, they found Phoebe waiting for them on the teak bench in the kitchen garden. Her cheeks were flushed red from the cold, almost exactly the same color as her shoulder-length mass of curly hair.

"You must be freezing!" Brook called over to her as she and Tilly climbed out of the car. "You should have gone in. You know where the extra key is." But even as she said it, Brook realized that Phoebe would never have entered the Bostocks' unoccupied house by herself. It was just one of those unspoken rules. One of those invisible lines that Brook kept stumbling upon, lines that seemed designed to separate her from so many people in Barnsbury.

"It's so pretty out here," Phoebe said, walking over to the car. She took a bag of groceries from Brook. "I've been watching the blue jays fight back the squirrels at the feeder."

"The forever war," Brook said, fumbling in her shoulder bag for her key ring. She looked up the hill to Michael's studio. The lights were still on. If he didn't come down in another half hour, she'd have to send Tilly up to get him. It took her a split second to register why she didn't want to go herself. Why she didn't want to face him. As she pushed open the kitchen door with her shoulder, she felt a little spasm of pain in the left side of her rib cage, as though she'd pulled a muscle. But it was nothing serious, she told herself.

❧

She was packing her overnight bag when she heard his voice downstairs. He'd come in through the kitchen, where Phoebe and Tilly were making popcorn. The festive, movie-night aroma had drifted up the stairs as she got ready, making her wish all over again that they didn't have to go to Rhinebeck. That they could just relax in front of the fire with Tilly and the popcorn and wait together for Liam to come home. That everything between Michael and her was the same as it had been when they'd first opened their eyes that morning.

"Brrr, your feet are cold," she'd murmured as he'd curled up against her back. He was nearly a foot taller and fifty pounds heavier than Brook. A bit like the custom-made pieces of furniture he created, Michael was solid but elegantly built. When he held her in his arms, she felt like the most delicate and precious thing in the world.

"How about these?" he'd whispered into her hair as his hands closed around her breasts.

"Freezing! But I know a trick or two that could help warm them up."

"I was hoping you would," he'd said, pulling her tighter.

Michael didn't like to have it acknowledged, but he was a remarkably handsome man. Movie-star, male-model caliber. Heads literally turned when he walked into a room. Tall, broad, dark-haired—he was all the clichés of masculine beauty rolled into one, with the added attraction of being clearly oblivious to the effect he had on others. It had taken Brook a while to realize that he honestly didn't know what all the fuss was about. Forthright and somewhat shy, he hated the flirty, come-hither way so many women acted around him. He had no patience for small talk—or for most talk—unless it was with Brook or his kids—and that balanced things out between them pretty nicely.

Brook talked and Michael listened. Brook's outlook was sunny, Michael was no stranger to gloom. But, as far as Brook was concerned, the underlying, unspoken equation of their marriage—the secret to its success really—was that she was rich and he was good-looking. For Brook it was simply a matter of physics, of opposites attracting, of two extremes finding the perfect gravitational balance in each other's orbit. But that whole rather crude theorem worked only because Brook believed Michael had been drawn to *her* at first, not to her money, just as she had fallen in love with his diffidence, the down-turning smile—his *essence*—not really registering how ridiculously handsome he was until later. Until it was too late for her to be put off by the fact that he was so obviously out of her league as far as looks went. But if there actually *had* been any sort of calculation on his part when he'd first approached her, then everything she believed to be good and true about her world was, well—

She heard him climbing the stairs and busied herself with the packing.

"Damn," he said as he came into the room and saw what she was doing. "I guess we're still going. I was hoping we'd get snowed in here."

"Too bad," she said, weighing his tone, listening for a false note, before she made herself stop. Oh, for heaven's sake! Was she actually going to start second-guessing him *now*?

"Did you pack for me, too?" he asked as he pulled off the wool hoodie he wore in the studio. He began to strip down. He liked to shower at the end of the day; he used a lot of natural stains and finishes in his work and often came in trailing the scent of turpentine or linseed oil.

"Yes," she said, surprised by how normal she sounded. She also felt sad and a little forsaken. This was the first time she could remember ever pretending to Michael that everything was fine when it really wasn't. He was the first, and usually the only, person she turned to when she felt as uncertain as she did at that moment. "I'm just about ready. I'll wait for you downstairs. I want to go over some things with Phoebe."

"Hey," he said, walking over to her and pulling her into his arms. "Is everything okay?" She breathed in the smell of him. She should just come right out and tell him what Alice had said. Ask him for an explanation.

"Well, as a matter of fact—" Her voice sounded a little breathy. Her heart was racing. She realized that she just wouldn't be able to bear it if she heard the slightest bit of hesitation in his answer. "I was talking to Alice before. She's getting the jitters."

"No big surprise there," he said, kissing the top of her head. "I won't be long."

∼

She knew, of course, that it was exactly the sort of thing Michael hated to hear. The kind of comment that made him look down, shaking his head. That actually made him blush. She'd long been aware that though her husband had an athlete's natural grace and lack of inhibition, though he was utterly at ease with his sexuality, the instant someone glanced at him sideways or commented on his good looks, he became self-conscious, almost shamefaced.

But the words seemed to fly out of her mouth of their own volition.

"Isn't he just the handsomest guy you've ever seen?" she said to Tilly and Phoebe as Michael, hair still damp from the shower and dressed in a wool sport jacket and turtleneck, came into the kitchen.

He stopped, staring at her, and cocked his head. She'd

always thought it was an endearing, kind of puppyish thing for such a big masculine guy to do. But then Alice had told her that's exactly how Michael had reacted when he'd first learned who she was. And she realized that the tiny seed of doubt that Alice had so thoughtlessly planted earlier in the day had, against Brook's will, already started to sprout. She felt Michael's scrutiny now, his speculation. She knew he was waiting for her to defuse the remark, add some kind of twist, or turn it into a joke.

But she didn't.

2

"Isn't he just the handsomest guy you've ever seen?" Mrs. Bostock asked Phoebe and Tilly as Mr. Bostock walked into the kitchen all dressed up for the party.

Phoebe smiled in reply, knowing it was not the kind of question she was supposed to answer. Which was good because, in her mind, Mr. Bostock was a little too old for her to honestly say. But she had noticed the boyhood photo of him that Mrs. Bostock kept on her dresser. In it he had on a red checked jacket and was carrying a gun across his shoulder. His long, dark hair was falling into his eyes, and he had a wicked grin plastered across his face. There was a wildness, a kind of daring, about him then that he didn't have anymore. In fact, he looked so much like Liam in the photo that, if Phoebe hadn't known Liam hated everything to do with hunting, she could easily have mistaken Mr. Bostock for his son. And, as far as Phoebe Lansing was concerned, Liam Bostock was the most wonderful-looking person in the world.

Phoebe couldn't actually remember a time when she didn't

feel that way about Liam. When she didn't know that she loved him. One of her first memories was playing on the swings with him behind the old elementary school. Phoebe lived right across from the school and thought of the playground as an extension of her own small yard. The Bostocks were new to Barnsbury then, had just finished building their beautiful house on Willard Mountain, and Mrs. Bostock often brought Liam and Tilly down to the playground to, as she'd told Phoebe, "get to know some people in town."

Which even Phoebe could have told her was a waste of time. Since the old elementary school had been shuttered, nobody but Phoebe ever really played there anymore. But she'd kept that piece of information to herself, which had allowed her to keep the Bostocks pretty much to herself that first summer.

She and Liam must have been around seven at the time, because Tilly had just learned how to walk. In fact, she'd somehow toddled over to the swing set without Mrs. Bostock noticing, and Phoebe, unaware of the little girl's approach and throwing all her weight into a back swing, had knocked Tilly right off her feet. There had been a lot of screaming and some blood. Though Tilly hadn't been seriously hurt, Phoebe found herself in tears. She felt guilty and responsible. Even then, she didn't just adore Liam—she was basically falling in love with the whole family.

"Don't feel bad," Liam had told her.

"I can't help it."

"I won't let you," he'd replied, and leaned over and kissed her right on the mouth. It was just a quick peck, the kind Phoebe's mom gave her when she said good-bye. His lips had been hot, a little chapped, the whole thing lasting no more than an instant, but the imprint he had left on her was permanent. Even during those first years at Deer Mountain when all the boys ran together in a pack, pointedly ignoring the girls, Liam would always break ranks to acknowledge Phoebe. Nodding or waving, with a little smile that she knew was telling her to *Wait. Just wait.* Her time was coming.

"I want to stay up until Liam gets home," Tilly told Phoebe as they loaded the dishwasher after their dinner.

"You heard what your mom told me," Phoebe replied, measuring out the dishwasher liquid and starting the machine, then stowing the detergent back under the sink. Phoebe knew the Bostocks' spacious, elegantly appointed kitchen as well as, if not better than, her own cramped and depressing one. She loved the entire Arts and Crafts–style house, with its golden oak wainscoting, art glass windowpanes, and high, beamed ceilings, but the kitchen was her favorite room. It was larger than her entire downstairs. The custom-made cabinets were cherrywood with pewter pulls shaped like oak leaves. The floor was covered in glazed earthenware tiles. The upper panel in the windows above the sink held a stained-glass depiction of wild birds—cardinals, blue jays, and chickadees—that a local artisan had created especially for the house. Phoebe cherished everything about the kitchen as if it belonged to her, and she was painstaking in its care.

"She said nine thirty at the latest," Phoebe added, wiping down the butcher-block counter abutting the sink, using a cloth dampened with mineral oil. She frequently had to remind Mrs. Bostock not to clean it with a wet sponge.

"She won't have to know," Tilly suggested. "We don't have to tell her."

"Yeah, but if she finds out, it's my butt in a sling."

Tilly giggled. The younger girl delighted in Phoebe's frank way of talking, the colorful expressions lifted—with a little necessary editing—directly from Phoebe's father. Everybody in town knew that Troy Lansing had a mouth on him and, especially since the divorce, he was not shy about turning it on his ex-wife and daughter. If there was often a note of aggression, a degree of bullying, in the way he spoke to them, Phoebe tried not to let it get to her. As Troy Lansing was the first to tell you, his life was not exactly a bowl of cherries. These days, it was a lot more like a load of crapola.

"Tell you what, though," she told Tilly. "Who's to say you can't wait up for him in your room? Your mom only said you had to be in *bed* by nine thirty. No one can tell you when you have to fall asleep, right?"

But Phoebe knew perfectly well that once Tilly's head hit the pillow, she'd be out like a light. When Tilly was younger and Phoebe used to read her a story at bedtime, her charge had usually drifted off to sleep before Phoebe had finished the first paragraph. And, in fact, when she went back upstairs a little after ten to check on Tilly, the younger girl was dead to the world, her arms flung above her head in an attitude of innocent abandon. Phoebe sat down in the armchair beside the bed, her heart filling with a familiar ache as she looked at Tilly—and then let her gaze roam around the prettily decorated bedroom. Sometimes, alone at night in her own dull box of a room, Phoebe pretended that she was actually here, nestled in Tilly's queen-sized bed with its ruffled pink-striped bed skirts and princess canopy, the walls decorated with posters from popular children's books—Beatrix Potter, Babar, and Madeline—the collection of American Girl dolls arranged just so on top of the hand-stenciled cedar chest.

Phoebe loved Tilly as if she were her own sister. But she also envied her—deeply and fiercely—the way she envied the whole Bostock family. For years, this love and envy had flowed together through Phoebe's heart in one strong, unstoppable stream. That she both loved them and wanted to *be* them seemed natural to her—simply her lot in life. But that she loved Liam above all others—including herself—was a secret she feared that, if known to the rest of the Bostock family, would upend the careful balancing act she'd undertaken. And so she'd kept the truth buried within her and had been able to move through the household—sitting right next to Liam at the kitchen table, or riding beside him in the car—like a thief carrying stolen goods that could never, rightly, be hers.

She had never expected more than that. She had never allowed herself to want more than that. It had seemed enough to simply *feel* the way she did—her love for Liam its own reward. That is, until last June, when everything changed.

Phoebe went back downstairs, stopping in the powder room adjoining the kitchen to check on her appearance. She'd put a lot of thought and effort into how she wanted to look that night. Her nose was a little too pert, her skin too freckled, to let her believe for a moment that she was beautiful. She was pretty enough, though, in a round-faced, red-haired kind of way. But she didn't kid herself. Grown men turned to stare after her, not at her smile or her wide green-gray eyes, but because of her full breasts and generous hips, the backside that, even packed tight inside hip-hugging jeans, still managed to jiggle and bounce.

If Liam noticed Phoebe's natural endowments, he'd never let on to her. Other boys tried to grope her breasts, but Liam wanted only to talk. And talk. She'd been amazed when he first opened up to her, confiding things that she knew he had never shared with another living soul. He'd kissed her a few times, but never more than fleetingly, never with more than the brotherly fondness of that brief buss the summer they first met.

"You're the only one who understands," he'd told her as they lay side by side under the stars, barely touching. "I couldn't go on without you."

But he had gone on. Or had been forced to go. And except for those three brief text messages over the course of the semester, he seemed to be managing okay without her. Though it was hard to tell. After all, she knew now just how convincingly Liam was able to hide his true feelings behind a bluff of humor and kidding.

It seemed like most of the time they had spent together over the summer was devoted to talking about *his* problems, *his* fears, and she cherished that closeness above anything else in the world. But, over the weeks and then months he'd been away, she found herself wanting something else, something more.

Phoebe eyed herself in the mirror. She thought the mascara she'd so painstakingly applied, together with the lavender cashmere sweater she'd "borrowed" from her mother, made her look special. She ran her hands down her sides, smoothing out the cashmere's downy folds. Tonight Liam Bostock was going to focus on *her*.

❧

She must have fallen asleep on the couch in the music room. She woke up slowly. Her sweater twisted around her waist, exposing a lightly freckled swath of stomach and hips. The last thing she remembered, right before she clicked off the television set, was the sound of Jon Stewart tapping his pen repeatedly on the top of his news desk. Now she was aware of a shuffling noise, a door opening and closing.

"Holy shit!" she heard someone say. A boy. Not Liam. She sat up, tugging at her sweater.

"No, leave it like that," the voice said. A light flashed on. It took her a moment to adjust her eyes to the sudden brightness. There were three of them: a tall, skinny boy with a spotted face; a taller, broader boy with a stubble of beard; and a heavy-lidded, grinning Liam.

"Hey," she said, raising her arm in a salute, and then running her hand through her hair. She knew by the way the tall boy was gazing at her that she looked okay.

"Brandon Cowley—Phoebe Lansing." Liam's voice seemed overly loud and emphatic. He didn't bother introducing the other boy, who had wandered across the room, sat down at the piano, and begun picking out the opening chords to "The Long and Winding Road."

"Hey," she said again, as Brandon collapsed on the other end of the couch. The pillows sighed under his weight. He was five or six inches taller than Liam, with the kind of solid build that made Phoebe think he lifted weights like her dad. He would have been very handsome if not for a slightly pug nose and a heavy jaw. But when he smiled at Phoebe, she knew he thought he was, as her dad would have put it, "really hot shit."

"So you're the babysitter, huh?" he asked, turning toward her. She smelled the alcohol on him then. Alarmed, she glanced over at Liam, who'd slid into one of the red leather chairs facing the couch. His face was flushed, his hair falling in his eyes. He looked shamefaced, actually. Of course—he'd been drinking, too. After everything they'd talked about. After all those promises he'd made! She felt crushed in a way that was entirely alien to her. Her hopes for the night were ruined. Worse than that, though, she had to face the fact that she'd failed Liam somehow. And that he'd failed himself.

"Yeah," she said, standing up. "I better get home."

"Oh, no, you can't go now," Brandon told her. He leaned over and dug around in the backpack he'd left on the carpet when he first sat down, and pulled out a bottle of Johnnie Walker Red.

"Heeeeeeeere's Johnnie!" he cried, waggling the bottle above his head.

Liam snorted. The boy at the piano shook his head.

"Thanks. But it's getting really late," Phoebe said, stepping around the table and the duffel Liam had dropped in front of him. As she moved past Liam, he reached out and grabbed her hand.

"Don't go, Phebe," he said. She looked down at him and felt her heart contract. His pupils were enormous. He seemed to be having a hard time focusing on her.

"Why?" she asked him, shaking her hand free. They'd gone over this again and again. How he'd dug himself into a hole but was going to pull himself out. Why he wasn't going to find himself by drinking or doing drugs. That he was better than that. Smarter and stronger without any of that. Someone he could be proud of. And, probably more important, someone his dad could be proud of. He looked back up at her, smiling crookedly. She fought an urge to slap him.

"The question is, Why *not*, Phebe?" Brandon said from the couch. She turned back toward him, ready to tell him not to call her that. It was Liam's name for her. One of their precious secrets. Brandon had twisted the cap off the bottle of scotch and was holding it out to her. His gaze moved up and down her body, taking her in with obvious appreciation. Just as she had imagined Liam would be doing. She had put a whole scenario together in her head about how things would go between them. The way he would first touch her hair, fingering it as if it were something priceless. Then he'd cup the back of her head and gently pull her to him. He'd press his body up against hers and look down at her and say: *You're beautiful—do you know that? You're so incredibly beautiful to me!*

All this time, she'd been so sure that she'd been helping him. Convinced that, by believing in him, she'd given him the strength he needed to take a stand against his problems. She'd felt so grown-up supporting him in this way. The love she'd always felt for him had only deepened with the conviction that he needed her. Because of her, he'd be able to make a fresh start. In spite of the distance and silence between them, she was sure he could somehow sense all the good, positive feelings she'd been sending his way these past few months.

Oh, what a fool she'd been!

She turned from Brandon back to Liam, hoping she would see something in his gaze. Something that would tell her she was wrong. But his eyes were closed. His mouth hung open. She felt her anger solidify into something she didn't recognize. Something hard and hurtful. She sat back down on the couch and reached over to take the bottle that Brandon was holding out to her.

❧

"Hmmm, you smell good," Brandon said as he buried his face in her hair. She'd stopped keeping track of how much scotch she'd choked down. The stuff tasted awful. It burned in her throat. But she was intent on showing Liam that she didn't give a damn. He was still slouched in the chair across from them, snoring lightly. She'd forgotten all about the other boy, until he suddenly materialized in front of the couch.

"I'm going up, bro," he said. "And I think you should, too."

"Thanks for the advice, *bro*," Brandon said, looking up at the tall, skinny boy who Phoebe now realized was Brandon's brother, Carey, Liam's roommate at Moorehouse. Tilly had told her about them, that she'd liked one but not the other. "We're doing just fine here."

"No, I mean it," Carey said. "Leave her alone. I think Liam was like, you know, just talking."

"And I think you should like, you know, just mind your own business."

Carey continued to stand there, hands thrust deep into the back pockets of his jeans, looking down at them. Brandon turned back to Phoebe, his lips traveling along her neck as his right hand started to lightly massage her stomach beneath the sweater. Embarrassed by Carey's disapproving gaze, she sat up, pushing Brandon's hand away.

"It's Phoebe, right?" Carey asked. When she nodded, he went on: "Listen, I just think you should know that my brother here has a way of—"

But before Carey could say another word, Brandon sprang up from the couch and pushed him in the chest.

"Mind your own fucking business, asshole!" he said as Carey fell back a few steps.

"Okay!" Carey said, regaining his balance. He put both hands up. "Okay. Whatever. Like I said. I'm going up to bed now."

─꧁─

"You're so beautiful," he was telling her. His voice seemed far away. She could almost pretend that it was Liam's. That he was Liam. And Liam was telling her exactly what she wanted to hear. She opened her mouth to say something, but suddenly his tongue was there, hot and probing. She felt nauseated. She tried to turn onto her side, but he held her in place with his left knee and then—in one swift powerful movement—pulled her down flat onto the couch and rolled on top of her.

"What?" she cried. "No, wait!" She'd never felt a boy's erection before. But what else could that thing be—digging between her thighs? And Brandon was so heavy! She could hardly breathe. It got even worse when he covered her mouth with his. She squirmed beneath him as he rocked into her. He was going to smother her, she thought. He was going to crush her to death! Panicking, she made a huge effort to push him off her, but she was barely able to move. His left hand dug into her throat, while his right tugged at her zipper. She felt the world darkening. Oh, God, why didn't Liam wake up? How could he let this happen to her?

"It's okay," Brandon was telling her, lifting off her for a moment. "You don't have to worry. I always come prepared, so to speak."

She took this opportunity to knee him—hard—and then scramble off the couch as he doubled over in pain.

"You fucking—," he cried, grabbing for her, but all he managed to get was a handful of cashmere. He yanked it, ripping the sweater nearly in half before letting go. She fell down, then immediately tried to get up, but the room swayed around her. She was terrified she was going to pass out. She took a deep breath and lurched to her feet.

"Hey, whoa?" Liam said, stirring in the chair. "What's happening, man?"

"You tell me!" Brandon said. "This stupid fat fucking cunt tried to castrate me."

"You—," Phoebe whispered, fighting back another wave of nausea. Whatever happened, she was not going to allow herself to get sick in front of this person. "You—tried to rape me."

"Fuck that shit. You were all over me. And what's the big deal anyway? Liam told me you've been putting out for him since seventh grade."

"Oh," she said, taking a step backward. She knew she'd been hit. She could feel the impact. She couldn't feel the pain yet, but she sensed it was coming. And she knew it was going to be terrible.

"No," Liam was saying, struggling to sit up. "Wait, no. I was just—Phebe, wait!"

But she turned and stumbled out of the room, her whole world spinning.

3

On the drive up from Connecticut, Brandon, Carey, and Liam stopped at a diner just off Route 7 for something to eat. It was the first time Liam had been able to spend any real face time with Brandon Cowley, though his presence loomed large at Moorehouse. Varsity football, ice hockey, lacrosse, student council—Brandon's achievements were many and varied, but it was more his personality that fascinated Liam. Brandon was a big, brash, in-your-face type of guy. He seemed utterly confident in any situation. Though often crude and cutting, Brandon possessed the kind of macho swagger and alpha male reputation that Liam longed to have himself. In every way, Liam's standing at school was more on a par with Brandon's younger, self-effacing, and socially invisible brother, Carey, who as Liam's roommate was his nominal best friend at the boarding school.

"So what's the deal with you two?" Brandon asked as he sat across the table from Liam and Carey, waiting for their orders to arrive. "You jerk off together at night? I never see you down at Ralph's or at any of the dances." Ralph's was the café and bakery in the small town of Moorehouse where students were encouraged to hang out and mingle with the locals.

"We get out," Carey told him. "We get around."

"Oh yeah?" Brandon laughed, looking from Carey to Liam. "Now, Liam here, I think, has a chance. But not you, pizza face. Jesus, your zits are just exploding all over the place right now."

"Thank you," Carey replied, biting the paper tip off a straw as a waitress distributed their platters and drinks. "I actually have a pretty good idea what I look like. I ran out of my medication."

"No, that's not the problem," Brandon replied. Then, shaking his head, he turned to Liam and continued: "You see, Carey's problem is that he likes to pick away at things. His pimples. Me. He really gets off on it. Pick, pick, pick! You should hear him complaining to our parents about me! *Brandon owes me money he won't pay back. Brandon's mean to me in front of my friends*. Jesus, what a whiner!"

"You do owe me money."

"And, actually, now that I think about it—how can I be mean to you in front of your friends when you actually seem to have only one?"

"Hey, c'mon," Liam said. "Could the two of you maybe lay off each other—at least while we're eating?"

"No, really," Brandon went on, looking at Liam over the top of the hamburger he was holding. "Carey was a total loner freshman year. I think you've got to be the only friend he has in the whole world. What's the deal there, anyway? Are you taking him on as a charity case or something? Because you actually seem cool enough to hang out with a better class of people."

Liam had long been aware that the Cowley brothers were not exactly close. For starters, they couldn't have been less alike. Carey was as awkward socially as Brandon was adept. A gifted pianist, Carey spent hours at a stretch holed up in Moorehouse's practice rooms, lost in his own world. Brandon was happiest surrounded by his posse of friends, most himself when he had an appreciative audience. Liam wasn't surprised to learn from Carey that, in fact, his roommate and Brandon weren't biological brothers. Both had been adopted at birth, two years apart, by a wealthy, socially connected couple in Syracuse.

"They're great parents. They're very loving and generous," Carey had told Liam. "But Brandon's really put one over on them. They've been led to believe that the sun shines directly out of my brother's backside." After months of being exposed to Carey's carping, though, Liam began to realize that the younger brother's feelings for the older were actually a very complicated mix of envy, disappointment, hero worship, and worry. Because, along with all his other leadership roles, Brandon was known to party harder than anyone else at Moorehouse, a prep school that prided itself on its zero tolerance policy.

"He thinks he can get away with anything," Carey explained to Liam. "Because my parents have always let him do whatever he wants. He's still like a little kid in that way. He just doesn't get the whole concept of consequences."

There was something about the wistful, concerned way Carey spoke about all this that made Liam finally break down and explain the facts behind his own recent run-in with consequences. One that had forced him to transfer from his local regional high school, where at least he was a well-known entity, to Moorehouse, where he'd spent the first half of his sophomore year in unhappy obscurity. It was not that he didn't like Carey. Though uncomfortably shy with others, Carey had learned to relax with and open up to Liam. And Liam had come to appreciate his dry humor, his quick mind, and his remarkable musical abilities. What bothered him was Carey's assumption that Liam enjoyed the role of outsider as much as he did.

The bickering between the two brothers continued right through dinner and ratcheted up when the check came and Brandon had to admit that he didn't have any cash on him.

"I blew the rest of my allowance on our dessert," he told Carey as his brother wearily reached for his wallet. "But wait till you see what I bought. I've got it in the car. And I have a feeling that Liam here is going to really eat it up."

In the parking lot, Brandon walked around the BMW and opened up the trunk. Liam, sitting in the back of the car, could hear him shifting things around before slamming the lid shut again. As he climbed behind the wheel, Brandon tossed a knapsack into Liam's lap.

"Go ahead and open it up, man," Brandon told him, turning on the overhead interior light before starting the engine. Secretly pleased that he was being singled out for this task, Liam unzipped the bag, felt around, and pulled out an unopened fifth of Johnnie Walker. His heart skidded.

"That's just the chaser," Brandon said. "There's something else. The special of the evening, so to speak." From the bottom of the sack, Liam fished out a small ziplock bag, containing an inch of white powder.

"Oh, Christ!" Carey said. "What is that shit?"

"OxyContin."

"Don't be an idiot," Carey said, turning around to face Liam. "You don't want to be caught even looking at that stuff."

"Don't listen to him," Brandon said, turning off the overhead light before reaching over and grabbing the bottle Liam had left on the seat beside him. "He's a total pussy. We're out here in the middle of fucking nowhere. Who's going to find out what we're doing? Unless this big crybaby goes and tells on us."

"Are you nuts?" Carey said. "You just got early acceptance to Brown. You can't keep doing this kind of shit! Don't you get it?"

"Yes, I get it," Brandon said, twisting the cap off the bottle. "I get that you only go around once in life, okay? Why not try enjoying yourself for a change, little brother? You'd be a lot more fun to have around." Brandon tipped his head back, took a long swig, then waggled the bottle in front of his brother's nose.

"No way," Carey said.

Brandon just shook his head, turned around, and held the bottle out to Liam.

"Okay, here you go, but take it easy. I don't want anyone puking in the back of my Beemer."

Liam hesitated. He'd spent the past six months staying clean, keeping out of trouble, and trying to listen, as Phoebe had counseled him, to his "own inner angels." But he could feel something start to give way inside him now. His resolve—easy enough to keep when there was nothing to tempt him—began to crumble. The bracing smell of scotch filled the back of the car. He could already feel the alcohol burning in his throat. Easing the tension he'd been carrying around with him for too long. Lifting the loneliness.

"Here you go, man," Brandon said again. "I say we get an early start on the holidays!"

It was Brandon's welcoming tone more than anything else that decided things for him. For months now, Liam had been watching the entitled way Brandon and his friends moved around campus, roughhousing, high-fiving, name-calling—as if they owned the place. That's what Liam wanted, to be part of a crowd. All Liam had ever really wanted—his whole life—was to fit in somewhere. To belong. Because the day his family moved from Manhattan back to his dad's hometown, Liam had been lost between worlds. He was neither a local nor a weekender. In the public schools in Barnsbury he was considered "the rich kid." Sure, he'd had a few friends. But he'd always been set apart. Up there on the mountain in that fancy new house. While the children of the wealthy second-home owners, who came up on weekends and holidays and went to private schools in the city, seemed to speak a whole different language than Liam did. They had their own, insular points of reference—and opinions. Whoever heard of living in the country and going to public school? He knew they thought something must be wrong with him.

Liam's mom had promised him that Moorehouse would be different. But, if anything, it had been worse. At least, until now. Until he reached over and took the bottle out of Brandon Cowley's extended hand.

❦

"A redhead, huh?" Brandon was saying. "I really get off on redheads. There's something so sweet—and kind of malleable—about them, don't you think?"

"Yeah," Liam said. Oh, man, was he flying! He felt weightless and wonderful. He couldn't recall how they'd gotten onto the subject of girls exactly. Or Phoebe in particular. No, that's right, Brandon had asked him if he was "getting any," and Liam—trying not to tip his inexperienced hand—replied that the boys-only Moorehouse was not exactly "the best place in the world to get laid."

"Tell me about it," Brandon had replied. "You got some girl tucked away at home?"

And so he'd offered up Phoebe. His own dear Phebe. His oldest and best friend in Barnsbury. The only person he'd been able to talk to about his self-doubts and confusion. His sense of being nobody inside. Phebe, his own personal confessor and counselor. The only person in the world who really *knew* him. But it was because he could count on her, he told himself, that he felt free to embroider on their relationship. She'd understand, wouldn't she? She'd probably laugh out loud if she heard the way he described her physical attributes as if he knew them intimately. In fact, the more Brandon questioned him, the further Liam embellished upon the truth.

"So she really puts out, huh?" Brandon asked.

"Oh, yeah," Liam said. "She's been putting out for me since seventh grade."

"Didn't you tell me that she was babysitting your sister tonight?" Carey asked. He'd hardly said a word since they'd left the diner, since Brandon and Liam had gotten their "early start on the holidays" by snorting a couple of lines of the crushed OxyContin in the parking lot. Instead, Carey had sat in disapproving silence as they drove north, staring straight ahead while Brandon and Liam passed the bottle of scotch back and forth between them.

"That's right," Liam said, though he'd forgotten all about it until that very moment. Until it was too late. Phoebe was going to be right there waiting for him! Oh, man, he'd really fucked up. The last thing he wanted was for Phoebe to see him in this condition. After all his promises.

"She's the babysitter?" Brandon said, slapping the wheel. "That's just too great! You don't mind if I give it a shot, do you, man?"

Liam opened his mouth to protest. Of course, he minded. And, besides, Phoebe wasn't his to give away. She was her own sweet, innocent self. No! He'd made a mistake. He needed to fix this, he told himself. But his thoughts kept slipping away from him, shimmering past like headlights. Blinding him. He needed to concentrate. He attempted to focus on the bright cold stars glittering above the mountains on the horizon, but they wouldn't stay still. They shot like tracers through the dark, leaving ghostly contrails in their wake. Something was very wrong. He tried to sit up. He needed to pull himself together. Clear his head. He had to set Brandon straight. There was something he wanted to clarify. Something he really needed to explain.

⟡

Someone was jiggling Liam's foot. He still had his boots on, though the laces on the right one had obviously become untied. Someone was tugging at them, pulling the boot back and forth.

"Hey!" Tilly whispered. "Are you still asleep?"

"I was," Liam said. Those two words alone took a tremendous effort on his part. His mouth was a furnace. His throat raw. He rolled over on the bed, blocking the morning sunlight with his arm. His temples pulsed with pain.

"So why are you already dressed?"

"I didn't—," he began to say, but then he stopped himself. The truth—that he'd never actually *un*dressed—would, of course, only lead to further questions on Tilly's part. She was always full of questions for him. Five years younger than he was, she'd been following him around her whole life, badgering him with a seemingly endless litany of *when*s and *where*s and *how come*s.

"What's the matter?" she asked now, leaning over the side of the bed. "Are you sick or something? Carey said you might not be feeling well. You and Brandon."

"Yeah," Liam sighed, closing his eyes. Jumbled pieces of last night floated around in his brain. The diner. The ziplock bag. Stars streaking across the sky.

"We cooked these really cool pancakes," Tilly went on. Her piping voice made his ears ache. "They're like everything pancakes. We put in blueberries and chocolate chips and walnuts and raisins. We made bacon and sausages. Carey's like the best cook. It's all ready. We're waiting for you downstairs."

"Okay," Liam said. He could smell the bacon now. It turned his stomach. He thought he might actually gag just thinking about the greasy strips of smoked meat.

"So, you're getting up, right?" Tilly said.

"Soon," Liam said, turning on his side. The room swayed.

"No, *now*, Liam!" Tilly insisted. "Or everything's going to get cold." He could hear the little quiver in her voice. She'd missed him a lot, he knew. She'd written him at least once a week the whole semester. Her loopy longhand filling page after page of yellow legal paper, reporting on her friends at school, her ice hockey team, the doings of Puff Daddy—their border collie—and their aging cat, JLo. She'd ended every missive with, "I can't wait for you to come home!!!!!" God, was he really going to start the holiday disappointing everyone again?

"Okay," he told her. "I'll be down in just a sec." But, after she left, he lay in bed for a while longer, staring at his bedroom ceiling, trying to piece together what exactly had happened the night before. He couldn't recall arriving home. Or climbing the stairs. Or falling into bed. His last, fleeting memory was of headlights swimming past him—and the sound of Brandon's voice.

⟡

"You were right about old Phoebe," Brandon said. Tilly and Carey had just left to take Puff Daddy for a walk, leaving the two boys alone at the kitchen table. Liam's plate sat in front of him, a pool of syrup coagulating around his half-finished stack of pancakes. He felt nauseated just looking at it, so he got up and cleared his plate. He stood at the sink, looking out the kitchen window. Tilly and Carey were playing catch with a tennis ball as they walked down the driveway, Puff Daddy racing between them, barking, and jumping up and down as he tried to intercept the ball. Every bone in Liam's body seemed to ache.

"What about her?" Liam asked, turning back to the table.

"She's got some incredible body."

"Yeah," Liam said. Phoebe. He remembered now. She'd been asleep on the couch. She'd been wearing a lavender sweater.

"But she's a fucking tease, man," Brandon said, crumpling his paper napkin and tossing it onto his empty plate. "I was like this close—" He lifted his right hand, thumb and index finger about an inch apart.

"That close?" Liam asked. Winter sunlight flooded the spacious kitchen, bouncing off the glass panes in the cupboards. Liam felt as if someone had attached a vise to his head and was slowly tightening the screws. He couldn't think in this state. He couldn't work out what Brandon was trying to say. Something about Phoebe. Oh, God! He realized now that she must have been there last night. She would have seen how totally out of it he'd been. *Why?* she'd asked him. He remembered now. She'd looked down at him with pity in her eyes and asked: *Why?* He needed to call her. No, he'd text her—it would be easier to explain things that way.

Puff Daddy started to bark. A car horn sounded outside. Liam turned back to the window to watch his mother's Volvo wagon pull in beside Brandon's BMW. Tilly came running up the drive with the dog, followed by Liam's tall, skinny roommate. He watched as his father and Carey shook hands, as his mom stood on tiptoe to kiss Carey on the cheek. There was the kind of son they deserved, Liam thought, someone trustworthy. Someone you could count on. Not the total screwup he was turning out to be. Michael Bostock loped toward the house, his overnight satchel slung over his shoulder. He was smiling, his step quickening with anticipation. Liam knew how deeply his dad cared about him. How torn his dad had been about the Moorehouse decision. How his father took pride in even the smallest of his son's accomplishments. But that morning Michael Bostock's love felt like a burden almost too heavy for Liam to bear.

4

*P*hoebe's mother totally bought her story: Phoebe had come down with the flu. She'd first felt sick at the Bostocks'. Her mom had been asleep by the time Phoebe got home, and she hadn't wanted to worry her. But Phoebe had spent the rest of the night going back and forth to the bathroom.

"Did you tell Mrs. Bostock you were feeling sick?" her mom asked.

Phoebe hadn't mentioned that the Bostocks, who normally would have driven her home, would be away overnight and that she planned to walk back. In the fantasy she'd spun for herself, she imagined Liam walking with her, the two of them holding hands.

"No," Phoebe mumbled, as her mom pulled the thermometer out of her mouth.

"Well, you should have," her mom said. "And you should have woken me up when you got home. You look like death warmed over. But at least you don't have a fever. Are you hungry at all?"

"Yuck, no," Phoebe said. She doubted she'd ever be able to eat again. What she did crave, though, was her mother's solicitude. Just having her linger at her bedside, straightening the comforter and plumping up her pillows, helped relieve the misery a little. She felt as soiled and torn as the cashmere sweater of her mom's that she'd stuffed in the back of the bathroom closet the night before. She suffered bodily, as well: her head felt swollen and her stomach churned. The marks that Brandon had left on either side of her neck and along her arms ached and she'd had to pull on a turtleneck to hide the darkening bruises. But her heart ached a whole lot more. She felt violated. First by Brandon and then—though she could hardly bear to think about it—by Liam. Her Liam! How could he have said that about her?

"Are you *crying*, honey?" her mother asked her, sitting down beside her on the edge of the bed. Mother and daughter shared many of the same physical attributes—though Wanda was a blonde—as well as a sweet, empathetic nature. "Is it really that bad? Maybe I should call Dr. Davis."

"No!" Phoebe said. "It's that—I usually feel so good, you know? I guess I'm just not used to feeling so awful."

"Oh, I know," her mom said, brushing back Phoebe's hair. "And I wish I could tell you that you won't ever feel this way again. I wish I could protect you better. But feeling bad sometimes? I'm afraid it's just something you're going to have to get used to in life."

As her mom left the room, Phoebe's eyes welled up again. Hot tears ran down her cheeks. Of course, her mom had been talking only about being sick. But her kind words made Phoebe wonder if her mom wasn't somehow able to sense that the true source of her daughter's distress lay in her heart. After all, this was emotional territory that Wanda Lansing knew all too well herself.

A little over four years ago, when Phoebe was eleven, Wanda discovered that Troy Lansing, her high school sweetheart and husband of nearly sixteen years, had been cheating on her. Not once, as he had first claimed when Wanda saw his battered pickup—how stupid and trite can you get!—parked outside the Mountain View Motor Inn. No, after some checking around—after discovering that well-meaning friends and family had been sheltering "poor Wanda" from the truth—it turned out that Troy was a serial philanderer. A longtime skirt chaser. A moral failing that, in a bold play on Troy's part for sympathy and forgiveness, he'd tried to turn into a personal affliction by claiming that *he* was the victim of a debilitating sexual addiction. Despite this last-ditch plea for understanding, Wanda—pretty much to everyone's surprise, including a stunned and repentant Troy—demanded and eventually received a divorce.

"The bastard," Wanda told her older brother, Fred. "He thought that—just because I loved him so much—I'd put up with anything. He was counting on me not making a fuss. To go along to get along, the way us Hendersons usually do."

Fred had told Wanda that he was proud of her. She knew he understood what a tough time she had standing up for herself. Hardworking, gentle-natured, and frugal, the first Hendersons had settled in the Barnsbury area over a hundred and fifty years ago and had quietly prospered. By the turn of the last century, Henderson Orchards had been one of the biggest apple growers in the western half of the state. Then, as farming began to die out, members of the extended family began to gravitate to desk jobs in insurance and financial services in the larger towns of Harringdale and Northridge. After the divorce, Wanda, who'd worked part-time as a bookkeeper before her marriage, took a position as an administrative assistant in the business office at the Deer Mountain public school system.

Fred, in fact, was the one anomaly in the current generation of Henderson pencil pushers. After doing a couple of tours of duty in Iraq, he'd come home to Barnsbury to find that the police chief had retired and that the position was up for grabs. Fred didn't hesitate when it was offered to him. It paid a little better than other career opportunities at the time and allowed him to continue to carry a gun and wear a uniform.

In a rural backwater like Barnsbury, law enforcement was pretty much a matter of ticketing traffic violators, investigating security-system false alarms, and mediating domestic disturbances—Saturday night drunken shouting matches and the like. What bothered him more, he'd confided to Wanda, were the kinds of social problems hiding in plain sight: the bullying teens, the alcoholic young mom, the half-blind grandmother who was still behind the wheel. And, though he didn't come right out and say it, she was aware that Fred was also concerned about her ongoing relationship with Troy.

"He spends more time at the house now," Fred recently pointed out to Wanda, "than he did when you two were married."

"Well, you know, he still can't find work," Wanda replied. "Construction's just dead, and he needs something to do or he'll go stir-crazy. So I asked him to fix up the basement. He's putting in a kind of den down there."

"For what? Who has time to enjoy a den besides him? You're not paying him for this bullshit, are you?"

"Don't worry about us, Fred. We're fine."

Phoebe, too, noticed how often her dad was stopping by the house these days. After a year or two of hardly seeing him at all, he now seemed to be around all the time: programming the flat-screen TV, putting up the storm windows, rotating the tires on her mom's car. And Phoebe's father was a man who made his presence felt. He wasn't shy about giving his ex-wife and daughter the benefit of his opinions and advice.

Phoebe's mother didn't seem to mind, though. True, there were times when Phoebe thought she saw Wanda flinch at something her dad said. Or when she sensed that her mom was retreating back into the shadows that had enveloped her after the breakup. But, for the most part, Phoebe got the feeling that her mother, by insisting on the divorce, had somehow gained the upper hand on her ex-husband—or, at least, leveled the playing field.

Despite the bad feelings and tough times, though, Wanda had never let her anger at Troy spill over and pollute Phoebe's own feelings toward her dad. And Phoebe really respected that about her mom: she tried like crazy to be fair. In fact, the first time Phoebe had fully registered her mother's strength of character was when she stood up for Phoebe's right to work for the Bostocks. It was just before her parents broke up, and Brook had asked Phoebe if she wanted to help out with Tilly in the afternoons. Troy had been dead set against it.

"I don't trust him," he said. "And I don't like them. I don't mind Phoebe picking up some extra money after school, but just not from the Bostocks."

"Well, I think that's *your* problem," Wanda said. "I know you've got this thing about Michael. But Brook is offering Phoebe three dollars more an hour than she's going to get anywhere else—and, besides, Phoebe *likes* Brook and the kids. I do, too, and I think you're wrong about Brook believing she's better than us."

"Well, you just don't see it," Troy told her. "You're never able to see the bad in other people." Which was a prescient statement, considering what Wanda was going to discover about Troy himself a month or two later.

Troy had his failings, for sure. Even Phoebe recognized that her father could be belligerent and overbearing. But he also doted on his only child. She was his pride and joy, his "sunshine." Though her dad didn't talk about it much, Phoebe knew that his younger sister had drowned when she was about the age Phoebe was now. She sometimes wondered if his tendency to be controlling and super protective wasn't wrapped up in that tragedy.

Troy often complained about his lot in life. He'd been forced to take whatever low-paying menial jobs he could find since construction had dried up when the recession hit the area. And he bemoaned his unemployed status to anyone he could buttonhole long enough to listen to him. But he ended every one of these litanies of woe the same way: "I've got the best little girl in the world, though. No one can take that away from me."

Phoebe gradually became aware that her parents were arguing. From the slant of sunlight through her bedroom window, she figured it was early afternoon. Still nauseated and exhausted from the night before, she drifted in and out of sleep, only half-hearing the rise and fall of her parents' voices down the hallway. Until the pitch rose abruptly.

"I've never even worn the thing! I've no idea why it's even . . ."

"Who do you think you're bullshitting here? I'd know that smell anywhere. . . ."

"And could you please explain what you're doing rummaging around inside my closets . . . ?"

"I had to turn the hot-water spigots off to work on the sink downstairs. You think I'm *looking* for fancy sweaters covered with your puke, for chrissakes?" Troy's voice now carried clearly down the hall. "You think I *want* to find out that my wife is dolling herself up to go out drinking—God knows who with and where—and getting so fucking drunk that she—"

"Shut your mouth!" Wanda hissed. "I'm your *ex*-wife! I do *not* go out drinking. And keep your voice down or Phoebe will hear you. She's sick as a dog, and I don't want you waking her up with your nasty, crazy accusations!"

"What's wrong with her?"

"She says she has the flu," Wanda replied. "But I think it's just a stomach bug. She came back last night from the Bostocks' feeling . . ."

In the silence that followed, Phoebe felt her limbs turn to pins and needles. Dread filled her with a kind of lethargy. This was too much for her. She couldn't handle it. By the time both her parents entered her room, she'd almost willed herself back to sleep.

"Phoebe?" her mom said. "We need to talk to you, honey."

Phoebe opened her eyes and stared at the low ceiling. The room was barely ten feet by twelve, a crummy little box. She hated the flimsiness of the house, with its chipped wood veneer cupboards in the kitchen and the spotted wall-to-wall carpeting everywhere. The air that was always slightly fetid with leftover cooking smells. Her mom worked her tail off, but there was never any money for extras. The cashmere sweater had been a birthday gift from Uncle Fred to her mom. It had seemed to Phoebe to be the one new, beautiful thing to enter the house in months. Now her father carried the soiled ruin under his right arm. Phoebe could feel his gaze on her. She flinched when he cracked his knuckles.

"Look at me," he said. Phoebe's turtleneck snagged on the blanket as she turned to face her father, exposing the ugly bruises.

"Oh, my God!" Wanda said. She sat down beside her daughter on the bed and peeled the turtleneck back farther. "Oh, Phoebe, honey, what happened?"

"Who did that to you?" Troy demanded. "Where were you last night?"

Phoebe shook her head. When it became clear that she was unwilling to speak, Wanda said, "I told you: she was baby-sitting. She was at the Bostocks'."

"What the hell went on there last night?" Troy said.

Phoebe shook her head faster. The sweater's sweet-sour smell filled her nostrils, and her stomach rebelled. She sat forward, weeping and retching at the same time, though there was nothing left to throw up. Her mom pulled her into her arms.

"It's okay. It's going to be okay," Wanda murmured, rocking her daughter back and forth.

"I'm going to leave the room, Phoebe," Troy announced. "And I want you to take that top off and let your mom see the rest of your body. Wanda, you need to ask your daughter some hard questions here. Do you understand me? I'm going to be standing right outside the door."

Phoebe fell back on the pillow as her dad turned to leave, then curled into a ball when the door slammed shut behind him.

"It's okay," Wanda said, rubbing Phoebe's back. "It's okay. We just need to know what happened. Were you drinking last night, honey?"

Troy had taken the sweater with him, but its stench still hung in the air. The lingering taste of scotch coated Phoebe's tongue. Surely, her mom could smell it on her daughter; it seemed embedded in her very pores.

"Yeah," Phoebe said into the pillow.

"Where did you get it from?"

"Liam's friend."

"So Liam was involved with what happened? Who else was there?"

"Liam and his roommate and his roommate's brother."

"So these boys offered you something to drink—and you just decided to take them up on it? I know this isn't the right moment to lecture you, Phoebe, but I am surprised. I mean I really thought we understood each other on this subject. Remember that talk we had last summer?"

A fresh wave of anguish swept through Phoebe as she thought back on the conversation her mom was referring to. It had been right after Liam first confided in Phoebe about his problems. Wanda, who periodically suggested that Phoebe "share anything that might be on your mind," had gotten an earful from her daughter about the dangers of teenage drinking. Oh, Phoebe had just been on fire with her love for Liam— thrilled by how much he was beginning to rely on her. How much he needed her!

"Liam asked me to stay," she told Wanda, turning around to face her mother. Her eyes were bloodshot from crying, her lips swollen.

"Tilly was already in bed?" Wanda asked, brushing back Phoebe's bangs. "So it was the three boys and you. Liam asked you to stay. And you all had something to drink. Is that right?"

"Liam's roommate didn't, but his older brother did. I think

maybe they all had been drinking on the way up from school. They seemed a little out of it when they got there."

"So when did Mr. and Mrs. Bostock come home? Did they see what was going on? Did they realize you'd been drinking?"

"Mommy," Phoebe said, fresh tears springing up. "They didn't *come* home. They spent the night with friends somewhere. I knew that they were planning to—but I forgot to tell you."

"You forgot? That's a little hard to believe," Wanda said, frowning as she took in her daughter's blotchy cheeks and swollen eyes. "But let's deal with that later. Sit up a sec. We're going to take this turtleneck off. Lift your arms up. That's a good girl." Wanda had to tug hard to get the top over her daughter's head. Phoebe had the pale, sensitive, lightly freckled skin of most redheads, which made the welts on her upper arms—the color and shape of fingerprints—appear that much darker and more vicious-looking.

"Oh, my God!" Wanda said.

"What?" Troy called from the other side of the door.

"Mommy!" Phoebe cried, as she looked down at herself and began to understand the full extent of her brutalization. Troy banged on the door.

"What's going on?" he said.

"Cover up a little, honey," Wanda said, rising from the bed. "I think we need to let your daddy see this."

⁀℮

Troy appeared to be in complete control of his emotions. He didn't curse or cry out when he gently examined his daughter's neck and arms. He sounded perfectly reasonable when he asked Wanda to get her digital camera. And when he took the many photos, from many different angles, of Phoebe's bruises, he was thorough and methodical. But it was this very composure that alarmed both Wanda and Phoebe. They knew his temper too well. Yes, he was calm—but they were both aware that it was a deadly calm.

"Okay," he said finally, turning off the camera and handing it back to Wanda, who'd pulled over the chair from Phoebe's desk and was wedged in next to the bed. Troy crossed his arms on his big chest and looked down at his dear daughter's tearstained face.

"Did he rape you?"

Phoebe shook her head.

"Are you sure? Would you have even known it if he had?"

"Yes," Phoebe whispered. "I would know. Because he tried."

"He *tried*? But—what? He couldn't do it? Or you wouldn't let him? What happened?"

"I—kicked him," Phoebe said, the memory of Brandon's tongue in her throat returning unbidden, along with that of Liam, passed out on the chair, openmouthed. "I kicked him where it hurts."

"Good for you, baby," Troy said with a mirthless laugh. "And I believe you. But your mom's going to run you up to the ER anyway and have you checked out."

"Oh, no, Daddy!" Phoebe said, pulling the covers around her. "I'm fine—really. I promise. I'm perfectly okay."

"Bullshit!" The word thundered around the little room. "You've been assaulted! You're covered with bruises. That Bostock kid tried to *rape* you, Phoebe! And, believe me, I'm going after that bastard. He's *not* going to get away with this."

"But, Daddy—," Phoebe began. Now was the moment to tell him that it wasn't Liam who had attacked her. He'd only sat passively by. But her father's outrage finally released her own anger— anger that until now had been covered over with layers of guilt, self-loathing, and shame. Brandon's *stupid fat fucking cunt* comment had been circling through her tortured thoughts all day, holding up a cruel mirror to her wounded psyche: Was this how Liam saw her, too? Dumb and overweight? *She's been putting out for me since seventh grade!* Liam had told Brandon. *That's what he really thinks of me,* Phoebe told herself. *He's just been using me. And then making fun of me to his rich friends. He's been laughing at me all this time!*

"There're no buts about this," Troy told her. "You've been wronged. You've been harmed. *Nobody* has the right to do what that boy did to you. I don't care if he's the Dalai Lama. We will not be humiliated. We will not be pushed aside. We will not stand for this. Do you understand me?"

"Yes," Phoebe said at last.

5

𝓑rook had overdone it again, Michael reflected as he trudged up the pathway to his studio. It was supposed to have been a simple family supper—an informal and relaxed preholiday get-together with Michael's mom, his older sister Lynn, and her husband, Alan Simonetti—but Brook had put together a buffet worthy of one her R.S.V.P. events.

"My goodness!" Michael's mom, Ethel, had said when Brook showed everyone into the dining room. There, arranged along the sideboard, and interspersed with gold-dusted pine-cones and delicate branches of white LED lights, was a tiered cake stand of tea sandwiches, platters of smoked salmon, steamed jumbo shrimp, and a spiral-cut glazed ham studded with cloves. Though never truly impoverished, Ethel had spent her married years pinching pennies and taking pride in making do with very little. "Who else is coming? The Queen of England?"

Beyond, through the double French doors, a large, elabo-rately decorated Christmas tree brushed the top of the great room's cathedral ceiling. Almost every mantelpiece, bookcase, and tabletop downstairs bore some evidence of the obvious pleasure Michael's wife took in the holiday season.

"No, it's only us," Brook told her mother-in-law. "But there's no reason we can't make it a special occasion, is there? Liam just got back from school. I feel like celebrating a little!"

"And the good china, too," Lynn said, picking up one of the gold-rimmed plates and turning it upside down. Michael glanced over at Brook, who met his gaze: *Don't correct her!* he telegraphed. *She doesn't need to know this isn't your best.* Michael himself couldn't keep track of how many different sets of plates they actually owned. Brook kept a "party room" down in the finished basement where she stored the extra cutlery, glasses, and china she kept accumulating. Though some of it was used for local R.S.V.P. events, Michael had resigned himself to the fact that his wife collected pretty tableware the way some women acquired expensive shoes.

Brook seemed to understand what his look was saying. Her smile faded a little. She didn't respond to Lynn's comment. She'd obviously picked up on his discomfort about once again having to mediate between her overly generous tendencies and his grudging family.

"Leave plenty of room for dessert!" Tilly instructed everyone as she piled shrimp onto her plate. "Mom's been baking for like the last two months!"

"Yes, but this is the kind of thing I do for a living," Brook said. It saddened Michael to think that he was responsible for making his wife apologize for her largesse. And he knew how proud Brook was of the success she had made of R.S.V.P. But she still didn't seem to understand that her in-laws considered her "business" something Brook did as a lark. Everyone knew she didn't actually *need* to work, Michael could just about hear his sister Lynn thinking, *Putting on big, la-di-da parties? Well, who wouldn't want to do that if you had the free time?*

"So how's the new school working out for you?" Michael's brother-in-law Alan asked Liam as people began to take their seats around the table.

"Okay," Liam replied, picking up and then putting down his fork. Michael tried not to stare too openly at his son. Ever since Michael had tried to hug him that morning when he and Brook got back from Rhinebeck and Liam had just stood there—stiff as a statue in his arms—Michael had been trying to figure out what was going on. Did Liam seem even more withdrawn than before? Sullen and withholding? *Oh, he was just being a teenager, for chrissakes,* Michael would tell himself one moment; then the next he'd know for certain that something was wrong. Liam's spark, that wicked sense of humor, was gone. Things were getting worse, not better. Sending Liam to Moorehouse had been, just as Michael had feared, a mistake.

"Maybe you could enumerate on that 'okay' a little," Michael suggested.

"Enumerate?" Liam asked.

"Yes. You know—fill in a few details for us."

"Oh," Liam said, looking down. "You mean elaborate."

"Right," Michael said, reaching for his water glass. *Don't react,* he told himself. *Don't show you're angry. Don't even let him know you noticed the put-down.* But, honestly, it felt like a slap in the face. And Liam's little jibe had landed squarely on one of Michael's sore spots—his tendency to fumble words when he was nervous or upset. Had Liam intended to hurt him in that way? No, Michael didn't think so. He couldn't allow himself to think so. For years, he'd thought of his son as his best friend, the one person he really wanted to hang out with. It was just that damned school, Michael told himself. Liam was surrounded now by rich, entitled kids who'd never been taught the importance of manners, let alone respect.

Brook had told him—with a resigned laugh—that the third-floor guest room where Liam's friends had slept the night before looked like a tsunami had come through. His dad would have slapped him halfway to kingdom come if he'd left a room that way, Michael knew.

It was probably just the time of year, all those sentimental Christmas carols and the forced cheer, but he found himself thinking a lot about his father these days. Old Jack Bostock. "Jack of All Trades," he used to call himself, "Master of None." His dad thought most careers were a joke. No, Jackie B. was smarter than that. He preferred the odd job, the short-term project, anything that freed him up to develop his gadgets and novelty items. The erasable magnetic memo pad. The reusable kitchen garbage bag. The never-fail squirrel-proof bird feeder. Surefire breakthrough inventions that were going to make them all millionaires. Michael thought about the endless hours the old man spent down in the basement, soldering scrap metal and filling out patent forms. Only to be one step behind, or a few inches too close to, someone else's design.

Not that Jack ever gave up. There was always another brilliant idea. The next big dream. In the meantime, he learned how to play the unemployment system like an accordion—squeezing it here, easing off a bit there, always with a grin and a ready one-liner. Because Jack was a kidder. He was a real card. Except when he drank—which he made a stab at keeping to just weekends and holidays. When he really let loose.

Christmas was one long, nonstop, riotous binge. Riotous to Jack, anyway. Not to his only son.

"You're looking so much like your dad these days," Michael's mom told him as he helped her carry Brook's presents and carefully packaged leftovers out to Ethel's car after supper. "I always miss him this time of the year. Oh, how that man loved a good time!"

Since Jack's early death from a heart attack—when Michael was just twenty-two—Ethel had devoted a good part of her energies to turning her late husband into a plaster saint. "The girls"—Michael's three much older sisters, who'd married and moved on before Jack's drinking turned mean—seemed perfectly happy to enable their mother in her mythmaking. But then, they'd never been exposed to the father that Michael had come to know all too well. Jack was the life of the party, all right, unless you were the one who had to scrape him off the floor when it was over. Oh, sure, everyone laughed at his jokes—except if you happened to be the butt of so many of them. Michael grew up acting as his father's punch line and punching bag rolled into one.

"Take Mikey, here," Jack would say, as the bar started to empty and Michael quietly urged his father to call it a night. "Big strapping guy, right? Thinks he's better than his dad. So I say, Mike—come on, take a shot at me. Why not? Show the old man what you've got."

Michael could hear the taunting words even now—and feel his stomach clench at the memory—as he pushed open the door to his studio. He flicked on the overhead lights and breathed in the scent of woodsmoke and tung oil that permeated the still air. He hadn't been completely honest with Brook when, after his family left, he told her that he needed to get some work done on his new commission. In fact, the enormous bird's-eye maple conference room table, which he was constructing from three separate lengths of wood, was well under way. No, what he needed was some time alone. To think about Liam. To get a grip on his feelings. Jesus, it was like he was still a boy himself. Stung by Liam's stupid, thoughtless comment. As though he didn't know what "elaborate" meant!

He started the fire in the woodstove. He donned his work gloves and goggles and began to sand. Moving with the grain. Feeling the satisfying give of grit under the heel of his palm. The sweet aroma of wood dust tickling his nostrils. The trouble was, unlike his own dad, who saw Michael as competition, he loved Liam, unconditionally, with all his heart. He had never raised a hand against his son, unlike his own dad, who'd whipped Michael with his leather belt on pretty much a regular basis. He had thought about that kind of thing a lot when he was a kid. How different he was going to be from his own father. How he was never going to repeat any of Jack's mistakes.

Michael's thoughts drifted back across the decades, as they so often did when he was working. It was one of the great things about the solitary, hands-on nature of his business that his mind was usually free to roam. Except when, instead of slipping gently over the surface of things, he found his thoughts swirling around and around in narrowing circles of worry and regret.

"How would *you* know?" Liam had demanded last June when everything blew up in their faces. "You've never done anything wrong. You're fucking perfect!"

And instead of responding to his son's cry of pain, instead of being honest and telling Liam the truth about his own terrible early mistakes, Michael had stupidly jumped all over Liam's swearing.

"Where did you learn to talk like that?" Michael had replied. "Not from me!"

"Exactly," Liam told him. "You're too fucking good to use bad language."

Michael knew what his son was going through, far more than Liam would ever be able to understand. He knew how much Liam wanted Michael to rise to the bait. He wanted him to strike out—strike back—help Liam redistribute the blame. Michael's father had been the same way: always coming out of his corner swinging, challenging any and all comers, but especially his only son. Which was exactly why Michael taught himself to hold his tongue and not fight back. He wasn't about to let Jack know how much his taunts got to him. He trained himself to be strong, determined not to give his old man the satisfaction of knowing he was actually bleeding inside. Though sometimes he felt like the Spartan boy he learned about in school who hid a stolen fox inside his cloak and allowed it to gnaw him to death.

For the most part, he succeeded in hiding his feelings from his dad. But that didn't do anything to stop the pain; it just concealed it. But what happens to bottled-up anger in a teenage boy? It's like any volatile substance under pressure. Eventually it's going to explode. *No,* Michael often wished he could tell his son, *I'm actually about as far from perfect as you can get.*

꧁

He'd been vaguely aware of a light *tick, tick, tick* coming from somewhere above him before he glanced up and saw that snow was accumulating on the skylights. Fat flakes swirled through the columns of light cast upward from the studio overheads into the night sky. He put down the sander and took off his gloves, flexing his fingers. He should go back down to the house soon. Brook would be wondering what had happened to him.

He stretched and then walked over to check on the Jøtul stove. Embers still glowed in the back, but it would be safe now to shut the vents and close the latch. As always when he finished for the day, he cleaned up and swept around his work area. Self-taught from workbooks and Internet courses, Michael had learned to be a stickler about neatness and attention to detail. Yes, he had a natural talent for what he did. But it was his dedication and meticulous work habits that really had gotten him to where he was today. Over the last twenty years, Michael Bostock Fine Wood Designs had grown into one of the most prestigious high-end custom-made furniture concerns on the East Coast. He had a team of eight woodworkers who turned out his designer chairs, tables, and lamps in a converted barn in North Barnsbury, while Michael handled new creations and one-of-a-kind projects in his mountainside studio. It was work that he loved, and which, especially since he'd signed on with a new dealer in New York five years ago for his custom-made pieces, was becoming increasingly lucrative.

His success had become a lot more important to him than he ever let on to Brook. He took pride in the fact that in the exceedingly unlikely event that the Pendleton Family Trust should suddenly collapse, he'd be able to keep his wife and children in the style to which Brook's inheritance had accustomed them.

"You know what I love about you?" Brook had asked him early on in their marriage.

"There's only one thing?"

"Of all the many, many things I love about you? I really, honestly think you don't give a damn about my having money."

But she was wrong. He did care. He'd fallen in love with someone whose name—along with the fortune that went with it—was almost as well-known as Du Pont or Vanderbilt. If you were any kind of a man, that level of wealth was a burden, a weight that was forever needing to be shifted and adjusted as you tried to establish a normal, loving marriage. And it only became more unwieldy and treacherous as you attempted to raise happy, well-adjusted children who understood the value of hard work and initiative.

"You lucky bastard," one of their New York friends had told Michael when Brook and he first announced their engagement. "You've hit the mother lode."

But, in fact, his only real luck had been in finding Brook. The Pendleton part? It was a curse, really. Brook's two domineering half sisters. The trust lawyers. The corporate board. The financial advisers. There wasn't one person—except Brook's father, who was a mere in-law, like Michael—whom Michael honestly admired or felt comfortable with. He would have been perfectly happy to donate the whole damned thing to charity. Except it wasn't his to give away. It was just his to have to deal with.

And as if the Pendleton money hadn't come with enough problems of its own, the trust had, as far as Michael was concerned, poisoned Brook's relations with his family before they even had a chance to meet her. It hadn't helped that the local Northridge paper had somehow gotten hold of the engagement news and run a piece on Brook's background, rehashing all the old society gossip about her mother and making Brook seem like some poor little rich girl with whom his family would have nothing in common.

"She's the kindest person I've ever known," Michael had reassured his mother when she confronted him with the article and her own fears. "Just wait until you meet her—you're going to love her, I promise."

But Brook never managed to break through to his family. Not for lack of trying—or was the problem that she tried too hard? He thought at least their hearts would melt—and their arms open—when he and Brook decided to move back to Barnsbury after 9/11. What clearer signal could they send that they wanted to be part of their lives and this town? But the family had remained standoffish. Judgmental. Like those little signals of disapproval Lynn kept sending Brook's way just that evening. With Michael's two oldest sisters, Jeannie and Beth, who came back to Barnsbury with their families only every other summer or two, it was easier. But that was only because those big family get-togethers tended to be such chaotic free-for-alls. Even then, Michael's sisters would keep to themselves, not making much of an effort to include Brook in their conversations. It infuriated Michael that they wouldn't give his wife a chance.

He was thinking about this and how he was going to spin the less-than-joyous supper to Brook as he checked the stove one last time. The skylights were now blanketed in white. He could hear the wind rustling through the hemlocks.

He opened the front door, then turned off the last bank of lights. It took a moment for his eyes to adjust to the darkness—out of which, after a moment, shapes began to emerge. The long ledge of the woodpile. The old oil drum where he stored the kindling. The stand of birches.

Down below, a door slammed. A moment or two later, he

saw a man climbing the steps to the studio from the parking area—two at a time—as though he couldn't wait to reach Michael. His heart leapt when, for a brief moment, he thought it was Liam—come to apologize or explain. But he soon realized the figure was too broad, his forward motion too purposeful. A moment later Michael recognized who it was. What exactly was coming at him.

"You've got a hell of a lot of explaining to do," Troy Lansing said when he reached the top of the steps, his breath coming out in ragged little puffs, his gloved hands balled into fists at his sides. Later, Michael would wonder why he hadn't been more surprised by Troy's sudden appearance that night. Of course, he couldn't have known then why specifically Troy had come, but the larger, deeper reasons for his angry outburst were never all that far from Michael's mind.

6

Brook lost her mother when she was nine years old, capsizing her world. For several years after Tilda Pendleton's death, Brook lived in a state of emotional vertigo. She moved through her daily existence with great care, keeping a firm grip on her feelings, for fear that the slightest vagrant memory would undo her. It was one of the reasons why, as she grew older, she worked so hard to keep her life upright and secure. Even as an adult, though, when faced with a real crisis, she tended to founder. Which was what had happened with Liam that past June. "Don't you think the real problem is that you've let him run wild up here?" her sister Peg had asked during the painful postmortem the morning after Liam had gotten drunk and disgraced himself at her daughter Kristin's wedding. Brook couldn't have been more thrilled when Kristin had asked to hold the wedding at the Bostocks' mountainside home—and that R.S.V.P. handle all the arrangements. Her fiancé's family lived in Albany, so it was a convenient location for both families, not to mention a lovely setting for the June nuptials.

Within a week of the invitations going out, all the best rooms at nearby inns and B and Bs had been booked for the weekend.

Though the ceremony and dinner had gone off without a hitch, the situation began to unravel when the Bostocks' closest neighbors complained to the Barnsbury police about the loud music and the cars that had been parked on their property without permission. When Chief Henderson came to investigate, one of the first things he saw was Liam passed out on the front lawn. It was a disastrous end to what Brook had hoped was going to be a proud affirmation of her decision to raise her family in Michael's hometown.

"We actually have a very regulated home life," Brook told Peg and Janice defensively at the start of the discussion. They were sitting in the Bostocks' great room. On the back lawn, the catering company was taking down the big white party tent and folding up the rented tables and chairs.

"We know you've tried to do your best," Janice told her. "But, honestly, we have to ask: why do you insist on stacking the cards against Liam? We understand you and Michael are determined to live a simple life and all, but you don't want your choices negatively impacting your children, do you? What kind of education is he getting, what kind of people is he associating with in—where is he enrolled exactly?—some public school up here?"

Janice was two years older than Peg, and both sisters were the products of Tilda Pendleton's eighteen-year marriage to the investment banker Howard Flatt. Brook, fifteen years younger than Peg, was the unexpected result of Tilda's midlife love affair with the left-leaning magazine editor Peter Hines. Peg and Janice had been teenagers at the time of their mother's well-publicized liaison and their parents' subsequent divorce.

Hurt and humiliated by Tilda's flagrant disregard for their own reputations, they had chosen to live with their father.

It seemed to Brook that her half sisters had overcompensated for their mother's transgressions by setting the strictest possible ethical standards for themselves. Even after Tilda Pendleton's sudden death—at forty-eight—they avoided mentioning her name. Having rejected the institution of marriage after the painful split from her first husband, Tilda had never married Peter, so Brook was quite literally a "love child." This stigma only added to Brook's many difficulties growing up. Peter Hines did his best to take care of Brook, but without Tilda, his best was really pretty bad, especially during the period when Brook needed him most. So Brook ended up as the odd little duckling, paddling frantically in the wake of the proper swans with whom Peg and Janice circulated.

It had taken Brook years before she stopped measuring herself against everything her sisters said and did. Starting her own business had been her first real attempt to stand on her own. Falling in love with and marrying Michael—something both sisters advised strenuously against—had, Brook believed, allowed her to finally break free and gain a real shot at happiness.

But Liam's behavior at the wedding had forced her to face the fact that the Bostocks' life in Barnsbury wasn't as perfect as she longed to believe. Though she made it seem to her sisters that her son's drinking had been an isolated incident, actually it was only the most recent. She'd first sniffed alcohol on his breath after an eighth-grade graduation party two years before. Michael and she had immediately sat him down and explained the dangers of underage drinking, but less than two months later she found three marijuana cigarettes tucked in the back of his sock drawer.

She'd lost track of the many times she'd discovered that he'd been drinking or smoking since then—and didn't like to dwell on the likelihood of other occasions when she hadn't found him out. She began keeping these episodes from Michael, who tended to react with anger and harsh disciplinary measures, which only made communicating with Liam more difficult. Instead, she began reaching out to Liam on her own. And her loving, concerned approach had appeared to be working. For six months or so, there'd been no new signs that Liam was misbehaving, allowing Brook to believe that their problems were behind them.

So Liam's backsliding at the wedding, made worse because it was so public, really shook her up. Frightened and at her wit's end, she listened attentively to the advice Peg and Janice offered. It had boiled down to one simple, very concrete suggestion: get Liam out of Barnsbury and send him to Moorehouse, the prep school in Connecticut that had educated the last four generations of Pendleton boys, including her half sisters' many sons.

"We actually wanted to suggest this last year," Peg had confided, "but we all know how sensitive Michael can be when we offer ideas."

Would Liam fare better once away from Barnsbury? Brook and Michael talked the question through. Had they made a mistake not giving him the very best education they could afford? Had they been selfish wanting to keep him at the center of their lives? Would he find the self-discipline there that he seemed to be lacking at home? They went over and over Peg's and Janice's arguments: *Just consider the connections he'll make, the much-needed confidence he'll gain, as well as the enlarged sense of the world and his own potential.* Michael seemed just as concerned and uncertain as Brook was.

"I don't want to hold him back," he told her. "But also I don't want him to feel that we're pushing him to go. I know what Peg and Janice think. What about you? Do you *really* think it's the right decision?"

Should she have told him the truth? That she didn't trust herself enough at that particular juncture to know for certain what was best for her own son? She'd always prided herself on the close, easygoing relationship she'd had with Liam. And she'd convinced herself that they'd reached a new level of understanding over the past few months. So his actions felt like a slap in the face. He'd turned inward and solitary in the days following the wedding, and she couldn't seem to break through his newly erected line of defenses—slumping posture, hair in his eyes, monosyllabic responses. She felt she'd already failed him somehow, that she didn't know how to begin to rectify her mistakes. She was aware that her youngest nephews, those closest to Liam in age, seemed to have flourished at Moorehouse.

The decision to go ahead had been a wrenching one. Far worse than she let on to Michael, who, she knew, still harbored serious reservations about the elite status of the prep school, its wealthy student body, and the demanding curriculum. Moorehouse, in fact, once Liam had been enrolled, became a subject they both tended to avoid. But Brook was counting on that changing over the holidays. Liam had told her on the phone recently that he felt he was finally "in a good place." Whether that meant Moorehouse or some temporary emotional state, Brook wasn't sure. Over the course of the fall, she sometimes worried about him so much she'd wake up in the middle of the night, her body rigid with tension.

❧

"Liam!" Brook heard Michael call as he came in from the studio, the front door slamming behind him. She was in the kitchen, cleaning up after the dinner with Michael's family.

"Liam! Get down here!" Michael called again, and this time Brook heard something in his tone—anger? fear?—that made her stop loading the dishwasher and head toward the front hall. "Liam!"

Michael was standing at the foot of the stairs, looking up. Troy Lansing, Phoebe's dad, was standing beside him.

"Liam—," Michael called again, then went up the steps. Brook heard Liam's footsteps in the upper hallway, what seemed like a terse exchange between father and his son, and then the two of them came back down, Liam first, pajama top unbuttoned, hair in his eyes. Michael followed behind, his mouth set in a grim line.

"What's going on?" Brook asked.

"I'm not really sure," Michael said, glancing from Troy to his son. "Troy has some questions for Liam."

As far as Brook knew, Troy Lansing and Michael hadn't actually exchanged more than a few curt words over the last twenty years. They'd been best friends once, but then something had happened that set the two of them against each other. Of course, Troy had a reputation in town for being difficult. Temperamental. Phoebe had never alluded to the situation, but Brook suspected that Troy wasn't all that thrilled when his daughter started working for them. On the rare occasions when he, rather than Wanda, picked Phoebe up at the

Bostocks', he never came to the door to let her know he was there. He stayed behind the wheel of his pickup and honked the horn.

"Troy has some bad news," Michael added when Troy, who was glaring at Liam, didn't say anything.

"Oh!" she said, looking from Troy to Michael to Liam. Nobody met her gaze. She suddenly resented Troy being in her house, filling up her front hall with whatever awful thing he had come to tell them. But it was Michael who once again broke the silence.

"Something happened here last night. Apparently there was some drinking. Apparently Phoebe had something to drink. And she was . . . assaulted."

"What?" Liam said. "Phoebe? What are you taking about?"

"Don't pull that innocent crap on me!" Troy said. "I know what happened. I made Phoebe tell me. The truth. She actually wanted to protect you."

Brook waited for Michael to leap to Liam's defense. But he just stood there, his eyes on his son.

"*What* truth?" Brook asked.

Troy looked at her. He pulled some papers out of the inside pocket of his parka. At first Brook thought he was showing her something Liam had sent to Phoebe. But when Troy handed them to her, she realized that they were actually a series of digital photos, printed out on regular laser paper, the color ink saturating the flimsy stock. She stared down at the photo on top, trying to make sense of the slightly blurred close-up. The shot was bisected diagonally by some kind of curve. She studied the shape for a moment—the curve was a cheek. A freckled cheek. And beneath that, slightly in shadow, but nevertheless quite clear: dark splotches. She brought the paper a little closer.

"They're bruises," Troy told her. "Along her neck. On her arms. Her stomach."

"Oh, my God," Brook said. She looked up and over at her Liam. He seemed stunned. He was blinking uncontrollably—the way he used to when he was much younger. And frightened. She felt her heart contract. She knew enough to realize that her son might very well have been drinking the night before. He might even have been smoking dope. But he'd never hurt anyone. Especially not Phoebe. Brook had absolutely no doubt about that.

"Liam couldn't possibly have had anything to do with this," Brook said firmly. "Tell him you didn't do it, Liam."

"I didn't," Liam said. It was almost a whisper. He licked his lips.

"Are you calling my daughter a liar?" Troy demanded.

"He told you he didn't do it," Brook said. "Please! Stop bullying him!"

Brook realized that Michael had come around and was now standing beside her. She felt his arm slide around her waist. Her throat ached. She'd been almost shouting, she realized. She couldn't understand how Michael could be so composed. How he could sound so reasonable and accommodating when he said:

"Listen, we're all pretty upset. But Troy has a right to be angry about what happened to Phoebe, every right to let off steam. I don't know why Phoebe would say Liam was the one responsible for this"—he looked down at the photos in Brook's hand—"this horrible thing. But she has, and we need to calm down and get to the bottom of it."

"*You* go ahead and calm down!" Troy said. "I won't be joining you, and I don't need to get to the bottom of this—

because I've already been there. I've already seen what happened firsthand. Phoebe came back from this house last night stinking drunk. She was wearing my wife's sweater, and she puked all over it. The sweater was torn almost in half by your son here. When he—when he tried to rape her."

Brook knew that she wasn't going to be able to reason with this man. He was trembling with rage: legs spread, fists balled, spoiling for a fight. He was in his element, she realized. He was beyond wanting answers; he was after blood. Michael obviously understood that, and was refusing to take the bait. But Brook couldn't stop herself. She couldn't let his awful lies go unanswered, spreading into the night, pooling down into the town.

Of all of them, Liam had had it the hardest when they first moved up to Barnsbury. Brook knew he'd been lonely and desperate for friends. In seventh grade, he'd started asking Brook to drop him off on the highway before the turnoff to Deer Mountain Elementary. She'd finally got him to confess that one of the kids in his class had looked up the list price of their silver Infiniti SUV. Liam's classmates had started calling it the Popemobile. She traded it in for a secondhand Volvo wagon two days later.

How ironic that she'd actually believed their move to Barnsbury would supply her family with a sense of community. That here, in the town where Michael was raised, where Bostocks had lived for four generations, she'd finally be able to find a home. Instead, she began to realize that Michael was being looked upon with distrust for marrying such a wealthy woman.

She'd made an effort to live with her disappointment and tamp down her anger. Except when she thought her children were being affected by her mistakes—singled out or harassed in some way. Like now. Like this foulmouthed Troy Lansing, who thought he could barge into her home and tell lies about her son. No! She'd put up with people talking behind her back for too long.

"No!" she said out loud. *Too* loud. She could feel Michael's grip tighten around her waist, but she paid no attention. "I'm sorry, but you are totally out of line—"

"Hold on," Michael began, but she pulled away from him.

"I don't know who you think you are," she went on, taking a step closer to Troy. She felt a rush of vertigo and knew she was losing it. But she couldn't stop. "I don't know why you think you can just come up here and say these terrible things about Liam. I'm sorry about what happened to Phoebe. I think she's the sweetest girl in the world, but this"—she waved the photos under Troy's nose—"is *not* our doing. It's *not* our fault. And you're *not* going to lay it on my son, do you hear me?"

"Stop it, Brook!" Michael said.

"No, let her rant," Troy said, nodding his head. He was smiling. "Let her foam at the mouth all she wants. Let her threaten me. It won't do any of you a damn bit of good. Because Liam here? Let me tell you: he fucked with the wrong person. And I don't care how rich you are or how much influence you think you might have—*nobody* assaults my daughter, leaves her black-and-blue, calls her a liar, and thinks for one minute that he's going to get away with it."

7

*S*till wiped out from the night before, Liam had gone to bed after dinner and was out the moment his head hit the pillow. He seemed to have dropped into the bottom of some endless well, when he felt his body jerk awake again for some reason.

"Liam!"

He sat up on one elbow and looked at the clock radio on his bedside table: nine thirty. He'd been asleep for less than an hour.

"Liam!" his father shouted.

Something was wrong. He knew every note and shading of his father's voice, and Michael Bostock didn't do anger. In fact, when he was most upset, his voice tended to flatten out and slow down. Things hadn't been right between them since the wedding, but Liam was still almost painfully alert to his dad's moods. He was able to discern levels of disapproval in Michael's slightest gesture. One sad shake of his dad's head was the equivalent to another father's reading the riot act. So the sudden urgency and lack of control he was hearing now set off alarm bells in Liam. Was the house on fire? He stumbled out of his bedroom and down the hall.

"Deny everything," his dad told him under his breath when they met at the top of the stairs.

"What?"

"Just do what I tell you," Michael said, stepping back to let Liam go in front of him. Phoebe's dad was standing in the front hallway, hands on his hips. He had one of those tough-guy stances, shorter than his dad by a couple of inches, but with the kind of bulk that meant business. Phoebe didn't talk about her home life much, though Liam knew her parents were divorced. He also knew that Troy Lansing and his own father didn't much like each other.

"You ever hit anyone?" Liam had asked Michael a couple of years back when they were on one of their camping trips. It was just the two of them. They'd hiked all day and had set up camp beside Half Moon Pond in the state forest south of Barnsbury. It was early May, the countryside just beginning to green out, the tree frogs keening across the mist-shrouded water. The question had been weighing on Liam's mind since February when he'd almost come to blows with Gavin Cooper, who was two years ahead of him at Deer Mountain. Liam had gotten used to kids giving him a hard time about being rich, but this thing with Gavin was meaner and more immediate than that. Liam had joined the ice hockey team that winter and had quickly shown his mettle as a defensive wing, managing to confuse Gavin and throw him off-balance a couple of times during pickup games, sending the older, stronger but far less agile center sprawling.

"You fucking with me?"

"No," Liam had told him. "You just keep getting in my way."

"You want to see me get in your way? Try pulling that again."

The opportunity presented itself a week or two later, and this time Gavin, from his prone position, whacked him across his shin guards so hard that Liam slid on his back across the rink. The school's assistant coach, who was reffing the game, threw Gavin off the ice.

"I got my eye on you, Cooper," the coach said. "I see that kind of behavior again and you can kiss varsity good-bye for the rest of the season."

The two boys kept their distance after that, but Liam knew it wasn't over. He could feel the anticipation humming through his body, like a low simmer, just waiting for the right moment to boil over, arms flailing, the taste of blood in his mouth.

"Why?" Michael had asked him. "You got someone in mind you want to hit?" Liam had told him the details of his escalating problems with Gavin. His dad didn't say anything for a while. He just poked at the fire, his expression difficult to read in the leaping shadows.

"Don't do it," he said finally, looking over at Liam. "Once you start fighting, it begins to feel like it's the solution to every-thing. It's okay to *want* to hit someone—like this asshole Gavin Cooper. Just never get yourself in a position where you *need* to. You ever feel that way, you come to me first, okay?"

"Yeah, okay," Liam had told him, delighted that his dad had used "asshole" with him like it was nothing. Like they were men. He'd listened to Michael's advice, too, and steered clear of Gavin for the rest of that semester. And he'd been rewarded when, a couple of days before school got out, he'd over-heard his former nemesis tell another varsity player in the locker room:

"That Bostock kid's crazy, but he's not afraid of anything."

It had been a big win for Liam. A rare triumph in Liam's otherwise fairly miserable career at Deer Mountain. The high point, actually. Looking back, Liam decided it was because he'd managed to channel his dad's spirit for a little while. He'd somehow been able to assume Michael's laid-back self-assurance as if it were his own. The feeling hadn't lasted long, but for a month or two he was able to pretend that he'd finally vanquished the dark thing in the pit of his being.

"What's going on?" Liam's mother asked, coming out of the kitchen just as he and Michael reached the bottom of the stairs. He didn't need to be told he was looking at trouble. His father's "Liam!" still rang in his ears. The air was charged with tension, though Phoebe's dad just stood there glaring at him. It was Michael himself who finally kicked the supports out from under Liam.

"Something happened here last night. Apparently there was some drinking. Apparently Phoebe had something to drink. And she was . . . assaulted."

The idea of Phoebe being attacked was bad enough. But then to hear that she said *he* had done it—that was totally insane. It wasn't the worst part, though. No, that came when he recalled what his dad had told him at the top of the stairs:

"Deny everything."

That meant his own father assumed Liam was capable of doing something this awful. It meant that, despite everything he claimed, Michael actually thought even less of Liam than he did of himself.

❧

"I want the truth," Michael said after Troy had gone. Liam was sitting across from his parents at the kitchen table.

"I didn't touch Phoebe," Liam replied, looking at his mom. "I promise." He was too hurt and shocked to look his dad in the face.

"Did you hear me?" his dad asked. "I want to know what happened in this house last night. From the beginning. Exactly what time did you get back here with those boys?"

"I don't know, *exactly*," Liam said. Self-loathing twisted in his stomach—along with a new kind of fear. If his dad believed he was that fucked-up, then maybe he really was. Maybe this wasn't a phase, like his counselor at Moorehouse had assured him. Something everybody went through. Maybe it was always going to be this way and he was going to be nothing but a loser for the rest of his life. "I don't know. We were drinking."

"You were already drinking on the drive up from school?" his mother asked.

"Yeah. In the car. And here. Brandon and me. And then Phoebe."

"Oh, Liam!" his mom said. "Why?"

"Listen," Michael interrupted. "Right now we need to talk about what happened last night. Liam, I want to make sure I understand: you're telling me that you gave Phoebe something to drink?"

"Brandon did."

"This is *your* home. What happens here is *your* responsibility."

"Okay, then," Liam replied. "I gave Phoebe Lansing something to drink. I gave her some Johnnie Walker Red. I handed the bottle to her and said, 'Heeeeere's Johnnie!' "

Liam still wasn't meeting his father's eye, but he could feel Michael staring at him from across the table. Though it felt more like his dad was actually miles away—and Liam a little speck on the horizon.

"And then what happened?"

"I don't really remember all that much. We were sitting around drinking. Brandon and Phoebe were together on the couch. I think he was like maybe kissing her a little."

"And you just sat there?" Brook asked.

"Where was Carey in all this?" Michael asked.

"He was around somewhere. We were all kind of out of it."

"And that's all you remember?" his dad asked. "Nothing else about Phoebe? This sweater that was torn in half? Her getting sick?"

"No," Liam replied. But as soon as he said it, he suddenly recalled—distant as an argument in another room—the sound of Brandon shouting and Phoebe crying. But the memory faded away before he was even sure where it was coming from.

"That's not good enough," Michael said. "Right now all we really have to go on is Phoebe's word against yours. You need to call Carey and Brandon and get to the bottom of this. *Now.*"

Liam didn't have Brandon's cell number or his e-mail address. In fact, until the drive up from Moorehouse the night before, Liam hadn't said a single word to Brandon, who, as a senior and a Moorehouse luminary, moved in circles that seemed as far away as constellations. As soon as he got back up to his room, he texted Carey: *Nd to talk to Brandon ASAP*. When he didn't hear back right away, he called Carey's cell and left a message.

"Something bad went down here last night with Phoebe and Brandon. I really have to talk to him. *Soon*, man. Please have him get back to me, okay?" He left his cell number again, though he knew Carey already had it. Then he texted him again just in case his roommate missed his first text.

He was too upset to sit still, so he practiced chords on his Fender acoustic, his free knee bouncing off-rhythm, his eyes fixed on his iPhone. His fingers shook. His mind was a mess. It was like he was trying to put together some enormous jigsaw puzzle and half the pieces were missing.

It had to have been Brandon who attacked Phoebe. Of course it had been Brandon. He remembered them sitting together on the couch. Liam closed his eyes and saw Brandon's left hand between Phoebe's thighs, his right moving beneath her sweater.

But she's a fucking tease, man, Brandon had told him that morning. *I was like this close.* Close to what? Raping her? What else could he have been bragging about? Then Liam found himself recalling the conversation he'd had with Brandon on the way up in the car. He was already flying high on the OxyContin-whiskey cocktail, pumped with a sudden, dizzying sense of invincibility. A part of it was the way Brandon had treated him. Like he really enjoyed hanging out with him. Like he knew he could share dope with Liam and count on him to be cool about it. Like he assumed Liam had done it for real, not just alone in his bed.

So she really puts out, huh? Brandon had asked.

Oh, yeah, Liam had told him.

A dumb lie! A stupid lie! Liam berated himself as he thought back on how he'd blown up his relationship with Phoebe to Brandon. The way he'd sacrificed her with hardly a second thought to get in good with Carey's older brother. And then, as though the puzzle pieces were falling from the sky on top of his head—but as heavy and hurtful as bricks—he remembered Brandon cursing at Phoebe and telling her:

What's the big deal anyway? Liam told me you've been putting out for him since seventh grade.

And then the look on Phoebe's face as she ran, hunched over and crying, holding her sweater bunched up around her waist, into the night.

The opening chords to "American Idiot" had Liam diving for his phone.

"Hey, man," Brandon said. "I hear you want to talk. What's up?"

"Phoebe's dad was here, claiming she was, like, assaulted last night." Some instinct kept Liam from saying whom Troy had accused of attacking her.

"That's kind of harsh," Brandon said. "I hope you pointed out that she was all over me."

"No," Liam said. "I did not. You don't know her dad. He's a total maniac. I didn't feel like having my head bashed in."

"Right," Brandon said, laughing a little. "Understood. But, come on! I didn't even get to close the deal. And she just about neutered me! I've been wearing my balls in a sling all day. So what am I supposed to do? Send her a bouquet from 1-800-Flowers?"

"This isn't a joke," Liam said. "This guy is really pissed off—and I don't know what's going to happen." But something was taking shape in Liam's mind. It was still too vague to call it a plan. "He said he wasn't going to let you get away with this. He wanted your number."

"Fuck, no!"

"Don't worry—I didn't give it to him."

"Listen, you have *got* to keep me out of this."

"You should have thought about that last night. Phoebe's dad said her sweater was ripped in half. He has photos of her with bruises all over her body. I'm not sure what he's going to do, but I don't think he's about to let things ride. Phoebe's uncle is the chief of police up here."

"Oh, no," Brandon said. "*Fuck*, no! I can't get messed up in anything like this right now. I just got into Brown. I worked my fucking *ass* off to get accepted—and my folks are totally thrilled. And, honestly, Bostock? I wouldn't have put the moves on her if you didn't green-light things for me."

"Yeah," Liam said. He felt queasy now that Brandon was reacting pretty much the way he had hoped. Calling him "Bostock" was a sure sign that Brandon understood just how much he needed Liam's help. How much Brandon would be in Liam's debt. For a second or two, Liam felt disgusted with himself all over again. The older boy was right—in some ways this was just as much Liam's fault as Brandon's. Just as much Liam's doing. So why shouldn't he just go ahead and take the blame? He'd only make matters worse for himself by telling the truth. He didn't want to even think about how Brandon would turn on him back at Moorehouse if Liam told anyone what really happened. He'd be merciless, Liam knew. But it wasn't the prospect of Brandon's wrath that made Liam decide what he did.

It was his father's "deny everything." Like, of course, he'd fucked up. Obviously, his dad had already decided what happened before he even asked Liam for an explanation. What bullshit! Hurt and shame pulsed through Liam. Well, he would show his dad what it was like to feel totally humiliated. To question where the hell you went wrong. To wonder how you could have let someone you loved so much . . . down so badly.

"Yeah, okay. I hear what you're saying," Liam told Brandon. "Don't worry. I think I know what to do."

8

Wanda drove Phoebe up to the emergency room in Harringdale, where, after an hour-long wait, they met with a middle-aged woman doctor who inspected Phoebe's bruises and then, at Wanda's request, performed a vaginal examination. Removing her gloves, the doctor looked from Phoebe to Wanda and asked:

"What happened? These are very nasty contusions and lacerations. Your daughter wasn't raped, but everything indicates she was sexually assaulted. If that's the case, we should alert the police."

"No!" Phoebe said. "Like I told my parents. A boy I know just got a little rough, that's all. Please, I'm fine. I want to go home."

"You're sure she wasn't violated?" Wanda asked.

"Yes, I'm quite sure, but I have a feeling she was very lucky. I'm going to ask that you talk to our social worker. And then I think you should seriously consider contacting the police."

"Mom, please, can't we just leave now?" Phoebe asked. "I don't feel well."

"I'm sorry, but you'll have to be interviewed by the social worker first," the doctor said firmly. "I'll go get her now. And I urge you to think about the next girl who runs into this friend of yours."

The interview didn't take long. Phoebe answered the mostly yes or no questions and once again downplayed her recent trauma, repeatedly saying that she just wanted to go home.

On the way back to Barnsbury, Wanda tried to get her daughter to open up a little.

"You've known Liam for so long," she said sympathetically. "You've been such good friends. You must be really hurt by what he did. But you should think hard about what the doctor said. It's not right for anybody—even people you really care about—to be abusive."

Wanda didn't need to add that she should know, though the pain Troy inflicted was strictly emotional. Phoebe's father had a quick temper, but he'd never laid a hand on either one of them.

"Yeah, I know," Phoebe said, closing her eyes and letting her head drop back against the seat rest. "But there's no way I want Uncle Fred or anyone else for that matter to hear about this, okay? I'm just so embarrassed."

"I'm really sorry, honey. It's a hard thing to have to learn, but a lot of men—and boys—can't be trusted."

But not trusting and no longer loving were too different things, and Phoebe was already regretting her lie about Liam. Yes, he'd hurt her—more than anyone else she'd ever known. But that's because she loved him more than anyone else. She'd spent endless hours daydreaming about him, making up in-volved scenarios between the two of them in which an idealized Liam would tell her how lovely she looked, how much she meant to him, how lucky he was to have her in his life. And when Liam actually started to talk to her last summer—and she got to know the sweet, confused, flesh-and-blood boy behind her fantasies—her feelings for him crystallized into something far more real and powerful. Something that now lay in ruins around her.

She lay awake for a long time that night thinking about what she had done and what she had lost.

⁓

Phoebe didn't know how word got out. It couldn't have been her mom. Wanda understood her daughter just wanted the whole thing to go away. More likely it was her dad. She was aware he'd gone up to the Bostocks' and had given them a piece of his mind. She was actually glad he'd gotten so mad. Impressed by the way he'd stood up for her. She knew he loved her more than just about anything. That's why she assumed he would realize that she didn't want the whole town talking about what she'd been through. Having everyone know she'd allowed herself to get drunk and be assaulted was the most humiliating thing she could possibly think of. That's exactly how she felt when she got the first text.

OMG! Just hrd. R U okay?

It was from Lacey Ripley, Phoebe's best friend for most of her life, who lived three blocks away in a house that was almost a carbon copy of the Lansings'. Lacey's parents were divorced, too. Both girls were only children, being raised by their moms. Having so much in common gave them the moral support they needed to navigate the social rapids of Deer Mountain High

School. They were also both somewhere in the middle of the popularity spectrum. Pretty but not knockouts (Lacey's complexion wasn't great), and too shy and uncertain to make it to the table in the far right corner of the cafeteria, that enviable epicenter of tenth-grade social life, where only the most popular kids were welcome.

They weren't in the same homeroom, but they sat together at lunch, during chorus and gym, and on the bus to and from school. And when they weren't together physically, they were texting or on Facebook. In fact, though they lived almost within shouting distance, they often texted more than they talked. So it had been easy enough for Phoebe to keep Lacey at arm's length for a full thirty-six hours after Phoebe's entire world fell apart, texting that she had come down with something and had to stay in bed for a day or two.

Only Lacey knew that Phoebe had loved Liam Bostock for just about forever. Only Lacey was aware of the fact that Liam and Phoebe had become really close last summer after he got in trouble. Only she realized just how eagerly Phoebe had been looking forward to his homecoming at Christmas. She even knew that Phoebe had borrowed her mother's sweater to look her best when Liam arrived back from Moorehouse. Staring down at Lacey's text message, Phoebe realized that lying about Liam meant lying to her best friend, too. Did she really want to keep this up?

Now the phone vibrated in her hand. She took a deep breath.

"Hey, Lace," she said.

"You're there! Why didn't you call me! Oh, my God, Phoebe! I can't believe what happened! And *Liam*—I can't believe that it would be Liam of all people!"

"How did you find out?"

"Tina Hibbert. Everybody's talking about it."

"What did Tina tell you?"

"That Liam put something in your drink—like one of those date rape drugs—and then attacked you. But you kicked him in the balls and got away in time."

"Oh, God."

"Are you okay? Do you want me to come over? My mom was wondering if we should maybe bring you guys a casserole or something."

"You do that when somebody dies," Phoebe said. "I'm still alive as far as I know."

"I just wanted to tell you how proud I am of you. That's what Tina thinks, too. Your bravery is awesome."

"Well, I don't feel brave, just really sick still. I will never, ever touch alcohol again. And, just so you know, Liam didn't spike my drink, Lace. I don't know where that came from."

"But he did try to, like . . . ?"

Lacey let the question trail off. Phoebe tried to figure out how to answer her. As far as she could remember, Phoebe had never kept anything important from her best friend. They knew each other's families and houses as well as they knew their own. Phoebe had lived at the Ripleys' for almost a month when her grandma died and her mom had to move her grandpa into a retirement community. The two girls shared every awful step of the divorces that tore each family apart. Phoebe made Lacey sleep in bed with her the night Lacey's father, just back from his second tour in Afghanistan, had threatened Lacey's mom with a gun. But the most precious thing Phoebe had ever shared with Lacey was her love for Liam. And, as of last summer, what Phoebe revealed of his love for her.

"So, like, you guys just talk and talk?" Lacey had asked when Phoebe told her about the nights she'd sneak out to meet Liam behind the old elementary school. "Doesn't he ever try to kiss you or anything?"

"No, he hasn't yet," Phoebe had had to admit. "I wish he would, though. I keep hoping he will." Lacey knew that, despite their growing emotional closeness, Liam and Phoebe had continued to keep their physical distance over the course of the summer. And Lacey was aware how much Phoebe was counting on that changing the night Liam came home for the holidays.

"It was that sweater, I bet," Lacey said when Phoebe didn't reply right away. "I think the problem was that he kept his passion like all bottled up inside for too long—and then when he saw how totally amazing you looked, he just couldn't help himself. Are you really bruised, though?"

"Yeah," Phoebe said, liking the idea that she'd driven Liam Bostock mad with desire. The fact that it was Brandon who'd actually attacked her was beginning to seem less important now. She was also buoyed by people thinking she was brave. Tina Hibbert was a year ahead of Phoebe and Lacey in school and a star forward on the volleyball team. Phoebe was surprised and pleased to learn that Tina even knew she existed. Suddenly the idea that everyone was talking about her seemed less horrible than she'd first imagined.

Phoebe's Facebook page soon filled with posts of outrage and support, and she received a dozen or so text messages along the same lines. It was Christmas break, which meant everyone had time to text and chat and voice their opinions. Phoebe was being praised for keeping her head and fighting back. The news that she'd *kicked him in the balls!* got a lot of play, as did the allegation that Liam had given Phoebe the date rape drug.

Liam was now remembered as that rich kid who thought he was so hot. A couple of girls who'd never actually spoken to Liam when he was still at Deer Mountain claimed he'd come on aggressively to them, too. Though up until that point, no one but Phoebe (and by extension Lacey) knew the circumstances behind Liam's transfer to Moorehouse his sophomore year, suddenly everyone was messaging about his "drinking problem."

Through all this, Phoebe kept thinking about Liam. Wondering what he was feeling. Why he didn't try to defend himself. Why didn't he just tell people Phoebe was lying? Apparently, he'd told her dad that he hadn't touched her, though Troy had said that he'd looked guilty as hell when he said it. She knew he was on Facebook. He had to be aware of the cruel things that were being written about him. But he wasn't responding to any of it. And his silence confused and troubled her.

Phoebe also worried about Mrs. Bostock. She, too, had made no effort to reach out to Phoebe. Usually at this time of year, Phoebe would be helping Brook at one or another local R.S.V.P. event, or putting in some extra hours up at the Bostocks'. She loved working for Brook, who was always so upbeat and kind to her, and it was really hard for her to have to face the possibility that she'd never step foot in that beautiful house again. Why should Brook let her? Considering what she'd accused Liam of doing, Brook probably despised her.

And Tilly! Dear, sweet, funny Tilly. Phoebe had lost her, too. She'd lost them all. The text messages kept coming in. She was beginning to think that it might be too late to change her story now.

"Well, I think you should tell her," Phoebe heard her mother say as Phoebe came down the stairs. Troy and Wanda were in the kitchen. Troy had bought a couple of Phoebe's favorite pizzas for dinner.

"Tell who what?" she asked. Her father was standing by the fridge, holding a freshly opened bottle of beer. He shook his head at Wanda before he took a swig.

"What's going on?" Phoebe asked, looking at her mom.

"Your father took it upon himself to contact your uncle Fred," Wanda said.

"Why do you have to say it like that?" Troy said. "I'm looking after my family. I'm thinking about the best interests of my little girl."

"I know you *think* you are," Wanda replied. "But would you be so eager to move on this if you didn't know that Brook Pendleton was loaded? You're looking after your own best interests, too. Admit it."

"Will someone please tell me what you're talking about?" Phoebe said.

"Okay," Troy said. "I went in and told the police chief of this town what happened on his watch. And I've been talking to a lawyer I know about the case."

"The *case*?" Phoebe said. "You mean a legal case? Against Liam? I keep telling you, Daddy, he didn't rape me. He didn't give me that date rape drug. I don't know who started that rumor!"

Troy set his beer down on the counter and folded his arms on his chest. In a firm, modulated tone, he said, "You were attacked, Phoebe. You were *this close* to being violated. You're still all black-and-blue. And I think you're still in shock. Or in denial. You do realize that what that boy did to you was *wrong*, don't you?"

Phoebe looked at the kitchen floor. She nodded.

"Okay," Troy said. "So I did what any normal parent would do. I went to the police and gave them a heads-up."

"This means your father is pressing charges," Wanda said. "It means that your uncle Fred and his deputies are going to have to investigate what happened, collect evidence, probably interview you and Liam and those other boys."

The words *investigate* and *interview* shook Phoebe. The truth was going to come out. Liam would certainly speak up now. She remembered Brandon's body grinding into hers, his fingers pressing on her neck. His pug nose, the smell of his breath. The idea of having to face him again made her feel faint. It was better to let it all go. Take it all back.

"No," she said. "It wasn't really so bad, I promise. It wasn't like you said, Daddy. Liam only—"

"You see, Troy?" Phoebe's mom cut in. "She doesn't want to relive any of this. And I don't blame her."

"That's because you're too damned soft, Wanda!" Troy shot back. "You let everyone walk all over you and never make a peep. Well, I'm sorry, but someone in this family has to take a stand. I'm sick and tired of people like us being given the shaft. How in the world could you think it's better to let something this bad go—to just sweep it under the rug? That's why this country is going down the tubes so fast. We're all too damn afraid to stand up for what's right. No one's going to keep me from talking truth to power."

"Well, last time I checked this wasn't about you," Wanda said. "It's about Phoebe, okay? And she wants to put this *behind* her. She just wants to get on with her life."

"Please don't do it, Daddy," Phoebe said.

"And let me remind you, Troy," Wanda went on, "that you are no longer my husband. You don't have the right to decide anymore what we're going to do."

"God—the two of you!" Troy said, throwing up his hands. "I don't get it. You've seen your daughter victimized, Wanda! And you, sunshine, you've been treated like dirt. Like something it's okay to just kick around. Well, it's *not* okay! I don't know how you can stomach it. I can't. And I won't. As far as I know, Wanda, Phoebe is *legally* still my daughter. My underage, innocent daughter. And I hate to have to tell you this, but I don't really need your permission to do what's right."

Part Two

9

"You're sure it's okay for me to go?" Brook asked again. It was two o'clock in the afternoon, the day after Christmas, and Michael was driving his wife down to Wassaic to catch the train to New York for a big R.S.V.P. event that evening. The fund-raiser at Cipriani in Midtown had been in the works for months, and Alice, who was better behind the scenes than out front, had sounded slightly hysterical when Brook implied that problems at home might keep her from being there.

"Yes, I'm sure," Michael said, glancing over at his wife. She seemed calm and composed, but he knew how alarmed she really was about what was going on with Liam. It would probably do her good to get away for even this brief period of time. She was planning on taking the train back later that evening, and Michael would be picking her up at the station. Brook didn't like driving alone at night.

Christmas had not been a joyous occasion at the Bostocks'. Liam was still unable to come up with a credible account of what had happened with Phoebe. The night of Troy's visit, Michael had waited up for his son to get through to his friends, sending a reluctant Brook up to bed at midnight. Around one thirty in the morning, Liam had come back downstairs and reported to his father, "They both say they don't remember anything. Brandon says he passed out. Carey was already asleep."

"This is bullshit!" Michael said. Without Brook in the room, he felt no compunction about speaking his mind to his son. "You're just blowing smoke in my face and you know it."

"Sorry, Dad," Liam replied. "You told me to deny everything. Maybe that's what Brandon's father told him to do, too."

"I told you that so you wouldn't give Troy any more ammunition. And that's what you should tell anybody else who asks. But I'm your father, and I deserve the truth. Now look me in the eye and tell me what really happened."

It wasn't until Liam met his gaze that Michael felt afraid. His son's face was emotionless, almost vacant, as if Liam had somehow managed to shed his inner self—and left this shell of a boy behind in his place.

"I don't remember," Liam said. "Sorry."

"Listen," Michael said, "you're too young for this. Drinking like this. Passing out. We've talked about it before. It's dangerous, Liam. Some people, they just can't drink. Can't handle it. At your age—or any age."

"Yeah, Dad."

Nothing much had changed in the three days since. They'd grounded Liam, though Michael got the sense his son didn't much care. When Tilly wasn't badgering him to play Star Wars Wii games or Brook wasn't insisting that he join them for meals, Liam stayed in his room. On Christmas Day, he'd made a small effort to seem engaged, unloading his stocking with the rest of the family and helping to take apart the mountain of presents Brook had assembled under the tree. Michael suspected the gesture was primarily for Tilly's benefit. His daughter, who had been heartsick when Liam left for Moorehouse, had been following him around like a lost puppy since his return.

With Liam's refusal to divulge facts, there was nothing much that Brook and Michael could do but sit and wait and hope for the best. Troy talked tough, but it seemed to Michael that he preferred nursing a grudge to actually acting on it. They'd both let what had happened between them sink into the past. *Let this go, too,* Michael mentally begged Troy. *We all make mistakes. Just let it go.* Brook wanted to call Phoebe, to commiserate and try to get her side of the story, but Michael advised her against it.

"It could make matters worse. I think it's better to keep a distance and pray this just blows over."

Every day, Michael braced himself for the other shoe to drop, but so far they'd heard nothing further from the Lansings. And when Michael drove into town for the papers and mail, everything seemed normal, the town hushed under the half foot of snow that had fallen on Christmas Eve.

After leaving Brook at the station, Michael decided to take the longer, scenic route home again. It was a bit foolhardy, as some of the back roads were not well plowed, but he needed the time alone—away from the house and his studio—to try to get some perspective on what had happened. Or might have. When Troy first confronted him with his accusations, he'd dismissed the idea out of hand.

"It had to have been one of the other boys," Michael had told him. The two men were standing outside Michael's studio, snow falling around them.

"Phoebe said it was Liam," Troy told him. "My daughter doesn't lie."

"Liam would never hurt her. He's a good kid."

"Yeah?" Troy replied. "Well, so were you, if I remember right."

Yes, everyone had liked Michael when he was Liam's age. He'd been thoughtful and soft-spoken. Maybe a little shy. Until he had something to drink, that is, which was something only Troy knew about him. Then nice Michael Bostock turned into someone else. Someone you'd hardly recognize. Someone Michael himself couldn't recall the next day.

That was the hellish part. Blacking out. Not knowing what you'd done or where or to whom. And that was what Michael dreaded had happened with Liam. That his son wasn't lying when he said he couldn't remember. That, drunk, he could have turned physically aggressive. He could have attacked Phoebe. Like father, like son. That's what Troy was thinking, Michael knew.

Together, Michael and Brook had talked to Liam about drinking and its consequences. Michael had also spoken to his son on his own. Trying to explain how some people were more susceptible than others. How sometimes alcoholism could be passed down through the generations.

"We never really talked about it in my family," Michael told him. "And I think your grandma's still in denial about it, but your grandfather was a really heavy drinker. Especially those last years. I think he died too young because of it. It can be a killer."

"Is that why you never drink?"

"Sure," Michael said. "It's one of the reasons." But not the real one. That he'd long ago decided to keep to himself. He'd stopped drinking at the age of sixteen before anyone but Troy realized he'd even started. He'd stopped cold. Stopped forever. And left behind the pathetic fuckup he had been. Someone he hated even now to acknowledge. As he came of age and everyone around him started drinking socially, he said alcohol gave him a headache. He almost came to believe it himself. By the time he met Brook, not drinking seemed like such a natural part of who he was, so organic to his nature, he decided she didn't have to know the truth. Besides, he had changed so fundamentally from that sixteen-year-old self, it was almost as though he had never existed.

But as Michael drove through the quickly darkening afternoon, he felt that boy's presence again. As if he were sitting beside him in the front seat of the pickup. That confused and angry boy. That boy who had never wanted to be anything like his father and yet, like in some kind of B-movie horror film, was turning into him right before his eyes. And he'd been so alone, so powerless to fight back!

For the first time in many years, he felt another presence, too. He remembered the unrestrained girlish laughter. The big grin with the crooked front teeth. The way she had of bumping up against him, finding any excuse to touch. Just as he once had to push her physically away, he now tried to force her out of his thoughts. But she lingered anyway, as she used to do, following in the shadows of the boy he used to be.

⁓

The police cruiser sat in front of the house, engine running, exhaust pluming into the frigid air. Michael parked his pickup by the garage and walked over to the driver's side of the cop car. The window came down.

"Hey, Mike," Fred Henderson said. "Your daughter said

you'd be back soon. I thought it would be best if I waited for you out here." Fred had been two years ahead of Michael in school and they'd run in different crowds, but Michael had always liked the older boy. It seemed to Michael that, even as a teen, Fred subscribed to a kind of patriotism and sense of honor that were rare these days. When Fred became Barnsbury's police chief, Michael made a point of telling him that he thought the town was lucky to have him.

"Do you want to come in?" Michael asked. There was no point in pretending Michael didn't know why Fred was there.

Fred rolled the window back up, turned the engine off, and hoisted himself out the cruiser. He had a clipboard with him. Though the Bostocks used the kitchen entrance, Michael led Fred up the front walkway, which was lined with snow-covered shrubs. Brook had decorated the potted evergreen topiaries flanking the entranceway with tiny white Christmas tree bulbs. A wreath of twined holly and mistletoe hung on the front door. Michael realized that he was hoping to send a message to Fred by coming in this way: *What a well-run household. Just look at these orderly, festive surroundings!* Too late, Michael remembered that it was only a dozen yards from here that Fred had found Liam last summer, passed out on the lawn. He tried to put that memory behind him, but he couldn't help but think that Fred was recalling the incident, too.

"I decided to wait until after Christmas to do this," Fred said when they'd gotten indoors.

"Thanks," Michael replied. "I appreciate that." For a moment he thought that Fred might be on his side. He recalled some crack Fred had made a couple of years back about Troy. But then Michael remembered who Phoebe was to the man standing in front of him.

"I just have to ask," Michael said. "Isn't there a conflict of interest here, considering Phoebe is your niece?"

"I ran it by the DA," Fred told him. "Preliminary questioning? I'm cleared. If the case goes any further, then he'll reevaluate. But, Mike, just so you know? My job is to remain unbiased. What I'm doing here is just gathering information. The DA's office makes the judgment calls. Okay?"

"Okay," Michael said, but he was rattled to learn that the district attorney's office was already even marginally involved.

"I'd like to talk to you alone first," Fred went on. "Then maybe you could ask Liam to join us. Your daughter said he was upstairs?"

"Yes," Michael said. "He's spent most of the holiday so far in his room. It's been a tough time for all of us. We're sorry about Phoebe. But—I have to be straight with you—I'm sure Liam wasn't responsible for what happened."

"I'm just here to get the facts," Fred replied, glancing around the spacious foyer with its cathedral ceiling and wrought-iron chandelier. It occurred to Michael that Fred had never been inside the house before; his professional call that past June could hardly be considered a social occasion. After the first couple of years in Barnsbury, Brook had stopped trying to have people from town up to the place. He and Brook had never managed to click with any of the local couples their own age. The people he'd grown up with treated him differently after he'd married her. Which was their problem, Michael had long ago decided.

Fred took a seat on the sofa opposite Michael's wing chair. He placed the clipboard on his lap, pulled out a pen, and began to ask Michael about the night Phoebe was assaulted. Michael patiently answered his questions. Why they had gone down to

Rhinebeck. What time they had left. How they'd hired Phoebe to babysit until Liam got back. Whether they were aware that their son was bringing two friends from Moorehouse up with him.

"Do you often leave your children alone in the house overnight?" Fred asked him then.

"No," Michael said, suddenly wary. "This was a rare exception." And it was. He and Brook had discussed it a couple of weeks ago and decided that Liam, going on sixteen, should be able to hold the fort for the few nighttime hours they wouldn't be there.

"Tell me about these friends of Liam's," Fred continued. "Their names. Where they live. Do you know their parents?"

It was because he was nervous, Michael knew, but he couldn't remember Brandon and Carey's last name. He'd never even spoken to their parents. He wasn't quite sure, but he believed they lived near Rochester.

"Do you let Liam drink in your presence?"

"Absolutely not! Brook only drinks socially, and I don't drink at all. What happened last summer, that was a misunderstanding. The hired catering staff didn't realize that Liam wasn't of age, and Brook and I were so busy—"

"But you usually keep alcohol in the house?" Fred interrupted him.

"Yes."

"You don't lock it up when you're not here?"

"No. I trust my kids."

"Even though Liam got into trouble with alcohol before this?"

There it was. Though a part of him had been bracing for this, he still didn't know how best to respond. Did he look as unnerved as he felt? Who else in Barnsbury besides Fred knew about Liam's drinking at the wedding? Was it something that he was obliged to share with the DA? The Pendletons had closed ranks after it had happened. Peg and Janice had told Brook and Michael to advise Liam not to talk about it to *anyone*, as the news could hurt his chances of getting into Moorehouse. Despite what Michael knew were their misgivings about his son, both of Brook's half sisters had mailed glowing letters of recommendation to the admissions office. That was how it was done, Michael told himself. You protected your own.

"It was a family occasion," Michael said. "And, like I said, an unfortunate mistake."

"And how was Phoebe supposed to get home that night?" Fred asked, once again throwing Michael off. He had no idea. Brook took care of the household details. Surely she'd worked out some sort of arrangement with Phoebe's mom. He hesitated. His mind had gone blank. Christ, he'd grown up with the woman! He could picture her so clearly. He was sure it must be obvious to Fred that Michael couldn't recall his sister's first name.

"I'm not sure, but I think Phoebe's mom was supposed to pick her up when she called."

Fred nodded, and made some notes.

"When you got back the next morning," he went on, "did everything seem normal to you?"

Sure, if normal meant a son shrugging off your embrace when you hadn't seen him for a month. Or the feeling that he couldn't wait to get out of your sight.

"Yes, as far as I remember. Everything was fine. The boys were up. Eating breakfast. They'd made pancakes. Brandon and Carey left for home soon after that."

"Okay," Fred said, looking down at his notes. He lifted a page briefly to check on something he'd written. "Could I talk to your son now?"

◦❧◦

Liam must have known who was there—and why. He came down right away, dressed in jeans and a flannel shirt that he'd actually tucked in. He'd even combed his hair. Michael felt a wave of relief. Liam understood how he had to present himself. What he needed to say. They were going to get through this.

Fred stood up. Liam walked over and shook his hand.

"I have a few questions for you about what happened the other night," Fred told him. "Your answers will be for the record. So I need you to take your time and try to remember everything as accurately as you can."

"I understand," Liam said, sitting in the chair Michael had vacated. Michael stood behind him, his hand resting lightly on the seat back.

It began routinely enough. Names and ages of his friends? When had they left Moorehouse? Had they stopped along the way? What time had they arrived at the house?

"I don't remember," Liam said.

"Approximately?" Fred asked.

"I was flying pretty high by then, so it's really hard for me to say."

Michael's heart stopped.

"You were what?" Fred asked.

"I'd started drinking in the car, so by the time we—"

"Shut up," Michael said.

"I was just trying to be accurate like—"

"Do not say another word, goddamn it!"

Fred Henderson looked down at his clipboard.

"Did you assault Phoebe Lansing?" he asked.

"He's not answering that!" Michael replied. The room swam. Ironically, he felt drunk, unable to make sense of his physical surroundings. "He's not answering another question."

"I'm not sure. As I said we were all pretty—," Liam began.

"No," Michael said, gripping his son's shoulder. "No, he did *not*."

But Liam talked right over him. "I was drunk. We gave Phoebe something to drink, too. We were all pretty wasted. Everything's a big blur. I *guess* it could have been me—it could have been any of us, honestly. I'm really not sure—but I *am* really sorry Phoebe got hurt. Please tell her that for me, okay?"

10

$\mathscr{B}$rook's reflection stared back at her from the train window, reduced to its basic components: halo of hair, oval face, eyes and mouth roughed in like a child's drawing. Beyond, through the hollows formed by her features, she glimpsed the nightscape flowing past: house lights, a jagged tree line, a long pale swath of frozen field. The car had emptied out after White Plains. Except for a young couple, asleep several rows ahead of her on the right, she was alone. When she'd first boarded the train, she had tried briefly to type up her critique of the Literacy International dinner on her laptop. But her mind kept wandering. As it had all evening. As it had been doing since Troy Lansing stormed out of her house.

He'd slammed the front door behind him when he left, and it seemed as though she could still feel the reverberations. For the last several days, she'd been exhausted and on edge. Troy's lies about Liam had entered her bloodstream like a virus. Her body ached with helplessness. She was someone who liked to get things done, to *act*, but there was nothing she could do to remedy this situation. She realized now that she shouldn't have stood up to Troy the way she had. She shouldn't have provoked him. She'd only made matters worse.

"I'm sorry," she'd told Michael as they waited downstairs for Liam to get through to Carey and Brandon. "But it makes me so mad to think Troy can just go around saying anything he wants."

"Phoebe told him it was Liam. I'm not defending him, but it was Phoebe who started this."

"Right, yes—I know. But why? I don't understand it. Why would she want to hurt Liam like that? And us?"

"It's the drinking that really worries me. I don't think they can do much with an attempted-rape claim, but Liam getting drunk again? If that gets back to Moorehouse, he's in real trouble."

"Oh, God, I hadn't thought of that." It surprised her how quickly Michael had processed what had happened and was already considering the consequences. Brook remained stuck on the event itself. She went around and around with it. The impossibility of Liam hurting anyone, but especially Phoebe. The shock of finding out she didn't really know Phoebe Lansing at all. For years, Brook had thought of the girl as almost another member of the family. She'd felt such a strong kinship with her—along with genuine affection. She'd secretly considered helping out with Phoebe's college education when the time came.

So her lies felt like such a betrayal! Perhaps Phoebe had always resented her, the way so many people in Barnsbury seemed to do. All this time when Brook had been so free and easy in Phoebe's company, flattering herself that the young girl looked up to her, maybe Phoebe was actually plotting how to get back at Brook for whatever wrong she imagined she'd done her. Was it simply a matter of her attitude? After Michael had pointed out that she could sometimes sound superior, she'd tried to lose the slightly plummy inflections left over from her upbringing, but she was only patchily successful. When excited, or under stress, she could hear her mother's fluting drawl escape unwanted from her lips.

Or was it something deeper and more insidious that kept her from forming any real connections in Barnsbury? She'd been blaming the close-minded town all these years, but perhaps it really was her fault. If someone as sweet and straightforward as Phoebe actually disliked her, there had to be a good reason. She stared out the train window, turning the possibilities over in her mind.

"You're such a Pollyanna!" the librarian at the Brearley School had told her when she was in the sixth grade there. Though Brook had never heard the term before, the librarian's tone was slightly mocking. When she asked her father what being a Pollyanna meant, he said, "Oh, it was a character in an old children's book who was always very optimistic and cheerful. It means you tend to see only the good in people."

Or tried to. More like *willed* herself to. Because she existed in the shadows for too long after her mother died. And her father, all these years later, still languished there. So, yes, she'd started to make a concerted effort to keep on the sunny side. Stay positive. And, gradually, that came to be part of her nature. It became her way of fighting back the dark. And taking a stand against the self-doubts that had troubled her for so long. Though nobody guessed how hard she had to work at it. *You're such a Pollyanna!* Maybe that's how people in Barnsbury, struggling through years of bad times, saw her. A smiley face.

Troy's slammed door reopened all these childhood insecu-rities. As well as the nagging question about Michael. The one that had first flared with Alice's little aside before Christmas and had been simmering in the back of her mind ever since. Had he ever truly fallen in love with her? Or had he been drawn instead to the Pendleton name, the promise of wealth and security and a life beyond anything a small-town boy could dream of? It was so unlike Michael to be seduced by money, and he often seemed to resent her family's influence, but Brook was also aware that her husband could tamp down his true feelings. There were parts of him that she knew he still kept hidden from her. Some-thing lurked behind his gaze at times—something she caught only glimpses of—that he didn't want her to see.

But Liam was her main worry. It was the one she woke up to each morning and lay awake with each night. Often, just when she'd finally managed to drift off to sleep, she'd wake up again so rigid with anger that she'd have to sit up in bed. Her son was already struggling with so many problems, Phoebe's accusation seemed particularly cruel. What would make Phoebe lie about Liam like that? She remembered what it was like to have people whisper behind her back. The shame and loneliness. The sen-sation of being isolated from the rest of the world, adrift and alone. That's how Liam felt now, she knew. She could read it in his blank look, in the closed-off, defensive way he moved through the house. She longed to reach out and draw him to her. But she knew if she tried, he'd only pull further away.

⁓

"There you are!" Michael said, taking her in his arms when he got out of his pickup to greet her at the station. It was late and cold, the parking lot slick with ice, but when she rested her cheek momentarily against the rough wool of her husband's winter jacket, her spirits lifted. She'd allowed herself to get ridiculously morose. Which wasn't going to do Liam or any of them a damn bit of good. She mentally squared her shoulders, and felt her equilibrium begin to return. Okay. That was better.

"Yes, here I am," she said, climbing up into the cab of the pickup.

"So, how did it go?" Michael asked, once they were on the highway. It was nearly midnight and the road was empty. The town of Dover Plains had closed down for the night.

"It was sleeting in the city, so we ended up starting half an hour late. And we never did catch up. I had to leave Alice to deal with the stragglers and the caterer or I would have missed the train."

"Good turnout?"

"Considering the weather, yes," Brook said, pleased that he'd asked. As the years went by and both of their businesses had grown, they tended to share fewer of the day-to-day details. In the beginning, he could name every event on R.S.V.P.'s roster and where and when it was being held. Now, with so many other things taking up their time and energy, their professional lives tended to get short shrift. She doubted Michael even knew who her client was that night, but it didn't matter. She was touched that he was showing an interest.

"Are you going to make your numbers?"

"We're on target at least," Brook said, thinking what a relief it was to talk to him about something other than the situation with Liam. She knew that he, too, had been worried sick about their son. The change of subject—and mood—was probably calculated on his part, but it was a good idea. She was grateful that he'd thought of it.

"You know Bank of America came in as a corporate sponsor at the last minute," Brook went on. She used to enjoy sharing this sort of shoptalk with him. She could feel herself beginning to finally relax. "That should put us over the goal."

"And Alice behaved?"

"More or less," Brook said. "She only referred to the board chair as the Dragon Lady once the entire evening. Though I'm afraid it might have been within earshot."

Michael laughed briefly, and they both fell silent. He'd turned the heat on full blast, and it was warm in the cab. Brook let her head fall back against the seat rest as she replayed the evening through in her mind. It was a good thing she'd been there. Alice was adept at the administrative side of their venture: watching budgets, managing databases and timelines, bargaining for the best terms and deals, and scouting new venues. But customer relations? Not so much. She tended to get defensive and brusque—and sometimes downright snappish—around R.S.V.P.'s more entitled clientele. When it came to the social milieu behind events such as Literacy International, Brook was the main liaison. She'd been raised in that world. Even after her divorce, Tilda Pendleton had been one of the city's most admired hostesses. And Brook, too, was naturally skilled at calming frayed nerves, soothing bruised egos, and generally making nice when the mood turned a little tense.

"So you'll have to go down for the postmortem?" Michael asked, startling Brook out of her reverie. She assumed they'd finished their conversation.

"We might be able to make it a conference call," Brook said, weighing the options. After every event, R.S.V.P. held a follow-up consultation with the client. This allowed Brook and Alice to evaluate how things had gone—finessing any missteps—and make suggestions for improvements in the future, helping to assure that there would be one.

As she let her thoughts work through the logistics, it began to occur to her that it was odd for Michael to be asking so many questions. This late at night. When they were both so tired. Something else was going on. She glanced over at him and felt her heart sink. His hands gripped the wheel. His mouth was set in a way she recognized all too well.

"How did the rest of your day go?" she asked, hoping she was wrong. But she already knew that she wasn't.

"Why didn't you tell me this right away?" she asked, pouncing on the easiest question. Her mind couldn't seem to focus on the real import of what he'd just told her. It loomed ahead of her in the dark, impossibly large and unscalable.

"I'm not sure," he said, looking across at her. "No, I am— I just wanted us to have a few minutes together. Before ruining everything."

"You realize, of course, that he knows perfectly well he didn't do it."

"Well, he claims he doesn't remember."

"He's covering up for one of them. Carey or Brandon." Brook tried to make sense of this latest development. How Fred Henderson had come to the house to ask questions. How Liam had suddenly confessed to getting drunk and had acknowledged that one of them had assaulted Phoebe. But why didn't Liam just come right out and say it wasn't him? Didn't he realize what a dangerous game he was playing?

"I asked him after Fred left," Michael told her. "Point-blank. He insists he doesn't remember a thing."

"I don't believe that, do you?" Brook said, turning to Michael. "We've got to find out which brother it was—we've got to figure out why Liam's doing this! It's crazy! What's he thinking?"

"I don't know, Brook," Michael said. "But no matter how crazy it is, how wrongheaded, that's where this stands."

"Oh, God."

"I decided we needed some legal advice. I put in a call to Larry McCarthy's office."

"Larry?" He was a high school buddy of Michael's who had a small practice in Harringdale. He was a contract lawyer. Handling real estate transactions. Business incorporations. He'd helped set up the legal framework for Michael Bostock Fine Wood Designs. Brook used him from time to time to look over local R.S.V.P. event paperwork. Larry was a nice guy. He coached his daughter's Little League team. You couldn't sit down in his office without him delivering some lame joke. The idea of turning to him for something so serious frightened her.

"I trust him," Michael said. He must have heard the doubt in her voice. "And we need someone we can really trust. Who's totally on our side. He's making some calls. He's going to get back to me tomorrow with some ideas. But he said not to worry. Liam's underage. He thinks it's mainly going to be a matter of damage control."

She tried to stay calm. She tried to listen to what Michael was saying. That Larry assured him everything would be okay. But then another part of her demanded, *What does* he *know?* Some one-man law office in the middle of nowhere? It was what Peg and Janice would ask. And she knew exactly what they would say: *Take charge of the situation! Get some top-*

notch legal guidance. NOW! She tried to fight down the voices in her head.

"I think we maybe need someone with more clout," she said carefully. Peg's husband, Stafford, was a partner at a big white-shoe law firm. He seemed to know everyone in the legal profession. "Let me call Staff tomorrow. You know he'll be able to refer us to—"

"Do you really want to go there?" Michael asked.

"You said we needed advice. Shouldn't we try to get the best?"

"Bringing in some high-powered New York lawyer is just going to raise everyone's hackles."

"You think?"

"Yes. We want to keep this low-key. We need to just find some way to quietly get Liam off the hook."

Brook hoped Michael was right. Because the last thing she wanted to do was run to her sisters for help again. Though Brook knew they'd willingly give it—and more. She'd already made a mess of things, as far as Peg and Janice were concerned. What pleasure they'd take swooping down with their opinions and connections and cleaning up after their hapless little sister! No, she'd worked too hard and for too long to gain her independence from them to cave in like that now. And she had to ask herself if Liam would be in this kind of trouble if she and Michael hadn't already done her sisters' bidding. If they hadn't sent him to Moorehouse, where he'd been forced to seek out new friends, one of whom was clearly a brute and a bully.

"Okay," she said, touching his arm. "Let's see what Larry says."

"Good," he told her, reaching over to take her hand. "Thank you, sweetie. We're going to get through this."

Though Michael called Larry's office the next day and the day after, the lawyer didn't get back to them until the afternoon of New Year's Eve. When the call came through, Michael said, "Hold on. I want Brook to hear this, too. I'm going to run upstairs and get on the other phone."

"Hey, Larry," Brook said, taking the receiver from Michael. "Hope you're having a better holiday than we are."

"Yeah," he said. "I'm sorry about all this. And I apologize for the delay. I've been back and forth with the DA's office, trying to get a handle on what's going on."

"I'm ready now," Michael said from the upstairs extension.

"Okay, here's the deal," Larry said. "It's actually kind of complicated. I've had to do a lot of reading up on this. Have you ever heard of something called the Social Host Liability law?"

"No," Michael said.

"I haven't either," Brook added.

"Well, frankly, I hadn't myself until these last few days. But it's a law that was enacted several years ago that holds parents legally and financially responsible if minors are found to be drinking on their property—and something bad happens."

"But we weren't even here," Brook said. "We had no idea what was going on, or of course we would have stopped it."

"Yes," Larry said, "I know, but that doesn't get you off the hook, I'm afraid. In fact, the DA's office is considering your absence a real factor in what happened. Especially in light of Liam's record with alcohol abuse."

"Record?" Brook asked, but she already guessed what Larry was going to say. She bowed her head, waiting for the blow.

"Yeah, some incident at your house last summer? During a wedding? According to someone who was interviewed, it was the reason Liam was sent away to prep school in Connecticut. So the assumption is you guys took it pretty seriously. Is that more or less correct?"

"Yes," Michael replied. "That's more or less right. So what happens now? Are we actually going to be charged with this thing?"

"Well, apparently that's what the DA's considering," Larry said. "There'll be a hearing with a magistrate in district court. Liam could be charged with attempted rape. And the two of you with this Social Host Liability thing. I'll be here for you, but you're going to need a criminal lawyer, too. One who really knows his way around the court system. I've been calling around, and I'll get back to you on that."

"This is kind of hard to take in," Michael said.

"I'm afraid that's not all. Troy Lansing has hired a Boston lawyer to pursue a civil action against you. This is a firm that's handled a number of cases like this before. One resulted in a pretty big settlement, I'm afraid. One hundred and fifty thousand dollars."

"Great," Michael said. "So that's what this is really about! Christ, I should have known! He's going to drag Liam through the dirt—and us along with him—just so he can get his hands on Brook's goddamned money."

11

Liam stared down at his iPhone, debating. He could hear the television in his parents' bedroom roaring with the crowds in Times Square. In another minute the New Year would begin. His parents had been arguing on and off all evening, but he could no longer hear their voices above the television. *Ten . . . nine . . . eight . . . seven . . .*

Quickly, before he could change his mind again, he thumbed the message to Phoebe:

> Sorry, sorry, sorry! Can we talk, pls? R old place? Hppy nu yr!

He sat back against the pillows, exhaling, clutching the phone. He knew that he had no right to hope she would message back. He had no reason to believe that he'd ever get to see her again. But he desperately needed to talk to someone. No, he needed to talk to *her*. Despite everything that had happened—all the lies and threats and accusations—Phoebe was still the only person in the world Liam could open his heart to. And he had to let her know that things had gone too far.

✧

"What's up?" Liam had asked Tilly that afternoon. He could hear his parents arguing in the kitchen while his sister hovered outside the swinging door in the dining room, her skinny arms hugging her chest. Tilly had to be aware that Liam had gotten into trouble again—and that it somehow involved Phoebe, who was no longer coming to the house. But Tilly pretended, to Liam at least, that everything was fine. They'd started a Ping-Pong tournament in the gym downstairs, and though she probably suspected he was throwing the games, she was clearly delighted when she ended up winning every other match. It broke his heart to see how grateful she was just to hang out with him. How hard she worked at getting him to laugh. She was the only one in his life at the moment who seemed not to realize—or care—that he was a total screwup.

"I don't know," Tilly said, shaking her head. "It's something Mr. McCarthy told them."

"What?" Liam asked, leaning his ear against the door. He could just barely make out what his parents were saying:

". . . why not just *talk* to him . . . explain how wrong-headed . . ."

". . . beyond that point now . . . Boston lawyer . . ."

". . . if you'd made more of an effort in the beginning . . ."

"I don't think it would have changed anything."

". . . but that's the real problem, isn't it?" Liam's mother's voice had turned strident. "You just can't get past this *thing* you have against him—"

Liam glanced over at Tilly and saw his sister's eyes filling with tears. Unable to stop himself, he pushed through into the kitchen.

"What's going on?" he said. His parents were standing about five feet apart, just outside his mom's work alcove. Brook was still gripping the phone receiver in her hand.

"It looks like we're facing criminal charges," Michael said evenly. "You're being accused of attempted rape, Liam. And your mother and me for allowing underage drinking in the house. I know, I know," he went on when Liam started to object. "We weren't here. We didn't know about it. But apparently we're still responsible for what happened."

"That's—just—" Liam was about to say "bullshit," but at the last second he changed it to "—bogus! This has nothing to do with the two of you."

"Yeah, well, the law sees it a little differently," Michael replied, running his hands through his hair. His face looked gray. The overhead lighting accentuated the lines bracketing his mouth and eyes.

"Let me talk to them," Liam went on. "Just tell me who to talk to!"

"No!" Michael told him. "You've already said enough. We're going to handle it. But, Christ, what a mess! Do you have any idea what a rape conviction would do to your future?"

"Listen," Brook said, turning to face him. "If you want to help, if you really want to help us—then be honest about what happened. I don't care what you said before. It doesn't matter to me that you changed your story. Now's the time, Liam, to tell us the truth. Before this thing goes one step further."

Liam looked from Brook to Michael.

"Your mom's right," Michael said, nodding his head. "These charges are deadly serious. It's not just about Phoebe anymore. And who did what to her. It's about everything that happened here that night. So let's at least use this opportunity to clear your name."

Liam felt his resolve start to waver. Hadn't he already given his dad enough to worry about without forcing him to believe that his son was a total prick in the bargain?

"Tilly?" Brook said, starting across the kitchen. "I think it's time for your bath, sweetie. Let's go upstairs, okay?"

"All right," Michael said once they heard Tilly and Brook on the steps. He went over and sat down at the round oak table, pulling out the chair next to him. When Liam was seated, Michael leaned in toward him, elbows on his knees, and said, "I've been thinking. All you have to do is recant the part of your statement about Phoebe. Say that you remember enough to know you didn't touch her. Go back to your first approach."

"My first approach?" Liam asked.

"Yes," Michael said. "When Troy was here, remember? You just flat-out denied it. That worked."

"Glad you thought so," Liam said, his heart hardening again. What was the point of reneging on Brandon and telling the truth, when his father would think it was all a lie anyway?

He must have drifted off, but the tremor of the cell phone in his hand jolted him upright. It was Phoebe:

OK. In I hr. But tl NO ONE!!!!

Liam loved being outside in the dark. Even on a night as cold and cloud-covered as this one, he felt his spirits rise as the frigid air hit his lungs. He slowly made his way down the slope of the roof, stopping when he reached the eaves above the garage, and looked out over the pale whitewashed world below. The snow-covered fields. The rickrack of evergreens running along the edge of the stream. And, beyond that, the mountains, swelling one behind the other like incoming waves, where he'd spent the happiest days of his life.

He was only seven the first time he and his dad had gone camping. It was the summer they moved up to Barnsbury, leaving behind a sweltering city still recovering from the 9/11 attacks the year before. His parents had enrolled him in Deer Mountain Elementary School for the fall, but he'd yet to discover he wouldn't be welcomed there. His new life in this new place still seemed full of promise. And a big part of that was exploring the Bostocks' sprawling property and the surrounding hills and fields. He hadn't spent much time outside the city before then, and he loved the sense of freedom and adventure the countryside gave him.

He built a fort made from fallen tree branches in the woods up behind his dad's studio. He spent hours watching the deer and foxes, the rabbits and wild turkeys, whose world he was slowly coming to know. He learned how to move through the underbrush as stealthily as an Indian scout. But it wasn't until his dad took him on an overnight hike into the state forest southwest of Barnsbury that he finally understood what it was that he'd been discovering about himself that summer.

They'd hiked all day, ending up on a limestone outcropping near the top of the highest mountain in the range. It had a ledge that jutted over the valley, giving a spectacular view of the whole region. Liam's father told him that he used to come up here when he was a kid, sleeping in the narrow caves that cut into the mountainside. He showed Liam where he'd carved his initials into the rock face. After their campfire dinner, Michael told Liam a story about an Indian maiden who, thinking mistakenly that she'd been abandoned by her white lover, leapt to her death from that very ridge. Liam's father fell silent for a while, watching the dying fire. Then he stood up and—without warning—howled into the darkness.

"Come on," his dad had told him. "Let your animal out." Liam had scrambled up to stand beside his dad, and together they'd howled for several long, thrilling minutes. Their voices had echoed and echoed into the night. How fearless and alive he'd felt! And he came to believe that, like his father, he had something fierce and untamable inside of him, something fighting to escape, that found an answering call in the restless night woods. Later that night, after they'd climbed into their sleeping bags, Liam said, "This is the best time I've ever had in my whole life."

It was a twenty-minute walk from his house to the little playground behind the old elementary school that had become Liam and Phoebe's meeting place. Liam knew the way like the back of his hand. How many nights had they met there last summer? Fifteen? Twenty? Soon after his cousin's wedding, he'd managed to overtake Phoebe one evening as she walked home from working for Liam's mom. It was near the playground where they used to play as kids, and on impulse he'd asked, "Want to go for a swing?"

He'd felt momentarily elated as he sailed up and back beside her, but there was something else that he was after. Some other impulse, unrealized until a little later, that drew him to his sweet-natured childhood friend. She was a great listener. Sitting beside her that first night as he poured his story out to her, he could feel her empathy and concern reaching to him across the dark. And, once he had her ear, once he sensed that she wouldn't judge him, he found himself telling her things that he'd barely been able to admit to himself. Night after night, he confided his unhappiness and fears. How he knew he'd never live up to his father's expectations. How lonely and adrift he often felt. How drinking and smoking dope helped him forget about his problems, but never for very long. How every once in a while, when he felt overwhelmed by despair, he thought about ending it all.

"You have to promise me you'll never do that," Phoebe had told him.

"I can't promise that."

"Then we have to make a pact that if you ever get to that point for real, you'll call me first, okay? You'll call me from wherever you are and give me the chance to talk you out of it."

He'd agreed to that, though he'd been embarrassed when she'd actually made him hold up his hand and promise. But it had helped him in the end. The pact had given him a kind of fallback plan, a safety net. During the bad times, when he was at his most vulnerable, he was able to imagine Phoebe standing there, blocking his way like some kind of guardian angel. But now, as he saw Phoebe waiting for him on the old cement bench, huddled into herself against the cold, it came to him that he'd probably lost not just her friendship but this one last stay against his own destructive impulses.

"Hey, there," she said, standing up as he approached, her breath coming out in quick white puffs.

"Phebe," he replied, digging his hands into the pockets of his North Face jacket. "Happy New Year?"

"Right," she said. He wasn't sure if she was being sarcastic. If so, it would be unlike her. It seemed to Liam that she always said exactly what she meant. It was one of the things that he admired about her, he realized now. One of the many things.

"So, I'm sort of freezing here," she went on, rocking back and forth in her worn imitation Uggs. "What's up?"

"I wanted to say I'm sorry," he began, just as he'd rehearsed all night, but he found himself losing his nerve in Phoebe's actual presence. With her standing right there he felt the full weight of what *she* had actually gone through. How hurt and humiliated she must have felt. He remembered the awful photographs that her father had shoved into his mother's face. And Liam had as good as told Brandon to go for it! "I'm really, really sorry about what happened."

"You know what I keep wondering?" Phoebe asked.

"No. Tell me."

"I keep wondering if you even *know* what happened. I mean, do you even remember?"

"Sort of," he said. "But not like totally."

"Okay, let me help you out a little, then. How about this? Your friend Brandon tried to rape me. And you just sat there—and watched."

"No!" Liam said. "I did *not* watch. I was *out* of it. I remember only bits and pieces. I was like blind drunk, Phebe. Really wasted. I don't remember him hurting you. Not really. It's hard to explain. It was weird. Like a dream."

"No," Phoebe said. "It was a nightmare."

"Right. Yeah, I know. I'm sorry. I'm really sorry."

"And there's something else I keep wondering."

"Yes?"

"Why you're covering up for Brandon. Why you're letting me get away with this. These things I've been saying about you.

The terrible things everyone's been saying. I mean, this whole thing is such a—"

"Yeah, I know," Liam said, reaching out and touching her hair with his glove. When she started to cry, he pulled her into his arms. She sobbed so hard that her shoulders shook. Her breathing was ragged with tears. He held her tight against him, until she finally seemed to cry herself out, laying her check against the front of his tearstained parka.

"Don't look at me!" she said as she tried to use her mitten to wipe her nose. "I always look terrible when I cry."

"I don't care," he said, kissing the top of her woolen cap. It was the most wonderful sensation holding her like this! He could feel her warmth through their layers of clothes, the soft pressure of her breasts against his chest. He trailed his lips down her cheek, searching for her mouth, but she turned her face away.

"No!" she said. "I look horrible. I'm covered with snot."

"Oh, Phebe," he laughed. "Who cares? Come on," he said, taking her hand. "Let's sit on the bench."

He put his arm around her after they sat down, and she rested her head against his shoulder. He took her mittened hand in his gloved one and squeezed it.

"Better now?"

"Yeah," she said. He was careful not to glance at her, but he could hear the smile in her voice. It made him light-headed to feel so good after being down for so long. Everything seemed possible again. He just needed to be honest with her. To lay it on the line.

"You blamed me because you wanted to get back at me," he said. "You thought I didn't care. That I didn't care what Brandon did to you. Right?"

"Yes," she said softly. "It seemed like he thought it was okay to do anything. Like he thought I was some kind of *slut* or something."

"I'm sorry. He's one of those guys who takes what he wants. Who's just used to getting his way all the time, you know?"

"So? Is he like making you *lie* for him?" Phoebe said, turning to Liam. Even in the dark he could see that her eyes were red-rimmed, her lips puffy. He fought back the urge to kiss her. He needed to stay focused. They had to sort this out.

"No, I decided to do that on my own," Liam said. "It's kind of complicated. But now—Phebe—what's happening now is just crazy, don't you think?"

"You mean about what my dad's doing?"

"Yeah, this lawsuit! Against my parents. They had nothing to do with any of this. It's just wrong to go after them—you know that. It's just not fair."

"There's a lot that's not fair," she said.

"Yeah, but come on! You know what this is really about."

"Do I?"

"It's about my mom's money, of course. Why else would anyone want to blame my folks?"

She pulled away before he knew what was happening.

"I should have known!" she said, getting up from the bench. "Man oh man, I never seem to learn. I'm such an idiot. You know what? I'm just an absolute total idiot when it comes to Liam Bostock!"

"Hey! Hold on!" Liam said when she started to walk away. "Where are you going? What's happening here?" He ran after her when she didn't turn around, and grabbed her wrist.

"Don't touch me!" she said, jerking her arm free. "I know

what you're trying to do. I know what you're thinking: 'Give fat, stupid Phoebe a kiss or two, and she'll do anything I want.'"

"That's not—"

"Well, I'm not a pushover anymore," she went on. "I've learned the hard way. I won't be manipulated. I won't be treated like some—"

"Where's this coming from, Phebe?" Liam asked. "What did I do?"

"Don't *Phebe* me anymore, Liam. My name is Phoebe, okay? And my father is planning to sue your parents because I was *brutalized* in your house. I was made to feel like shit! And you know the worst part of it? It wasn't actually when your friend Brandon tried to force his stupid dick into me. It was when he said, 'What's the big deal? Liam told me you've been putting out for him since seventh grade.'"

"Phe—"

"Tell me that's a lie, too. But you can't, can you? I know just by looking you in the face. I know because I know you better than you know yourself sometimes. And it's sad. It's really, really sad. Because the fact is I used to love you so bad it hurt. And now I don't love you anymore, but it *still* hurts. Worse than ever."

12

*P*hoebe didn't want to go to the hearing, but her dad kept at her.

"You won't have to say a word," he told her. "But your being there will send a message to the magistrate and the Bostocks and their lawyers. You'll be putting a face on the crime—and that's important."

"Where are you getting all this from?" Wanda asked. "You're sounding more and more like some lawyer yourself these days."

"I'm not ashamed to admit that Cranston and Cranston has been giving me advice," Troy said, referring to the Boston law firm he'd hired to pursue civil charges against Liam and his parents. "And I refuse to apologize for trying to make sure that justice is done here."

"Whatever," Wanda said. "You do what you need to do. But I'm not going to let you talk Phoebe into going to this thing against her will."

As Troy's words sank in, though, Phoebe began to seriously consider what her father was saying. How her presence in the courtroom would make it clear that she was the innocent victim—and that she wasn't afraid to stand up for herself. Phoebe's fight with Liam on New Year's was still raw and painful, something she tried hard to keep bandaged away in the back of her mind. But it kept cycling through her thoughts anyway. How Liam had made it sound like this whole thing was just her dad's attempt to get his hands on the Bostocks' money. How what Brandon had done to her—what Liam had *let* him do—was nothing. How her pain and suffering didn't even count. She began to picture herself walking into the courtroom and everyone turning to look at her—admiring her courage and the new Forever 21 jacket her dad had bought her at the mall.

❧

With its wide granite steps and Federal-style pillars, the Harringdale district courthouse looked imposing, even majestic, and Phoebe felt goose bumps rise on her arms as she and her dad walked across the domed rotunda, their footsteps echoing on the inlaid marble floor. She'd been given the day off from school and was beginning to feel nervously excited about what lay ahead. But the courtroom where the "show cause" hearing with the magistrate was to be held turned out to be a disappointment. Phoebe imagined it would be like the one she'd seen in old *Law & Order* episodes: a sunlit, spacious chamber with murals on the walls, a witness box, and an impressively elevated bench for the judge.

Instead, the room that Troy and Phoebe were directed to had a dropped soundproof ceiling and was lit by recessed energy-saving LED grids. The paneled walls had a prefab look, as did the nondescript raised desk in the front of the room, which was flanked by tired-looking flags. Two tables faced the desk, each with three ordinary office chairs, one of which was occupied by the familiar bulk of Phoebe's uncle Fred. Five wooden pews behind the tables were divided by a center aisle. Scattered in the first couple of rows were half a dozen people Phoebe didn't recognize, including a man who turned as they entered and walked toward them with his right hand out-stretched.

"Troy," he said, clapping Phoebe's dad on the shoulder as he reached them. He was a tall, fit fiftysomething, dressed in a charcoal gray suit.

"This is Henry Cranston," Troy said, giving Phoebe a little nudge. "Go ahead and shake his hand. He won't bite."

"And you must be Phoebe. We've heard a lot of great things about you from your dad." His grip was firm and dry. She could feel him sizing her up.

"Hi," she said, suddenly shy. She saw herself through Henry Cranston's eyes. The new white leather fringed jacket that fit her snugly, the black tights and short denim skirt. The curly red hair that, despite the clips, she could do little to control. She'd dressed herself up when, she realized, she probably should have toned herself down. Her dad didn't know any better, but she guessed that if her mom hadn't left for work before Troy picked her up, she would have sent her daughter back upstairs to change into something less revealing.

"Your dad told us that you didn't want to be here today," the lawyer went on in a confiding voice. He had a tan, leathery face that crinkled around the eyes as he smiled at her. "I really appreciate that you changed your mind and overcame your concerns."

"Thanks," Phoebe said, feeling better. "But I don't have to say anything, right?"

"No, you don't. And because you're underage, your name won't be mentioned. A 'show cause' hearing is just what it sounds like. The police present all the evidence they've gathered to the district magistrate and he or she decides if it seems like enough to go ahead with the cases—the attempted-rape case against Liam and the Social Host Liability charges against his parents. Do you understand what all that means?"

"Pretty much," Phoebe said. "My dad's been kind of coaching me."

"Great," Cranston said, turning his smile on Troy. "Why don't you two come sit with us? I brought two associates with me. We're in the third row back. But, wait—there's something I want you to know."

"What's that?" Troy said.

"While doing a little preliminary legwork, we learned that Chief Henderson is Phoebe's uncle. I'm sure you would have mentioned this, Troy, if you realized it was a problem. Because it's a major conflict in our book. I took Henderson aside earlier and suggested that someone else on his team present the evidence. I pointed out that it could look prejudicial if he did it. And negatively impact not just these proceedings, but our efforts with the civil suit. Believe me, the Bostocks' lawyers are going to try to do everything they can to get these cases thrown out of court before they even get started. And the chief's relationship to Phoebe is one big red flag."

"Right," Troy said, nodding. "Of course. You did the right thing."

But Phoebe wasn't so sure her uncle agreed. As she took her seat between her dad and Cranston, she noticed that Uncle

Fred was sitting ramrod straight, his back to them, his neck flushed a deep red. She knew from conversations she'd overheard between her uncle and her mom how much time and effort he'd put into the investigation.

"We appreciate all your hard work," Wanda had told her brother when he dropped by the house the day before to wish Phoebe luck.

"Hey, it's my niece we're talking about here," he said. Phoebe was aware how protective her uncle was of her mom and her, especially since the divorce. She knew he took pride in keeping an eye out for them, cruising past the house whenever he was out on patrol.

More people filed into the room from its back entrance and from a side door. An older, gray-haired woman with round horn-rimmed glasses entered from the side and sat down behind the raised desk.

"We lucked out," Cranston said, leaning over Phoebe to whisper to Troy. "The magistrate's a grandmother and, from what we learned, super tough on crime."

Phoebe caught her breath as Liam and his parents walked up the aisle right past her to the front row. They shook hands with two men who were waiting for them there. It was the first time that Phoebe had seen Liam in a jacket and tie. He'd recently had a haircut, and his ears stuck out in a boyish way. Her heart ached as she watched him take his seat between his parents.

Phoebe only half listened to the proceedings. It began with a lot of legal mumbo jumbo she didn't understand. Dates and dockets and blah blah blah. She couldn't help but wonder what Liam was thinking. How he was feeling. He must have spotted her as he came into the room, but he didn't turn around or even glance her way. It was as if he were already a prisoner. Cut off from her and the rest of the world. He looked so alone and vulnerable. She hated that she couldn't let herself love him anymore. It hurt too much to think about that for very long. So she tried instead to concentrate on Uncle Fred's young male deputy, who was delivering the report to the magistrate. He seemed uncomfortable in his unexpected public role, stumbling over his words.

". . . establish evidence of a pattern of parental negligence . . . underage drinking on the premises the night of the wedding both by the accused and at least three other invited guests . . . the accused so intoxicated he had to be carried into the house by his father . . ."

It was Phoebe who had told her uncle that Liam's transfer from Deer Mountain to Moorehouse had been the result of his passing out at his cousin's wedding. At the time it had seemed to Phoebe like a harmless enough piece of information, but now she heard it turned into another black mark against the Bostocks:

". . . concerned enough about his behavior to remove him from the local high school he'd been attending and send him to a private prep school in Connecticut. It was from there that he returned home the night in question with two prep school friends. The Bostocks were aware that the boys would be staying overnight without adult supervision. They had invited them, even as they themselves planned to be at another house party over fifty miles away. They had asked the victim to babysit for them, knowing that the three boys would be arriving later that evening to a house equipped with an unlocked liquor cabinet and wine cellar in the basement. The boys, who had already been drinking in the car on the way up from Connecticut, continued the party at the Bostocks' residence. The victim, alone in the house with her charge asleep upstairs, was coerced into drinking with them. . . ."

The deputy walked up to the magistrate's desk and handed her a sheaf of papers.

"These are printouts of photos the victim's father took the day after the incident. As you can see, there is heavy bruising on her neck and arms and stomach area. . . ."

Phoebe closed her eyes, remembering. Brandon's braying laugh. His body pinning her down. His tongue exploring her mouth. The taste of whiskey on his breath that would later make her so sick. That memory alone almost made her gag. She leaned forward, bowing her head.

"Are you okay?" her dad whispered.

"Phoebe? Do you need some air?" Henry Cranston asked, his concerned voice carrying across the courtroom.

The magistrate stood up, raising her hand to silence the deputy, her gaze scanning the crowd until it rested on Henry Cranston, who had half risen from his seat as he leaned over Phoebe.

"Is there a problem?" she asked.

"I'm fine," Phoebe whispered, sitting up again, her face flushed with embarrassment. She hadn't meant to cause a disturbance, and she was upset that the lawyer had made such a big deal out of it.

"No, everything's okay," Cranston said. "And we apologize for the interruption." But the room's attention had, for the first time and at a critical moment, focused on Phoebe. She could see several people craning their necks to get a better look at her. That round-faced, redheaded teenage girl. Who else could she be but the unnamed, underage victim?

⁂

Martin Freston, the Bostocks' lawyer, seemed to be on good terms with the magistrate. They exchanged some private words before he took his turn addressing the courtroom.

"Before I begin," Freston said, "I need to go on record stating my concern that the police investigation into this incident was led by the victim's *uncle*. It's impossible not to believe his findings would be prejudicial, which I very much believe they are."

"Your concerns are duly noted," the magistrate said.

"Thank you," Freston replied. "Now, I'm sure we're all very sorry about what the victim went through. But we have to ask an important question: Can she substantiate her accusations? What do we actually know about what happened that night? A group of underage teenagers was drinking— and one of them got hurt. Not raped—but unfortunately roughed up.

"Yes, the photos are disturbing," Freston continued. "But I think we need to remember that everyone bruises differently and the victim is quite fair-skinned. I'm not in any way dismissing her suffering, but I do think it's important to try to put it in perspective. I go back to what we actually know about what happened that night. An underage girl was drinking with a group of underage boys—willingly, I need to add. The police claim she was coerced—which is, like so much else in that so-called 'report,' a biased opinion. No one *forced* alcohol down her throat. She was underage and she was drinking—so much so that she made herself sick. The boys involved claim they were too out of it to remember who did what to whom, though the victim has accused just one of the boys. As it happens, it's the one boy she knows well. In fact, a boy she knows very, very well."

Phoebe didn't like this man's tone of voice. She didn't like the snide way he said the word "victim" or the way he made it sound like she was some kind of a party girl. But her anger turned to alarm when he brought up her relationship to Liam.

"What are you implying?" the magistrate asked Freston.

"I interviewed the other two boys," Freston said. "One of them told me that it was well-known the victim and the accused had had sexual re—"

"Bullshit!" Phoebe's dad cried, jumping to his feet. "That's a damned lie! And I—"

"Quiet!" the magistrate cut in, pointing at Troy. "You will sit down immediately and not say another word or I'll have to ask you to leave this courtroom."

She then turned to Freston and said, "I thought you were making a point about what we actually know, but you've just introduced inflammatory hearsay of your own into the argument. I suggest that you, too, stick to the facts from now on."

"I'm very sorry," Freston replied, though he seemed anything but, as far as Phoebe was concerned. He then went on to detail the Bostocks' standing in the community. How deeply Michael's past was rooted in Barnsbury. How Brook came from a prestigious family whose philanthropic endeavors touched cultural institutions across New England.

"But, despite their wealth, the Bostocks lead a simple, quiet life. In fact, after 9/11 they decided to leave New York City and return to Mr. Bostock's hometown to raise their children in a less stressful and more nurturing environment. They are very loving and involved parents. They will be the first to tell you that they made a miscalculation when they decided not to be home on the night in question. But they did *nothing* to abet or encourage what took place under their roof. They were as shocked and upset as anyone to learn what happened to the victim. Laws are written to protect the innocent and punish the guilty, but in this case the Social Host Liability law is being turned against two caring, responsible people who made an error of judgment. What parent doesn't make some kind of error every day of the week?"

The magistrate motioned for the deputy and Freston to join her at the bench and, turning away from the microphone, conferred with them for several minutes. After directing the men to return to their seats, she leafed back and forth through the police statement and her pad of notes.

Phoebe's stomach ached. She knew it was Brandon who had repeated the lie about her to the Bostocks' lawyer. But the fact that it was Liam who'd started it made the blatant falsehood hurt even more. She leaned forward a little, trying to catch a glimpse of Liam, but her view was blocked by Mr. and Mrs. Bostock, who sat flanking their son.

"This is a disturbing and confusing case," the magistrate said, dropping her pen and looking up from the desk at last. "Clearly, a young girl has been abused physically—and no doubt emotionally, as well. But it is indeed one built primarily on hearsay, not facts. It seems impossible to determine with any degree of certainty which of the boys assaulted the victim. I strongly suggest that the Bostocks as well as the parents of the victim have very serious conversations with their teenagers about the dangers of underage drinking. I assume the Bostocks will learn from their mistakes and start to practice better parental oversight."

The magistrate looked down at the papers on her desk again, then back up at the courtroom, before adding:

"I'm dismissing the charges for lack of evidence."

13

❧

"*I* saw a notice in the post office this afternoon," Brook told Michael two days after the hearing. "Fred Henderson is holding a meeting tomorrow night at the town hall. It's on the dangers of underage drinking."

"I don't like the sound of that," Michael said. They were in the kitchen, getting dinner ready. Liam and Tilly were watching television in the music room. Brook had been so relieved when the charges were dropped that she refused to pay much attention to her husband's prediction that the ruling would only make matters worse with Troy.

Brook had her own misgivings about how the hearing had gone. When she'd asked Liam on the ride home from the courthouse about Freston's claim that Phoebe and Liam were involved sexually, he'd quickly denied it. But there was something about his answer that had unsettled her. His "No way!" had seemed overly vehement. She'd tried to press him, but he retreated into himself, and she decided to let it go. *Ease up on him,* she told herself. *He's just had the scare of his life!* She could be more forgiving now that she knew he was out of harm's way. And her relief was buoyed by the thought that this close call would finally motivate Liam to turn his life around.

"I think it's a good idea, actually," Brook said. "This is a great opportunity for people to air their concerns and get some professional advice about how to deal with a very serious problem."

"It's a great opportunity for Troy to bad-mouth us," Michael said flatly. "He's been going around town telling everyone that Liam only got off because we threw our weight around."

"Honestly, Michael!" Brook said, dropping the silverware in a noisy heap on the table. "Henderson's called the meeting, not Troy! And I'm getting fed up with the way you keep going on about Troy. The man has a right to be upset with us, okay? I feel terrible about what happened to Phoebe under *our* roof. I think I'd be saying some pretty nasty things, too, if Tilly had gone through something like that."

They'd been having more and more disagreements like this one. It seemed to Brook that most of their arguments arose from the fact that she was ready to put the incident behind them—and Michael wasn't. He was holding on to his anger in a way she'd never known him to do before. And the frustration he was feeling toward their son was an almost palpable presence in their home these days.

"God, you're so naive sometimes!" Michael told her.

"And you're so damned negative. We've been exonerated, for heaven's sake. I don't see why you don't try to reach out to Troy tomorrow night. Take him aside. Say that we really hope we can let bygones be—"

"I'm not going to that witch hunt and neither are you."

"I'm sorry?" Brook said. "Since when is it okay for you to

order me around? Of course I'm going. We've got nothing to be ashamed of. We've got nothing to hide. In fact, having gone through what we just did, I think we've got a responsibility to share what we've learned with other parents."

But Brook could tell by Michael's grim expression and the way he folded his arms across his chest that he was having none of it. God, he could be so pigheaded at times! If only he'd let down his defenses a little. Make an effort to bridge his differences with Troy. Why couldn't Michael see that he was giving up the chance to engage other parents in the town? It was the perfect forum for them to explain what had happened—and acknowledge that they'd made a mistake they now really regretted. And they needed to reach out to Troy in particular. They had to win him over! If Michael wasn't willing to help, then Brook would have to do it on her own.

⹋

She arrived late, and the parking lot outside the town hall offices was nearly full. As she walked around to the front entrance, Brook glimpsed Fred Henderson through the windows, standing behind a lectern. Rows of people faced him on metal folding chairs, while others stood along the side walls.

". . . and we were celebrating his seventy-fifth birthday," a woman in the third row was saying as Brook slipped into the back of the auditorium. "So, of course, my husband broke out the champagne for his dad. All the grandkids were there. We gave each of the teenagers a sip or two to toast him with. So what we did was illegal?"

"The short answer is *yes*," the chief responded. "Obviously no one got hurt at Dick's birthday celebration—so no harm done. Technically, though, if one of the teenage cousins had somehow managed to drink more than that sip or two and hurt himself or someone else? The parents could hold you liable. Knowing your family the way I do, Claire, I'm sure that would never happen. But the worst-case scenario is you could be sued for damages. And those are just the legal ramifications. That's not even addressing how drinking of any kind is harmful for teenagers—physically and mentally."

"I've got a twenty-year-old serving in Afghanistan," a man toward the back called out. "You telling me I can't give that soldier a beer when he comes home on leave?"

Brook heard someone in the crowd say, "Of course you can! That's ridiculous." But then the chief held up his hand and, reading from the clipboard he was holding, said:

"The law states that you cannot serve alcohol to persons under twenty-one years of age. Or allow them to consume alcohol in your home even if exceptions permit minors to consume alcohol in other places. Now, I know that as a parent you think, 'Hey, I've got the right to let my teenagers have a beer or two if I'm keeping an eye on things. They're in my house, right?' But what happens if, say, your kid—or a friend of his—has a beer or two or three, gets behind the wheel of his pickup, and plows into someone else's car? That's one of the reasons the state of Massachusetts tightened up the law to make parents responsible for whatever happens if minors drink in their home."

"It's a shame it takes a law to tell certain people how to parent," said a woman in the middle of the audience. Brook had seen her around town with a couple of school-age children, but she didn't know her name.

"Was that a question?" Fred asked. "Remember this is a Q and A, folks, okay? Please keep your opinions to yourself. Anyone else? Yes, Ted?"

"In this case, the parents weren't at home when things got out of hand," said a man standing against the wall near the front. Brook had only a partial view of him, but she thought she recognized the speaker as a fellow Deer Mountain parent. "I think it's kind of crazy to blame people for something that happened when they weren't even there."

"Yeah, but they knew these underage prep school kids would be spending the night," said the same mother who'd spoken up before. "What did they think was going to happen? I mean, honestly—"

"And that's really the point of the law," Henderson said. "To encourage you as parents to think about what might happen with your kids even if you aren't there. Maybe especially if you aren't there. If you know you're going to be held responsible for what goes on under your roof, then it's my guess you're going to lay down some stricter rules. And you're probably going to make sure you don't have kegs of beer lying around, right?"

Brook decided this was the moment to speak up. Stepping forward and raising her hand, she called out:

"Excuse me? Hi, everyone! I'm Brook Bostock. It was my son and his friends who were involved in this recent incident and—" Her words were drowned out for a moment by the noise of dozens of chairs squeaking on the hardwood floor as people turned in their seats. Brook recognized many of them— the librarian at Deer Mountain, a couple of women from her book group—but she was met with mostly curious stares.

"Go on, Mrs. Bostock," Henderson said.

"We actually have a very regulated home life," Brook began again, trying to remember how it was she'd intended to explain things. "And I want to make it clear that we're really very caring and involved parents. We don't allow or condone underage drinking, and we were just as upset as everyone else when we learned what happened in our house that night. And I just wanted to say that if we had to do it all over again, we would certainly—"

"Well, you don't get a redo on this one," Troy said. Brook hadn't seen him sitting in the front row next to Wanda, but he rose now and turned to face her across the suddenly hushed room.

"I understand that," Brook replied, determined to hold her ground. She wasn't going to let herself get into an argument. She was just going to explain and apologize. "It happened. And I'm sorry. *We're* sorry. That's really what I came here to say."

"You're *sorry*," Troy said, nodding. "You're sorry *it* happened. I'm just wondering what you mean by that."

"Troy," Wanda said, tugging on her ex-husband's sleeve. "Come on. This really isn't the place to—"

"No, I think it is," Troy replied. "I think we have the right to ask Mrs. Bostock what exactly she's sorry about. Is she sorry that she left our daughter alone in her house knowing three prep school boys were going to arrive later that night? Is she sorry she left Phoebe there without any adult supervision—"

"Okay, that's enough," Henderson interrupted, clapping his hand on Troy's shoulder. "It's time to let some of these other folks have the floor."

"Fine," Troy said, though he continued to stand there, staring back at Brook. "But I just want to add one last thing. As far as I'm concerned about you saying you're sorry? It's an insult."

"Sit *down*!" Wanda said, pulling on his arm until Troy reluctantly took his seat. Henderson opened up the floor again for further questions and the meeting went on, but it seemed to

Brook that her exchange with Troy had unsettled the genial atmosphere of the gathering.

"This has always been a good, caring community," said Devon Lowell, one of the town's selectmen, when no further hands were raised. He stood up in the second row and turned to face the crowd. "Understanding the law's important and all that, but I say let's try our best not to forget the values that've always made Barnsbury such a great place to raise a family."

"Okay, folks," Henderson added, as people started to get ready to leave. "Thanks for coming. I've got a handout up here that goes into more detail about some of the issues we covered. And a good article on how to talk to your teenager about drinking and drugs. Feel free to take extra copies and share them with your friends."

As Brook began to zip up her parka, a middle-aged woman who'd been standing near her in the back walked over and said, "Troy's known for holding a grudge. I'd just let what he said roll off your back, if I were you."

"Thanks, I'll try," Brook said, smiling as she tried to remember where she'd seen the familiar-looking woman before. "Weren't you a teacher's aide at Deer Mountain?"

"I still am," she said, holding out her hand. "Trish Blondel. I'm a friend of Wanda's, so I know what I'm talking about when it comes to Troy. And I thought it was great that you came tonight."

"Thanks again," Brook said as the two of them were separated by the press of the departing crowd. Several other people nodded at Brook or said hello as she made her way out the door and into the parking lot. But she also overheard a woman say, "When kids act like that, I'm sorry, but it's got to tell you something about the way they were raised."

It was another frigid night and most people hurried to their cars, but Brook took her time, going over the meeting in her mind. She was sure that she'd been right to attend. Even though Troy and some of the others had been tough on her, she felt she'd come through it okay and maybe even made a good impression on some people. It was with this renewed sense of confidence that she approached Troy when she saw him about to climb into his pickup.

"Listen," she said as she came up to him. "I know you're upset. And I think you have every right to be."

"That's big of you," Troy said.

She remembered what Wanda's friend had said about Troy holding a grudge. She couldn't let herself be put off by his attitude. She took a deep breath and tried hard to find just the right, conciliatory tone. "I'm terribly sorry about what happened to Phoebe. She's a wonderful girl. I've gotten to know her pretty well over the last couple of years, and I've really started to think of her as family. So this whole terrible thing was—"

"You think of her as *family*?" Troy said. "Is that why you had your lawyer say Phoebe was having sex with your son? My daughter is a virgin, by the way. We took her up to the ER after the assault and a doctor confirmed what we already knew. So, I have to tell you, if that's the way you treat your *family*, I'm not surprised that your son is so totally messed up."

"I had no idea the lawyer was going to say that," Brook replied, taking a step back. "And we didn't tell him to say anything of the sort. I was shocked by it, too. Liam denied it to me afterward. One of the other boys obviously got the wrong impression about Phoebe and made that truly unconscionable statement."

"And I asked Phoebe about it, too," Troy said. "You know what she told me? She said that Liam told his friends my daughter quote unquote *really puts out*!"

"That can't be true. Liam would never—"

"Oh, please," Troy said, throwing up his hands. "I'll tell you what's true: you have absolutely no idea what your son did or didn't do. You were fifty miles away! He got drunk. He assaulted my daughter. And then you proceeded to smear her in public like she was nothing! Like she was some kind of a slut! Well, you're not going to get away with it!"

"I'm sorry, Troy," Brook said. "That should never have come out. But, I promise you, Michael and I had no idea the lawyer was going to introduce it. What happened was awful. But it's time we all tried to move on. The magistrate already—"

"Oh, screw that hearing! It was obvious to everyone there that your lawyer had the magistrate eating right out of his hand. This time I'm going to get a fair hearing. This time we're going to put together a case so damaging that no amount of money and influence in the world is going to be able to whitewash it."

"This time? What do you mean?"

"My lawyers are filing a civil suit against you tomorrow. We're moving on, all right. We're moving right back to court."

14

*M*ichael got up early the morning after the town hall meeting, made his usual thermos of coffee, and headed out to the studio. He hadn't slept well. He'd had some kind of a dream or nightmare just before waking that he couldn't quite remember—but that had upset him badly. Well, there was plenty to be upset about.

Brook had come back from the meeting in a terrible state. As she explained what had happened, Michael could feel his anger mounting. She'd made a public apology to Troy! And now he was hitting them both with a civil suit. Why the hell hadn't Brook listened to his warning? Michael was too pissed off to comfort her. It took all his willpower just to hold his tongue. She had no idea what she was dealing with when it came to Troy, but she still thought she knew better. Just as Michael feared, the dismissal of the criminal charges had only goaded Troy further. And now he was bound to use Brook's apology against them. He was going to use everything he could find against them.

The walk up to the studio cleared Michael's head a little. The sun was rising above the mountain ridge, tingeing the snow-covered tree line shades of pink and gold, then blazing across the frozen expanse of fields. The clear winter morning forced him to take a hard look at himself. He didn't much like what he saw. He had to get his temper under control. He had to get a grip on his emotions. Underneath all these other problems, he could feel a deeper anxiety shifting and stirring. Fragments of the bad dream he'd had kept resurfacing. What was it? The lake again? The image of Sylvia wading into the water? No, he just couldn't deal with that now! He needed to focus. Be aggressive. Get out in front of the fight that was coming with Troy.

By the time he opened up the studio, got the Jøtul stove going, and turned on his computer, he'd decided to work out a plan of attack. He was making a mental list of the steps he and Brook needed to take when he saw the headline on the *Harringdale Record*'s online site. It was under the local-news banner: "Civil charges citing Social Host law expected to be filed this morning against Barnsbury couple . . ."

He set down his coffee cup and stared at the computer screen. There was something about actually seeing his and Brook's names in print that stopped him cold. But he shouldn't have been surprised. Of course, the Harringdale paper was going to carry the story. And there was bound to be more local coverage. The question was, could they contain the damage? Could they keep it from being picked up by other media outlets and spreading to Moorehouse—and beyond?

His son was Michael's first concern. He'd hoped for some kind of reconciliation with him after the hearing went their way, but Liam had remained as cool and closed off as ever.

He'd just shrugged when Michael asked if he wanted to go back to Moorehouse that semester. Despite Michael's misgivings about the prep school, he knew Liam couldn't possibly return to his old life in Barnsbury and Deer Mountain at this point. But if the civil suit became public knowledge, Moorehouse might object to Liam's return. And then what? Michael saw his son drifting, from one school to another—lonely, unhappy, and further and further estranged from them.

Michael needed advice, and he needed it *now*. As he considered his options, he began to wonder if he'd made a mistake not listening to Brook when she suggested they ask her family for help. How much of his resistance had just been a matter of his own damned ego? Well, to hell with the anger and humiliation he so often felt when dealing with the Pendleton clan. If they could help Liam keep his place at Moorehouse and out of the limelight during this new legal battle, Michael was more than willing to swallow his pride.

⸙

He heard only Brook's side of the telephone conversation with Peg, but that was enough.

"Yes, I'm aware of that. But, as I said, all the charges were—no, you're right. Of course, it's still a matter of perception. . . ."

Brook frowned, her hair falling into her face as she looked down and shook her head. He couldn't read her expression, but he did hear her voice grow softer, almost meek.

"No, I think we can handle that side of things. Michael's found a very good local law—yes, of course, we'll keep Staff's people in mind. But I'm actually calling to talk to you about

Moorehouse and what you'd advise. We thought perhaps we should contact the headmaster, let him know what's happened. Yes . . . I remember you saying you were on the committee. So you know him well? Would it be too much to ask . . . ? Yes, of course, I'm aware of that—I know you moved heaven and earth to help get Liam in last summer . . . and you know how much we appreciate . . ."

Brook held the receiver away from her ear, allowing Michael to hear his sister-in-law's response. It was in the tone of a lecture, though Michael could make out only snatches:

". . . did try to warn you . . . understand the importance . . . Pendleton name . . . honestly worry . . . feel it essential . . . family first . . . frankly embarrassing . . . but owes his job to me . . . see what I can do . . ."

When it was over, Brook hung up the phone with a sigh.

"There goes at least a pound of flesh," she said. "But it was worth it. She's going to call Foster Norwood now. She was on the search committee that ended up recommending him for headmaster five or six years ago."

⁂

"Here, let me just—," Brook said, standing on tiptoe to smooth down Michael's hair after he pulled off his wool watch cap. He wished now that he'd kept it on. The entrance hall in Foster Norwood's house was freezing, which only added to Michael's general unease. He tried not to show it, but he never felt particularly welcome at Moorehouse.

The white clapboard nineteenth-century buildings on the 250-acre campus had been meticulously restored to retain their old New England quaintness, but behind the famous chapel, where teenage boys had been attending services for nearly two hundred years, sprawled a new ultramodern sports complex underwritten by a billionaire alumnus. Michael and Brook had met the headmaster once before when they dropped Liam off at the school last September. He'd spoken reverently about the school's fine academic reputation, but it seemed to Michael that Norwood's voice only came fully to life when he mentioned the school's ice hockey team.

"The Warriors were in the New England prep finals eight years in a row!" he'd told them. "I was delighted to learn that Liam seems to know his way around a puck."

The mood today was bound to be decidedly less jovial. In just three days the winter term at Moorehouse would commence. The piece in the *Harringdale Record* had been fleshed out the next day with a longer story that described the civil case in detail, named Brook as "an heiress to the Pendleton fortune," and, though not revealing Liam's name, mentioned that the boy in question attended "a prestigious prep school favored by the very wealthy" in Connecticut.

Peg had made the initial call to Norwood, but reported back that the headmaster wanted to talk to them directly.

"Sometimes I think it's best to discuss these sorts of issues in person, don't you?" Norwood told Michael when he called. But it sounded more like a command than a question, and Michael had arranged to meet with the headmaster the very next day.

On the ride down in the car, Michael and Brook had debated what, if anything, they should say about Carey's and Brandon's role in what had happened. Brook was all for voicing her suspicions, but Michael pointed out, "As long as Liam refuses to tell us what really happened, what's the benefit? We incriminate the other boys without really gaining anything from it."

"I just hope that you made it clear that Liam's innocent," Brook insisted.

"Yes, of course. But I think the best approach is just to say that *we're* to blame for what happened. I say we go down there, plead mea culpa, and say how much Liam wants to put this behind him."

Though the middle-aged woman who'd answered the door said the headmaster would be ready to see the Bostocks "in just a couple of secs," when the seconds stretched to nearly twenty minutes Michael began to suspect that Norwood was keeping them waiting on purpose. Letting them know who controlled things. God, how Michael hated power plays like that! He was reminding himself that he had to stay cool and focus on Liam's future, when Norwood finally emerged from his ground-floor study, right hand outstretched.

"Sorry to keep you folks waiting," he said with a gap-toothed smile. A former marine, the headmaster appeared to be almost bursting out of his blue blazer and sweater vest, the Moorehouse blue and gold striped tie noose-tight around his neck. He was probably around Michael's age, though he came across as younger—clean-shaven, round-cheeked, thick fair hair tamed by a brush cut. He radiated boyish, can-do enthusiasm.

"I've been stuck on the phone with maintenance," he went on, ushering them into his office. "Sorry about the subzero temperatures. The boiler system's acting up again."

They took the two leather armchairs facing Norwood's walnut desk. Michael guessed that this was where the troublemakers routinely sat—all those high-spirited, hormone-fueled teenagers—awaiting the headmaster's punishment. How he wished Liam's problems were as simple as those Norwood probably routinely mediated: a prank gone wrong, a one-too-many missed curfew. Group photos lined the walls: students dressed in the Moorehouse colors taking the playing field, a handful of boys skiing across the snow-covered fields, a chorus lined up in rows in the chapel, mouths wide with song. Michael knew that the students were required to wear blazers and ties during school hours. That they addressed their teachers as "sir" and "ma'am." It was a place that seemed as unreal as Hogwarts to Michael, one where he'd never belong. Even now, as he tried to mentally organize his arguments on his son's behalf, he felt handicapped by who he was or, more to the point, who he wasn't.

"Thanks for seeing us," Michael began, "at such short notice."

"Please!" the headmaster said, leaning back in his swivel chair. "I don't need to tell you how indebted we are to the Pendleton family. And, frankly, I'm grateful that Mrs. Jeffries reached out to me about this—and that you both obviously understand the seriousness of the situation. Too many parents simply look the other way when it comes to teenage drinking. During breaks and weekends, of course, the students get to do whatever their individual families deem best. It's one of those tricky areas for us at Moorehouse. An open, honest discussion like this one is very welcome."

"Just to be clear," Michael said. "We don't condone underage drinking at our house. What happened was not something we would have turned a blind eye to if we'd had any idea what was going on. And we realize that it was a serious error of judgment on our part not to be there that night. As I told you on the phone, we were cleared of any criminal charges. But the father of the girl involved has decided to go after us in civil court."

"Right," Norwood said, nodding. "I understand. And there's already been some publicity. But it was just this local girl's word against Liam's, right? The other boys weren't involved."

"Yes," Michael said quickly.

"Because I see from the sign-out sheet," Norwood continued, looking down at a manila folder that he had in front of him on the desk, "Brandon Cowley drove Liam home. Brandon's a sixth-form prefect. A student leader. One of our top athletes."

"Yes, Brandon and his brother, Carey, brought Liam home," Brook said. "They did so earlier in the year, too."

"But they are *not* named in this new litigation, correct?" Norwood asked.

"No, just Liam," Michael repeated. "And there's no question that he's very sorry about what happened."

"He's still—," Brook began, then hesitated before going on. "He's a little young for his age. And we want to keep him from suffering any lasting harm from all this. We want to make sure he's safe here at Moorehouse."

"Safe?" Norwood asked, leaning forward. "In what sense?"

"He *was* drinking," Michael said. "There's no denying that."

"Yes," Norwood said, looking from Brook to Michael. "But, as I explained, Moorehouse can't dictate what happens in the privacy of your family. As long as it was Liam *alone*, and in your own home, I don't believe that the matter falls under the school's purview."

"That's a relief," Brook said, smiling for the first time since they sat down.

"However," Norwood continued, "I do think the circumstances dictate some sort of disciplinary action. I'll discuss the matter with his dorm family and prefect, but it's my guess that we're going to want to institute some stricter oversight measures. And, of course, I think it goes without saying that if Liam finds himself in hot water again this coming term, we may have to consider expelling him."

∼

"You were right about protecting the Cowley brothers," Brook said as they walked across the parking lot to the car.

"Yeah," Michael said, digging his hands into his jacket pockets. He felt chilled to the bone. Chilled in even deeper ways than that. The more he thought about it, the more it felt as though they'd cut a quiet little deal with Foster Norwood: *Keep our star senior out of it, and we'll keep your son in school.*

"He did seem to worry more about Brandon's role in the whole thing," Michael added, "than Liam's. Makes me wonder if he knows something about the kid we don't."

"I don't care," Brook said. "As long as Liam's allowed to go back. I never thought I'd say this, but I think he'll be better off away from us and Barnsbury for a while."

"Yes," Michael said as they reached the car. But they were sending him back to the school under a cloud. And worse, they were sending Liam away without understanding what he was thinking or feeling. It was a temporary solution at best. Too often these days Michael found himself making choices he wasn't proud of. How many times in the last week or so had he felt that he'd been forced to compromise, to bargain, to downright lie? And the most frightening thing about it was the realization that he'd go to any lengths to help his troubled son.

15

Three days after the Bostocks drove Liam back to Moore-house for the winter term, a story about the lawsuit appeared in the *Boston Globe* and was picked up by the Yahoo! news feed. It went into greater depth about the Social Host Liability law than the *Harringdale Record* had, describing similar court cases that had been tried—and often settled—in Massachusetts and other states. Brook was described as being a Pendleton heiress, and the Bostocks were said by neighbors to keep aloof from the Barnsbury community.

Michael handed Brook the paper across the breakfast table, while Tilly sat between them, dawdling over her oatmeal.

"We'll talk about that later," he said, tilting his head sideways at Tilly, whom he was dropping off at school. "Let's go, Tiddlywinks. We're already late."

That morning, Brook fielded calls from Alice and a number of other friends in the city who had somehow caught wind of the story and contacted one another. Though they all expressed concern and support, Brook kept hearing an unspoken question in their voices: *How in the world could you have let this happen?* But it was the call from her father, who disliked the phone and sometimes went for days without returning her messages, that upset Brook the most.

"What the *hell* is going on?" he demanded. It was nearly noon. Brook had been awake for hours, but she knew her father's habits well enough to suspect he'd just rolled out of bed and was having his usual meager breakfast of black coffee and toast while devouring a gluttonous intake of news, both print and digital. Michael and Brook had had Peter's Riverside Drive apartment wired for high-speed Internet, and he was slowly coming to terms with the digital age, checking for breaking news online, and tracking everything he cared about through Google Alerts.

Most people thought of Peter Hines, if they thought of him at all these days, as a gruff, opinionated old-school left-leaning crank, sunk in the political past and his own sad personal history. His professional heyday—when *The Liberalist,* the magazine he edited, was averaging over 150,000 weekly subscribers—had been at the tag end of the George H. W. Bush administration. Despite his submitting long, bristling editorials on a regular basis to every news source he knew, Peter Hines's voice had been pretty much stilled for the past twenty years.

Brook was one of the few people who understood that just beneath the surface of her father's often terse and crotchety exterior lay a deeply caring person. To many, he appeared resigned to living a lonely, almost hermetic existence in a city where he'd once been at the political and social epicenter. But his daughter knew that he actually kept a very close eye on the few people he loved, and would leap to their defense like the firebrand he once was if anything appeared to threaten them.

"I just read this crazy *Boston Globe* story online and—"

"I know," she said. "I've been meaning to call you about it." But she just hadn't been able to find the quiet stretch of time that would be required to explain the whole thing to her father. The former investigative reporter would have undoubtedly demanded all the facts, wanted the history and background on the Social Host law, asked for a blow-by-blow account of the court hearing, needed to grill her extensively on how Michael and she planned to proceed, and then gone on to second-guess, analyze, and/or demand more information on just about every statement she'd made. He'd gotten worse as he'd grown older, and his friendships had narrowed to a few old newspaper cronies who tended to reinforce his quarrelsome ways. The very thought of picking up the phone to call him had seemed exhausting.

"Well, why didn't you, then?"

"It's been kind of a madhouse here. Michael and I have our hands full."

"I've still got a contact or two at the *Globe*," Peter said, "and I'm going to tell them what I think of this so-called reporting. I counted at least four unnamed sources. And then to go and haul in that goddamn Pendleton business! I'll tell you what I think: as far as I'm concerned, that's the only reason this thing is considered newsworthy. If you were a Smith or a Doe or a Hines—"

"Dad," Brook said. It was one of the few sore points between them that Brook hadn't eventually taken his name after her mother died. Brook believed that his resentment masked his own regrets that he wasn't able to talk Tilda into marrying him and becoming a Hines. By doing so, they would have legitimized both their marriage and their daughter's lineage. That Peter had come to dislike and distrust Peg, Janice, and everything Pendleton didn't much help his daughter's position.

But Brook, who had so little to remember Tilda Pendleton by, hadn't been able to bear the thought of giving up the one tangible thing that still connected her to her mother.

"Okay. All right. I'm sorry," he said. "How are you holding up, Brooklet?"

"I'm fine," she told him, but her voice quavered. Because that was what he used to ask, using Tilda's own term of endearment for her, when he tucked her into bed at night. During the years when it felt as though Peter Hines and Brook Pendleton were two refugees from some terrible natural disaster, wandering lost and alone through a world that seemed a wasteland without the woman they had both loved so completely.

⟜❦

"Then let's sit the judge next to the senator's wife," Tilda Pendleton said, conferring with Beatrix Walsh, who acted as Tilda's majordomo, memory bank, and social secretary all rolled into one tightly wound ball. Brook sat across from them in the breakfast parlor, following the conversation closely while pretending to be engrossed in her chapter book. The two women were in the midst of finalizing the seating plan for the fundraising dinner Tilda and Peter were holding at their lower Fifth Avenue penthouse that evening for a friend of Tilda's, a tough, savvy federal prosecutor who had her eye on higher office.

Though mid-October, the weather looked warm enough to serve cocktails on the wraparound terrace with its unobstructed views of the West Village and the Hudson River. Dinner itself would be held inside, the louvered French doors opened to combine the living room and formal dining area into one large elegant space.

"No, not a good pairing," Beatrix replied, tapping the

eraser end of a pencil against her teeth. Though Beatrix reeked of cigarettes and spoke in a Boston lockjaw, Tilda often declared she'd be utterly lost without her. "The senator's wife is a strict Roman Catholic, and the judge just ruled on that gay bias case. It would be safer to go with Kitty. Let's move the wife over here—to table nine where we have the monsignor."

"You're right," Tilda said, her gaze moving over the seating chart. The twelve round banquet tables of ten were all filled. The phone had been ringing off the hook for the past couple of weeks as Tilda's vast Rolodex of friends fought for one of the thousand-dollars-a-seat places. A year or two before this, when Brook was just beginning to discover how much she loved watching Tilda put together these magical evenings, she'd questioned her mother the morning after such an event.

"Why are all the seats still here?"

"What do you mean, sweetie pie?" Tilda had replied, as they watched the party-supply crew untie the cream-colored cushions from the gilt chairs that were scattered around the apartment. "Where would they have gone?"

"People paid so much money for them! Don't they get to take them home?"

It became one of Tilda's favorite anecdotes, repeated with loving amusement again and again. But at the dinner that evening, for the first time that Brook could remember, Tilda actually tried to tell the story twice. Brook, as usual, had been allowed to join her parents for dessert and, perched on Peter's knee, was trying her best to follow the animated political conversation at her parents' table. When the waitstaff started to serve the chocolate tart with raspberry sorbet and almond tuiles, the honoree held up her hand and said:

"None for me, thanks. I'm afraid I have to watch my girlish

figure. But you certainly don't need to," she added, handing her plate across the table to Brook. With the spotlight trained suddenly on her daughter, Tilda told the chair anecdote, and the whole table, several of whom already knew the story by heart, laughed appreciatively. The conversation soon shifted to weightier matters, and when the coffee service began, Brook rose dutifully from her father's lap to take her leave. Tilda drew Brook to her side as she moved past, hugged her tight, and said, "Sleep well," and then, just as her daughter was pulling away, "Oh, wait! You don't mind if I tell that funny story about you and the chairs, do you?"

"Mom?" Brook said. She saw her father's quick frown and the exchange of looks around the table. Tilda, too, obviously sensed something was wrong.

"No, not right now, I think, Brooklet," she said, smiling at Brook and patting her cheek as if the idea had actually been her daughter's. "We need to leave plenty of time for any long-winded types at our table."

Hours later, after the speeches, after the brandy, after the last lingering guests had finally gone, Brook heard her mother getting violently sick in the bathroom down the hall. Then she heard Peter banging on the door and shouting, "What is it? What's the matter? Tilda, open the door!"

But Peter eventually had to rouse the super and his son to pry the door off its hinges. By then Tilda had already slipped into the coma from which she would never emerge. And Brook's happy childhood came to its abrupt end.

ℓℓ

With no other role models at hand, Brook grew up following in the footsteps of her half sisters: attending Brearley, spending a month every summer at the Flatt compound in Maine, where she learned to hike and ride, and two weeks every Christmas holiday at their place on St. Bart's, where she picked up snorkeling and sailing. During the school year she studied dance at the same Lincoln Center studio Peg and Janice had attended, and received private voice lessons from a teacher who had tutored both Flatt sisters. Brook didn't exactly shine in any of these endeavors.

"She has a sweet voice," the voice teacher commented. "But Brook lacks the necessary passion." She was well aware that she was just going through the motions, doing what was expected of her, without getting any real pleasure from it. She kept a resolute smile on her face, but her heart was empty. She knew of no other way to be. No clearer path to follow. Wasn't it safer and easier just to go along to get along? She even applied this philosophy to the boys who began to ask her out: the age- and class-appropriate teenagers from Dalton and Trinity, whose groping hands she was constantly having to move back to neutral territory, whose soggy kisses she endured for as long as was polite, counting to twenty in her head.

But every night she came home to her father, breathing a huge sigh of relief. He was the only person in the world who understood her craving just to be left alone. They'd moved to a co-op on Riverside Drive because the Fifth Avenue penthouse held too many wonderful memories that made them both miserable. The two of them lived together like enlightened Buddhists: wanting and expecting nothing.

At Vassar, though she maintained her usual cheerful front, Brook's sense of ennui deepened. She'd chosen the college in the Hudson Valley so she could get back to the city and be with her dad on weekends. Since walking away from *The Liberalist*, he'd stopped keeping any sort of regular hours, reading all night and sleeping through the day. Brook worried about him. He worried about her.

"You're supposed to be making lifelong friends in your college years," he told her. "You can't do that if you spend all your free time holed up here with me. Now, don't come back until Christmas. I'm not going to up and die on you, okay?"

She switched her concentration from film to women's studies to English, trying to find something that grabbed her interest. She started going to the college-sponsored "Conversation Dinners." She made some friends—or at least found herself being asked out to concerts and movies, or back to someone's dorm room for take-out pizza and beer. But nothing and no one really penetrated her inner gloom, until she overheard a girl in her residence hall talking about a party the English department was mounting for a beloved professor's retirement at the end of the term.

"I hate these things. It's always the same cheese cubes and sugary Chardonnay. Professor Hyatt deserves better. Her class on Emily Dickinson just about changed my life."

"You should have everyone come dressed in white," Brook suggested. "And serve like—sherry, maybe. Didn't she describe her eyes as the color of 'the sherry in the glass that the guest leaves'?"

"What a great idea," Brook's fellow student said. "What else would you do?"

It wasn't long before Brook became known as the "party girl," coming up with creative ideas for birthday, Halloween, New Year's Eve, even Presidents' Day celebrations. She was always on the lookout for wacky, inexpensive party favors. Where to score lots of designer paper plates and napkins. She kept her ear to the ground—almost literally—and found the hottest local bands and coolest DJs. She didn't fully realize it until after graduation, when her Vassar friends began to fight over her availability to help orchestrate their engagement, shower, and wedding parties, but she'd managed to put herself in business. A part of her realized that what she'd actually done was find a way to channel her mother's spirit—and re-create the happiest moments of her life. *Well, so be it,* she thought. She'd found her calling.

As R.S.V.P. began to take on professional stature, with a growing reputation and roster of clients, she brought her college friend Alice on to handle the business side of things. They leased a one-room office in Midtown. They were soon both so busy that they had to hire an assistant and then a part-time bookkeeper. There was only one fly in the ointment. Well, two actually. Peg and Janice. Though they were indulgent when they learned Brook was helping her own friends with their events, they became alarmed when they learned she was beginning to do so for *their* friends, as well.

"Don't you think it's going to be a little awkward?" Peg had asked her. "I mean, I'm actually going to be attending the Lightman wedding, and you're going to be there as the hired help."

"But I love what I'm doing," Brook told her. "And I'm really good at it. You don't have to acknowledge me at the Lightmans'. I won't find it awkward. I *want* to do this."

Handling the wedding accounted for Brook's first real rift with her older sisters. The only time in her life so far that she didn't follow their example or bow to their better judgment. It made her feel sad and a little anxious, but at the same time, she couldn't help but feel that Tilda would have been pleased—no, she would have been proud.

Without exactly meaning to, she started to break free of her sisters' gravitational pull and was finally able to see how circumscribed their lives were. While Brook was meeting new people every day and dealing with everyone from busboys to heads of major nonprofits, Peg and Janice tended to see only the same staid upper tier of New York society into which they'd been born, raised, married, and into which they were now indoctrinating their own children. Brook felt comfortable enough joining the Flatt side of her family for birthday celebrations and various holidays, but she now had other, more interesting places to go.

"This is just so impulsive! You know, you're turning out just like Mom," Janice told her when Brook announced that she and Michael were getting married. They'd been dating for less than six months at that point—with Janice's and Peg's growing disapproval.

"Thank you," Brook said.

"No, I mean that you're letting your wild—"

"I said, thank you," Brook repeated. "I couldn't think of a higher compliment."

⁓

The call Brook had been bracing for all day came later that afternoon while she waited for Tilly to finish up ice hockey practice. She was parked outside the Deer Mountain sports complex, heater going full blast, when her cell rang. The caller's name was displayed on her iPhone.

"Hello, Staff," she said.

"Peg asked me to get in touch," her brother-in-law said. "She filled me in on what happened—and I read that awful *Boston Globe* piece. It's a shame this made its way onto the Internet. It's definitely going to be more costly to settle now."

"Settle?"

"Don't tell me you were actually thinking of letting this thing go to trial."

"Well, yes, I guess—"

"That's out of the question."

"But, Staff, the criminal charges against us were thrown out of court. This is just some—"

"I can't believe we're actually arguing about this, Brook. I had an associate run a background check on the law firm involved. They're tough and aggressive. They're going to be looking for the biggest possible payout—and they're not going to give a damn who they hurt in the process. I've been in touch with a firm in Boston that—"

"Michael and I are already in good hands. The lawyer who helped us before is—"

"No! You need some top-notch specialized legal advice and you need it immediately. Don't you understand? This firm knows how to milk this thing. They're already pushing the envelope, turning public opinion against you. They're calling the shots. Who do you think's behind all this press?"

"I told you, Staff, we're dealing with it."

"Just how are you dealing with it when your name's getting dragged through the mud day after day?"

"Whose name are you and Peg really worried about?"

"Oh, for heaven's sake, Brook. I would have thought that growing up the way you did would have made you a bit more sensitive to how painful this kind of publicity can be. If you refuse to think about your own reputation, at least consider what this might do to Liam."

"Thanks for your advice," Brook replied, barely able to keep her voice steady. She'd escaped nothing. She was not free.

Her father was right. None of this would be happening if she were a Smith or a Doe or a Hines. Because she was a Pendleton, she'd brought the whole damned thing down on their heads.

"Give it some thought," Staff said. "I think you'll soon see the wisdom in what I'm saying."

16

"*H*ey, fucking good game, man!" Brandon said, clapping Liam on the back as the Warriors made their way off the ice and down the brightly lit corridor to the locker room. Liam was sweat-soaked and exhausted—and more than a little stunned that he'd been invited to play with the Warriors in the first place, even if it was just an intramural matchup. The assistant coach, who worked with the younger boys and new recruits, had told the second- and third-string players to stay out of the way of the varsity team.

"They rule, okay?" he'd explained the first day of practice. "They're in the running for the prep finals for the ninth year in a row. That's Moorehouse history in the making. They don't wait for the showers. They have first dibs on the steam room and sauna. They tell you to lie down and roll over like a dog—you just say 'woof, woof' and do it."

"When do we get to be them?" someone had asked.

"Probably never," the coach had replied. "It's basically a senior privilege—and even then you've got to be the best of the best."

Liam knew he was a damned good player. Isolated as he'd been at Deer Mountain, he'd spent hours alone at his old high school's rink, obsessively honing his skating and shooting skills. Hard work and natural ability had shaped him into one of those rare defensemen who, while creative, swift, and agile, were also combative and physical, tenaciously guarding the goal area.

But even if he was a star in the making, he was still a lowly sophomore and pretty much a nonentity at Moorehouse. He'd seen Andy Mason, the varsity coach, glance his way from time to time, but he had no illusions. Moorehouse took great pride in—and put a lot of capital into—its ice hockey team, recruiting the best young talent and carefully bringing its players up through the ranks. At the very least, Liam knew that he was on a two-year waiting list. Which was actually fine with him. Since the start of winter term, all he really wanted to do was keep his head down—and get by unnoticed.

He knew from talking to his folks that news about the lawsuit had been picked up by the national media. Because he was a minor, his first name was being kept out of the coverage, and most of the pieces concentrated on the Pendleton side of his genetic makeup. More than three weeks into the new semester, nobody seemed to connect the story with Liam Bostock. But then Moorehouse, like most prep schools, was a world unto itself, with its attention fixed primarily on its own affairs. During the winter months, the doings of the Warriors— one of the leading lights of the New England Prep School Ice Hockey Association—totally eclipsed any interest that might be generated by a *Boston Globe* article on underage drinking.

Carey knew, of course. Carey knew and couldn't get over Liam's decision to take the heat for Brandon. In fact, Carey and Liam kept arguing about what had happened the entire first week that they were back on campus. It didn't help that Liam was so down about other things, as well. He felt bad about what he'd already put his parents through. Worse as he watched them try to deal with these new legal problems. They were at each other's throats. It was like Liam had developed a way of making everyone he loved miserable.

He couldn't stop thinking about how badly he'd fucked up with Phoebe, too. He kept remembering how great it had been to hold her in his arms. How, so briefly and for the first time in months, he'd felt really good about himself again. But then, how everything had suddenly gone wrong. How she'd turned on him and said: *The fact is I used to love you so bad it hurt. And now I don't love you anymore, but it still hurts.* The painful words turned in his gut. And then to have that stupid lie he told Brandon about her used against her at the hearing! He hadn't even been able to look at her after that.

Just when Liam was pretty sure that he'd finally been able to blot out Phoebe's face and voice and put what had happened behind him for a little while, Carey would say something like:

"I don't get it. I don't get any of it. Why Phoebe blamed you—and why you didn't stand up for yourself."

"Listen, I have my reasons. Let's just leave it at that, okay?"

"There's only one possible explanation I can come up with, but I just refuse to believe you did this to get in good with my big brother."

"Can't we drop the subject? I'm sick of the whole thing."

"What's going on with you? Why can't we talk about this?"

"Why can't we *talk* about this? You sound like a girl! I'm

not interested in *sharing* my emotions with you—so will you please just shut the fuck up?"

Liam hated the hurt silence that followed and that had now solidified into a thick fog of unhappiness that filled their small dorm room. Stilted politeness replaced the oddball camaraderie that had defined their first term together. Liam began to spend all his free time at Moorehouse's enormous new sports complex with its state-of-the art exercise machines, Olympic-sized pools, and two ice-skating rinks, the old one that was used for practice, and the other—a new slick, gleaming arena that any professional NHL team would have been proud to call home—set aside strictly for the championship Warriors' varsity games.

Liam bulked up with weight training. Strengthened on the Nautilus machines. Built his stamina swimming laps. And, any time the practice rink was free, skated and practiced his shots and maneuvers. Occasionally, he'd come across Brandon and his fellow Warriors in the locker room or sauna, but he'd find a way of slipping past them without comment. Once Brandon caught his eye—and gave him a curt nod—but there'd been no further communication between the boys since the night on the phone when Liam told Brandon: "Don't worry. I think I know what to do."

Until that afternoon when the Warriors clomped onto the rink for a practice game, forcing everyone else off the ice. Intimidating behind their red and silver masks and outfitted with custom gloves and skates—their blades flashing, sticks raised high in pregame salute—they looked like an invading alien army. But there was an underlying uneasiness in the air. They were facing a tough game against Westminster Academy that coming Saturday and four of the first-string players had come down with the nasty winter flu that was spreading through the school.

Liam skated off the ice, sat down on one of the benches just outside the rink, and started to unlace his skates. He tried to find Brandon's number 16 in the confusion of circling uniforms. But he didn't see him. God, Liam thought, it would be a disaster for the Warriors if Brandon was out sick, too. He was their championship goalie—tough, demanding, loud-mouthed, with a kind of defensive radar that made him one of the most revered and reviled players in the league.

Since his falling-out with Carey, Liam had been trying to figure out how he actually felt about Brandon. He was afraid of him; there was no point in denying that. It was a big part of the reason he'd decided to cover up for the older boy. But his reasons for protecting him were complicated by other, more confusing emotions. He envied Brandon his outsized confidence and sense of entitlement. He was awed by the charismatic force field he seemed to generate, one that helped him bend friends and foes alike to his will. In many ways, Brandon as a person was not all that different from the way he was as a player. He loved to compete, and he'd do just about anything to win.

Liam had no illusions about Carey's older brother. He would have raped Phoebe if she hadn't managed to fight him off. He was a brute and a bully, and Liam knew that he should hate him for it. But the truth was, Liam felt himself drawn to Brandon—enthralled by his ego and swagger. Carey was right: he did want to "get in good" with Brandon. He wanted to impress him. Wow him. Prove to him—and himself—that he was just as tough and smart as Brandon. No—that he was tougher and smarter. He wanted to both *be* Brandon—and beat him at his own game. Liam didn't like this about himself. It was one of many things he didn't like. But he felt powerless to do anything about it. And how fucked-up was that? Sometimes Liam could almost hear a drip, drip, drip of self-loathing pooling down into the darkness inside him.

"You! Bostock!" Coach Mason called from the center of the rink where he was surrounded by a sea of Warriors. "Lace up!"

"What?" Liam asked, rising off the bench in his stocking feet. He glanced behind him to make sure the coach wasn't talking to someone else.

"Lace the hell up and get out here. We need some warm bodies."

It was just an intramural practice game. And Liam had been invited to participate only because the coach was obviously desperate for at least twelve players to fill out the two sides. But that didn't take away from the fact that Liam had played well. He'd been in the zone. His lonely, relentless conditioning had paid off in ways that surprised even him. Stamina, timing, pacing, aim—he seemed to have had everything down to a science. No, an art. He skated like the wind. He handled the puck like a pro. He feinted easily around the Warriors' top left wing. Forced the center to commit three penalties. He badgered, provoked, and in general made himself indispensable to his side of the Warriors. And the whole time, he felt Brandon crouched behind him. Watching him. Weighing his performance. And finally, toward the end, when Liam managed to get the right wing to trip over himself as he charged down the ice, lifting up his goalie mask and yelling:

"You sic 'em, boy!"

He was breathing so hard by the time the game ended, he had to gulp in air before he was able to respond to Brandon's congratulations.

"Thanks," he said. "It was like the best thing that's happened to me all year."

"Yeah?" Brandon asked, looking over at him. "Well, don't repeat that kind of crap to the other guys, okay? They'll think you're a total pussy."

Following the game, and to his great surprise, Liam was picked by the coach to join the varsity Warriors. Though relegated to the back bench and rarely given the chance to play, he was allowed to dress for every match—donning the red and silver uniform that he'd come to love—and to travel with the team on the bus to away games. Initially he was reserved and almost mute around the other players, but he gradually began to relax and feel more a part of things. Especially after Brandon began to single him out: bad-mouthing him, giving him a hard time about some screwup on the ice, in general making it clear he was worthy of notice.

At Coach Mason's request, Liam had his hair cut even shorter than his mom had made him trim it for the hearing. It now looked a little like the business end of a utility broom. One day, before an important home game, Brandon grazed his knuckles across the top of Liam's head on his way out to the ice. When Brandon made a number of spectacular saves that afternoon, he attributed his luck to Liam.

"You know, I think it's a little like rubbing a rabbit's foot. Only for me, it's Bostock's fucking brush cut." After that, everyone on the Warriors would file past Liam and run their gloves over his head before hitting the ice. As the Warriors' undefeated streak continued, Liam became the team's unofficial mascot. They started to call him "Bossy." And not just

Brandon, but everyone now began to routinely make Liam the butt of crude but good-natured jokes. It bothered Liam from time to time, but not nearly enough to overshadow his pleasure at being a part of something at last. And not just *any*thing—he was one of the Warriors! He found himself living for the team, for the games, and the bright, flattering glare of Brandon Cowley's attention.

It was far better than trying to find a way of living in any degree of comfort with Carey. The more Liam was consumed by the Warriors, the colder and more withdrawn Carey became. Like Liam, Carey began to spend less and less time in the dorm room the boys shared, instead haunting the music house with its solitary, soundproof practice rooms. Carey had turned into a real prick in Liam's estimation. Judgmental and full of himself. It seemed impossible now that they had actually been pretty good friends just a few short weeks ago.

Liam began to sit at the group of tables the Warriors commandeered in the dining hall. He trailed along with the team after practice when they tramped en masse down to Ralph's café in town. He even began to accompany them to the dances that Moorehouse sponsored with girls-only prep schools in the area, sitting with the team in the middle rows of the bus where Brandon held court. One night, driving back through the winter darkness, his fellow Warriors were grossly sizing up the girls they'd just met. One of them asked Liam, "Think you'd give it up for that Nisha chick, Bossy?"

"Sure."

"What? Bossy's giving up his cherry for a Chink?"

"Jesus, you asshole, she's like Indian or Pakistani, right, Brand?"

They all deferred to Brandon when it came to questions

about girls. He seemed to have an encyclopedic knowledge of sexual positions and practices, both foreign and domestic, as well as a kind of sixth sense about which of the girls they met "clearly wanted it real bad."

"I hate to disappoint you guys, but Bossy can't give it up for anyone—'cause it's already gone."

"Fuck no!"

"Bossy? How do you know? Were you there?"

"Let's just leave it at that," Brandon replied, as Liam felt his heart begin to pound. He was glad the bus was shrouded in darkness, because he could feel his face burning. What was Brandon up to? Was this his way of thanking Liam for what he'd done? Making the team think Liam was already in Brandon's sexual league. Or was it Brandon's subtle way of reminding him to keep his word—and his mouth shut? Liam felt buoyed and threatened by Brandon at the same time.

Later that night, lying awake in bed, Liam wondered if his recent streak of tremendous good luck—making the Warriors, being taken up by the team, becoming known around campus as a player—wasn't in fact the result of Liam's natural abilities. Perhaps it was all due to Brandon's influence—over Coach Mason, his fellow Warriors, nearly everybody on campus. Maybe this was just his way of paying Liam back—or paying him off. Liam hardened his heart against the possibility. *No!* He was earning his own way on the team. He was liked for who he was as a person, what he could do as an athlete. It took him over an hour to calm his fears and finally get some sleep.

17

Phoebe and Lacey were both in the drama club at Deer Mountain, though neither one had worked up the courage to try out for an actual show. They were happy enough to serve on the production crew and watch from the wings while the likes of Malina Simmons and Justin Finkleday—two of the most awesome seniors—faced the stage lights and basked in the applause. The two girls had almost taken the plunge together that past fall when the school mounted *Our Town*, reasoning that they could at least handle the pressure of standing motionless among the dead of Grover's Corners, but at the last minute Lacey had chickened out.

"What's the point?" Lacey told Phoebe. "I get stage fright so bad, I feel sick to my stomach just *thinking* about being up there."

"Yeah," Phoebe agreed. "I get butterflies, too." But, for her, it was a good kind of nervousness—one mixed with an undercurrent of excitement. Though Phoebe didn't think of herself as particularly outgoing, she was nevertheless strangely drawn to the idea of climbing onto the stage and taking on the persona of someone else. A made-up character. What fun it would be to step out of herself for a while and into the skin of someone entirely new, someone larger than life! She had the memory for it, too. She didn't tell Lacey, but by the time the auditions had rolled around, she knew almost the entire play by heart. So she was really disappointed when Lacey changed her mind about the tryouts, but she knew she couldn't say anything. They had an unspoken pact as best friends. They prided themselves on doing everything—or not—together.

But something had shifted in their relationship since the news about the lawsuit hit. Where in the past Phoebe and Lacey had gone about their days lost in the crowd of the nearly three hundred high schoolers who jammed the halls of Deer Mountain, now Phoebe was starting to be noticed.

"The principal would like to see you, Phoebe," her homeroom teacher, Mrs. Rubino, had told her about a week after the town hall meeting. Just that morning, her dad had called to tell her mom to check out the *Boston Globe*, which had run an in-depth story on the lawsuit he'd filed against Liam's parents. She could feel the eyes of the whole class follow her as she stood up and walked out of the room. Phoebe had been in the school's offices on many occasions—her mom was an administrative assistant in accounting there—but this was the first time she'd ever had a face-to-face with Principal Gunther.

Balding, in his mid-sixties, Gunther projected the world-weary acerbity of one who had been disciplining teenagers for over three decades. Phoebe had always been a little afraid of him. He tended to be gruff, and his humor had a sarcastic edge. He made a point of reminding his students that he wasn't afraid to "tell it like it is." So Phoebe was surprised and relieved when, in a gentle tone, he suggested she take a seat.

"I understand you've been going through a pretty tough time," he said. "I'm sorry to hear about it. And I just wanted you to know that all of us here in the administration stand behind you and your family one hundred percent." He took her in over his bifocals, but the look seemed kind and a little sad.

"Thank you," she said.

"Now, if it's okay with you, I'd like to say a few words at the student assembly this afternoon about the situation—and your courage."

"Oh!" Phoebe said, her face reddening. She was getting better and better at repressing the fact that she hadn't told the truth about what had happened that night. But when caught off guard, as she found herself to be at that moment, she realized how ashamed she actually felt deep down—and trapped by a situation that was only getting more complicated every day. It frightened her how quickly her one stupid lie had spawned other lies and then spread seemingly overnight into the overheated reality of law offices, courtrooms, and the media.

"No, don't worry," Gunther said, misinterpreting her expression. "I won't mention you by name. I plan to keep my remarks very general. But I do think it's important to address the issue directly, as well as make it clear that Deer Mountain has a zero tolerance policy when it comes to physical abuse of any kind."

The principal was true to his word. He didn't single out Phoebe or any one person or incident. But, for those who already knew what had happened over the holidays, there could be no doubt whom Gunther had in mind when he talked to the special assembly about underage drinking and aggressive be-havior.

"Never be afraid to do the right thing. There are going to be times in your life when people will try to make you do what *they* want. What *they* say is right. Sometimes they'll be bigger, older, or more powerful than you. You could very well be tempted to give in—and be a victim. But don't! The first step in becoming a great human being is learning that you have to *fight* for what you know is right. You have to learn to stand up for yourself. No matter what the circumstances."

Word spread quickly. Immediately after the assembly, stu-dents who had previously looked right through Phoebe in the hallways now started nodding and smiling at her when she and Lacey passed by. After a year and a half of blending in to the point of total camouflage, Phoebe Lansing was becoming visible.

"Hey, Phoebe."

"How you doing, Phoebe?"

"Yo." A few days after Gunther's talk, she actually got a high five from Tommy Redmile, Deer Mountain's star bas-ketball forward.

Lacey would lower her head and scurry past when these relative strangers greeted her friend. But Phoebe began to nod and smile back.

"Hey!" she said. "How's it going?"

"What are you doing?" Lacey asked after Tommy Redmile sauntered away down the hall.

"What do you mean?" Phoebe asked, her smile fading.

"It's almost as if you really *like* all this attention."

"What am I supposed to do?" Phoebe asked. She was be-ginning to resent Lacey's increasingly judgmental tone and the way her friend seemed to assume that Phoebe shouldn't *want* to be more a part of things at school. "People are just being nice."

"Is that what you think?"

"Yes," Phoebe said. "I think people are trying to show their support."

"You didn't see the way Tommy was looking at you?"

"Why don't you just come out and say whatever it is you're trying to say."

"He was looking at your *boobs* when he talked to you, Phoebe. These guys look at you and all they're thinking about is how you somehow put yourself in a position where—"

"Where *what*? Are you saying I was *asking* for what . . . for what Liam did?"

"No! Of course not," Lacey replied. But in the brief silence that followed, Phoebe couldn't help but remember how she'd told Lacey she was borrowing her mom's lavender cashmere sweater the night Liam was coming home. How she was going to *force* him to make a move.

"Then . . . what?" Phoebe asked when Lacey just stood there biting her bottom lip.

"I'm just . . . I just know what a hard time you've been having," Lacey replied. "I just want you to think about who you should be trusting right now. Who really knows you—and cares about you. That's all."

But it wasn't all. In fact, it was just the beginning of Lacey's little asides and complaints about Phoebe's behavior. She suggested that Phoebe was "friending" way too many people on Facebook.

"Do you even know half these guys?"

"What's your problem?"

"I'm just saying . . . there are a lot of creeps out there. And you're kind of in the spotlight right now."

Lacey also didn't like having to wait for Phoebe in the school bus while Phoebe lingered after drama club. Lately, Phoebe had been sticking around to chat with Mara Junge, a senior who was in charge of the drama club's winter production of *As You Like It.*

"Sorry," Phoebe said, sliding into the seat Lacey had saved for her. In the past, they were usually two of the first students on the bus and always sat together on the right, fifth row back. Recently, though, Phoebe had to run to make the bus at all. "You know how Mara is when she gets talking."

"Actually, I don't. But I guess you do. The two of you seem to have an awful lot to say to each other these days."

Phoebe tried to ignore her friend's hurt tone. She tried to tell herself that Lacey would be as thrilled as Phoebe was when she told her what Mara had just suggested. In fact, Phoebe was so excited by the news there was no way she couldn't share it with her best friend:

"Mara has this kind of crazy idea I should try out for the role of Phebe in the play!"

"What? The shepherdess? Why? Because your names sound alike? That's kind of lame, don't you think?"

"No," Phoebe said. "Actually, I think it's pretty cool."

"Well, good for you," Lacey replied, turning her face to the window as the bus shifted into gear. "Break a leg."

✧

Lacey was just jealous. Lacey was way too shy and self-conscious. She didn't know how to get beyond her own insecurities. But that wasn't Phoebe's fault, was it? In fact, Phoebe felt

sorry for Lacey when she dropped out of drama club the following week. Rehearsals kept Phoebe at school until late afternoon, so they were no longer taking the bus home together—
and they avoided each other on the morning route. But wasn't
it really for the best? Lacey had always been a little too needy.
And kind of controlling. Besides, Phoebe was busy now with
the play, her fellow thespians, and a couple of boys who had
started to show an interest in her.

One, Neil Steinbeck, was on varsity wrestling and had
dark hair like Liam. Though he had a spray of acne scars across
his cheeks and a prominent Adam's apple, something about
him reminded her a little of Liam. Or maybe it was just that she
compared him to Liam so often in her mind that bits of Liam
couldn't help but rub off on him. Neil began to wait for her
after school when he wasn't at practice or a match. He invited
her to hang out with his friends at the Harringdale mall one
Saturday. She tried hard to concentrate on the good things
about him—varsity sports, a short, compact build that could
be described as muscle-bound, the dark hair. It wasn't until he
kissed her at the movies that she realized she was kidding
herself. His tongue felt as thick and slippery as a frog in her
throat. She almost gagged.

She began to let herself dream about Liam again. She
started to build the same kind of elaborate scenarios she used
to construct involving the two of them. Only now she had real
story lines to work with, as well as serious, dramatic plot
points. She'd lie awake in the dark, long after her mother had
turned out the downstairs light and gone to bed, acting out
both their parts in her imagination. Over and over again, Liam
would beg her forgiveness for what had happened.

"I want to kill Brandon," he'd tell her. "I should never

have brought him home—or let him anywhere near you. You're so beautiful, guys just can't help themselves. You know that, don't you?"

These late-night fantasies were once again becoming the high point of her day. She didn't want her mom to know, but between the rehearsals for *As You Like It* and the time she was spending with Neil and her other new friends, her grades were beginning to suffer. And Lacey wasn't around anymore to help out with her algebra assignments. Though she now had dozens of new numbers on her cell phone, there was no one she really wanted to call. Even the play was turning out to be something of a letdown. She'd been fitted for the shepherdess costume. It had bell sleeves and an elaborate hoop skirt. She felt like an idiot wearing it. So many people seemed to think they knew her now. But she was having a hard time recognizing herself.

One Sunday at the end of February when Wanda and Phoebe arrived home from church, they found Troy waiting for them in his pickup truck. He followed them into the house.

"How about a day trip to Boston next weekend, sunshine?" he asked Phoebe, helping himself to one of the bagels Wanda had left out on the kitchen counter.

"What's going on?" Phoebe's mother asked.

"Cranston and Cranston want to interview Phoebe," Troy said.

"I can't go," Phoebe said. "I think I have rehearsal."

"Well, you'll just have to skip it," Troy said. "They need to get this done. They've hired a PI to do some of the legwork and they need your full statement ASAP."

"PI?" Wanda asked. "Why don't you just say private investigator? Do you have any idea how full of yourself you—"

"Could you please cut me a little slack?" Troy said. "I'm juggling a lot of balls right now and the last thing I need is—"

"Mom?" Phoebe said. "Can I talk to Daddy by myself for a minute?"

Wanda crossed her arms on her chest. She looked from Phoebe to Troy and then back to Phoebe again.

"Don't let this big deal here try to push you around," she said as she walked out of the kitchen.

"Well?" Troy said, leaning against the kitchen counter

"Daddy?" Phoebe said, her eyes welling. Ever since the hearing, she'd been feeling awful whenever she thought about Liam. The prospect of repeating her lies to a roomful of lawyers made her sick to her stomach. Phoebe's anxiety had been building for days—no—for weeks. It had been building from the moment Troy had put the words into her mouth. And now she needed to spit them back out.

"Hey, don't worry about this meeting, okay?" Troy told her. "I'll be right there. You've already met Henry Cranston. It's no big deal."

"It's not that," Phoebe said. "I have to tell you something: it wasn't Liam. It was Brandon—Liam's friend from school."

"What? What are you talking about?"

"It wasn't Liam who attacked me."

"I'm sorry—but I'm not getting this. What's going on?"

"I'm trying to tell you, Daddy, it wasn't Liam—"

"Did he get to you somehow? Has he been texting you?"

"No!" The fact that she hadn't heard a word from Liam since New Year's actually weighed heavily on her heart.

"Then why are you changing your story?"

"I'm not. I'm telling you the truth. *You* made me say it was Liam, remember? *You* were the one who blamed him right away. I was so upset I just—I just went along. It was Brandon who—"

"Wait, hold on!" Troy said, holding up both hands. He stared out the window for a long moment, obviously turning something over in his mind. Then, in a lowered voice, he asked Phoebe: "Does your mom know about this?"

"No. I haven't told anybody."

"Nobody? You sure? None of your friends at school? Not even Lacey?"

"No."

"Then listen to me and listen good: you're going to keep this to yourself. Your statement is already on record, Phoebe. Cranston took the case based on what you claimed. You start accusing someone else now—someone nobody around here has ever even heard of—and you know what's going to happen? Do you have any idea?"

"No," Phoebe said shakily.

"People are going to stop believing in you! They're going to start to question the whole thing. They'll wonder, what's she going to say tomorrow? That maybe it was all three of those boys together? You start to backtrack now and you'll lose everyone's sympathy. You'll look like a liar and an idiot—and worse. And this is not the optimum moment to put our credibility in doubt, do you understand me?"

"But I *will* be a liar," Phoebe said, tears rolling down her cheeks.

"Oh, sunshine," Troy said, crouching down beside her. "Don't forget that the Bostocks' lawyer felt it was perfectly okay to claim you'd had sex with Liam. That was the ugliest lie I've ever heard. You sticking to your story is nothing compared to that as far as I'm concerned."

"So you don't think it's wrong, Daddy?"

"No," Troy said, looking into his daughter's eyes. "What that boy did to you was wrong. And if Liam wants to protect him, that's his problem. What you're doing is standing up for yourself. What you're doing is right. And I couldn't be more proud of you."

18

Michael turned the windshield wipers to their fastest speed, but the sleet had frozen solid to the outside glass, and the wipers slid uselessly over an icy patch that was obscuring his view. When he reached a flat, straight stretch of Route 99, he slowed the pickup to a crawl, wound down the window, and tried to scrape the sleet off with his gloved left hand while steering with his right. No deal. He pulled to the side of the road and turned off the engine.

Darkness had fallen during the drive back from his workshop, and the view to the west was a study in black and white: the snow-covered cornfields and hills set against the starless backdrop of oncoming night. For a while he just sat there, listening to the sleet tapping against the windows and the slow *tick-tick* of the engine as it cooled down. He should have left the shop an hour earlier. But just as he was getting ready to head home, his foreman, Terry Lonnegan, had knocked on the open door of his office.

"Got a sec?" Terry asked, stepping into the cramped room.

It had once been a horse stall in an old barn that Michael had converted into the beamed, open-plan workshop where a crew of eight now turned out Michael's line of custom chairs, tables, and lamps. Since he conducted most of his business from his studio at home, this office had become something of a repository for promotional brochures and catalogs for Michael Bostock Fine Wood Designs.

"Sure, take a seat," Michael said.

Terry had been Michael's first hire nearly twenty years ago when Michael finally faced the fact that he had more business coming in than he could handle on his own. Terry was over a decade older than Michael and lived in nearby Covington, but they shared a hard-nosed work ethic that bordered on perfectionism. It was Terry who'd advised Michael on finding local talent as the business continued to grow—and Terry who now oversaw the seasoned team of woodworkers. Michael paid a good wage and offered benefits. Like Terry, Michael's employees tended to stay put.

"What's up?" Michael asked when Terry just stood there.

"Don't want to butt in where I don't belong," Terry said, looking past Michael out the window.

"Doubt you could."

"I've been hearing some stuff. Thought I better pass it on to you."

"Okay."

"This is from a niece of mine who's at Deer Mountain. Claims Liam used to drink and smoke dope a lot when he was going to school there."

It took Michael a moment or two to absorb this information. Then he asked, "Did she say if she ever actually *saw* him doing any of this?"

"No—and I asked her that question. As far I'm concerned, it's just the usual 'everybody knows' kind of bullshit. But it's out there."

"Thanks for telling me."

"Yeah, sure," he said. "You guys are going to fight this thing, right?"

"I believe that's the plan, if we have to," Michael said. "We're lawyering up. We're going to have a meeting next week with some Boston firm that's handled this kind of deal before."

"Good," Terry said. "I know what a lot of people are saying, but not everybody thinks Troy Lansing's in this for the right reasons. Me included."

"Thanks, Terry."

"And I told my niece to put a sock in it."

As Michael sat in the darkness, he thought back on Terry's aside: *I know what a lot of people are saying.* But what *were* they saying exactly? That he and Brook were negligent parents? That Liam had real problems? That Troy was right to stick it to those entitled Bostocks? Though Michael had been making a concerted effort lately not to let the case bring him down, Terry's little heads-up had done a number on him. He felt both empty and exhausted. It was the same reaction he'd had the week before when Brook first suggested they meet with a law firm her brother-in-law Staff had lined up.

"What happened to our decision to stick with Freston? He did pretty damn well by us last time. And I thought we agreed that it looked better to have someone from the community."

"Troy's lawyers are from Boston," Brook pointed out. "And Staff made a pretty persuasive argument for dealing with people who know this area of the law. But I'm not saying we've got to go with them. I see this as a kind of information-gathering session."

"Right," Michael said. Though he meant *wrong*. He meant: *You're buckling under to family pressure again*. He'd agreed to at least meet with the firm, but he sensed this was just the first step in Brook's family's attempts to seize control of the situation. He knew from firsthand experience how thoroughly Brook's half sisters disliked having the Pendleton name in the news. They were probably furious about the kind of negative media coverage the family was getting now. And they were no doubt blaming him, whispering their usual entitled venom into Brook's ear. It depressed him how quickly Janice and Peg could exert their old influence over his wife. How easily they could manipulate her, especially when she was feeling so vulnerable.

Some things never changed.

⁓

Wayne Dwyer, Michael's dealer in Manhattan at the time, had talked him into it. A charity auction for a fancy private school in Manhattan that would feature, among other high-end items, a couple of Michael's pieces.

"You're just starting out, so we need to build up your name recognition," Wayne had told him. "And this crowd is your target customer base. Superrich, but also young and hip enough to be open to your work. They were brought up on chintz and Chippendale, and they're eager to set their own design agenda."

"That's fine. I'm okay with you donating an item or two, but why do I need to go down there?"

"To mingle, for heaven's sake! To shake a few hands and flash that shy, seductive smile of yours. Come on, Michael:

you're this handsome, mysterious backwoodsman type—those mothers are going to be all over you!"

Michael assumed Wayne had been exaggerating about the attention he was likely to receive. But, in fact, from the moment he walked into the Skylight Ballroom of the Puck Building, where the preauction party was in full swing, he found himself surrounded by a group of young, extremely fit, expensively turned-out women who appeared to be fascinated by the custom-made pieces of his that were on display.

"This is so beautiful," one of them said, running her fingers over the surface of the mahogany table with its bird's-eye maple inlays. "Do you think of yourself as an artist?"

The women were sipping from flutes of champagne. Michael was drinking San Pellegrino and trying hard to respond with more than his usual monosyllables.

"Well, I wouldn't—"

"An artist whose medium is wood?" another of them suggested, gazing up at him. They were all so petite! He felt like a clumsy giant. He glanced around the room trying to work out an escape route, and his gaze fell once again on a woman who'd been wandering in and out of his line of vision all evening.

She had soft brown hair held back in some kind of a clip, though a strand or two had come loose. As opposed to most of the other women, who wore tight bright dresses and towering heels, she had on a simple navy pants suit and flats. Even without the heels, she was taller than the others and heavier, though in the way Michael preferred. The businesslike cut of her suit only accentuated the generous curves of her hips and breasts. Michael watched her cross the room and realized she was talking intently into a headphone set—and walking directly toward him!

"The auction is starting in five minutes," she said as she reached him. "And we're putting you on first." Her voice was low and intimate. He felt like she was sharing a secret with him.

"Great," he replied, smiling down at her. The other women had started drifting away to the seating area.

"So you'll have a couple of minutes—but no more—to do your thing."

"What thing?" he asked, suddenly alarmed. He glanced over at the stage where two workmen were positioning his chairs at an angle to the coffee table.

"Oh, you know, to talk about your work—the materials, your method. Whatever you usually say."

"I don't usually say—anything," Michael replied, his heart-beat accelerating. She was so lovely, and he was sure he was coming across like a total idiot.

"Oh?" she said, looking up at him. Her eyes were hazel with gold highlights, the color of the woods on a warm autumn day. He wanted to lose himself in them.

"I'm not a very good public speaker."

"I'd be happy to do it for you, then, if you don't mind. I read over all the material your dealer sent, and I love your things."

"That would be—" Was he even more tongue-tied than usual, or was it just that he wanted to be having a very different kind of conversation with her? Somewhere far removed from this crowd and chatter.

"I'd appreciate it," he finally said. He watched her wend her way back through the audience, stopping here and there to talk to one of the guests or kiss someone's cheek. She welcomed an older man to the stage, and then a series of people came and went from the lectern. The auctioneer introduced himself. Then the woman stepped back up to the microphone and said some things about Michael—"using time-honored techniques . . . every detail rendered by hand . . . outrageously creative designs . . . by far the most exciting new furniture maker of our generation"—but he wasn't really paying attention to what she said. He was too busy admiring the sweet, poised way that she was saying it. The bidding began, but his thoughts were elsewhere.

"Congratulations," said a dark, curly-haired woman—also wearing a headset—as his furniture was being taken off the stage. "That was twice the floor."

"Sorry?"

"Your furniture went for a record price. Didn't you even notice?"

"I was wondering who that woman is," Michael said, nodding toward the stage. "Do you know her name?"

"You mean my partner?"

"Partner?" Michael asked, confused. "As in . . . ?"

"Oh, no! Don't worry," the woman said, laughing. "We're business partners. We own R.S.V.P.—the events firm that's handling the auction tonight. I'm Alice Lerner. Her name is Brook Pendleton."

"Nice to meet you," Michael said, holding out his hand.

"She's Brook *Pendleton*," Alice said. "One of the Pendleton Pendletons?"

"Oh," Michael said.

"I'm only telling you this because I couldn't help but notice that you haven't taken your eyes off her all night. And I just thought you should know that she happens to be one of the kindest, most generous, and all-round best people in the world."

"I'm not surprised."

"But she has this thing about her money. She has a difficult time with a lot of men she meets, okay? The money thing gets in the way. And she's trying hard to make it on her own terms. It's terribly important to her."

"I understand what you're saying," he said, turning to Alice. "And I really appreciate it."

"Good," Alice said. "I don't usually go around talking about her, by the way. And please don't ever let her know that I told you what I just did, okay?"

Sometimes Michael wondered what would have happened if Alice hadn't tipped him off. Without it, would he ever have found the courage to continue to pursue Brook once he'd discovered how wealthy she was? But knowing she saw her fortune as a burden made it easier somehow for him to overcome his own concerns. Rather than feel threatened and overwhelmed by her background, he longed to protect her from it. If she wanted to stand on her own two feet, as Alice had said, then Michael would do everything in his power to make sure her footing was secure.

He got an R.S.V.P. business card from Alice and called Brook the next morning. They had lunch. And then, because they still seemed to have so much to say to each other, they had dinner that same night. He loved the way she looked, the sound of her voice, her uninhibited laugh. When he first kissed her, he understood finally why people talked about being head over heels. He felt dizzy and disoriented and in some kind of exhilarating free fall. Things progressed pretty quickly from there.

For the first three or four weeks they were together, he allowed Brook to think he knew nothing about her privileged upbringing. Not that she didn't talk about her family, but it tended to be in vague terms and most often in the afterglow of their lovemaking, when every piece of information they exchanged seemed designed to reinforce the magical nature of their newfound happiness.

"I can't believe you have three much older sisters. . . ."

"Why?"

"Mine are much older, too! I have two of them. They're half sisters, though."

"Are they like Cinderella's stepsisters? Mean and jealous?"

"No—but they can be pretty difficult."

"Families," he said, leaning over to kiss the little indentation at the base of her throat. "They're all difficult in some way."

Michael had intended to stay in Manhattan for only a week or two—to attend the auction and meet with some potential corporate clients that Wayne had lined up. He'd been crashing with a friend in the West Village, though he was spending most nights with Brook at her loft in Tribeca. But work was beginning to pile up in North Barnsbury, and he knew it was probably time that the two of them start to face reality. When he told her that he really had to head back up to the country again, she began to cry.

"Oh, please don't go," she said, tears sliding down her cheeks. "I'm sorry, but I have these abandonment issues."

"Hey," he said, pulling her into his arms. "I'll be back. You know I'll be back."

"Do I know? How can I know?"

The words had just slipped out of his mouth—before he fully realized how much he meant them:

"Because I think we should get married. I want to marry you."

"You do? Do you really?"

"Yes."

"Oh, Michael, so do I! But there's something about me you don't know."

"Is it a communicable disease?"

"No," she said, laughing. "But it might be worse, as far as you're concerned. It complicates things a lot, I'm afraid."

"You're already married? You have ten kids?"

She hugged her knees and told him. She'd apparently been terrified that the news would scare him off. That he would suddenly feel different about her. He'd start seeing her as some kind of freak. Once again, Michael silently thanked Alice for warning him, because he'd been able to think through his reaction long before he actually had to deliver it.

"So what's the problem exactly? Are you worried that I'll give up my work—forget who I am—and live off of you like some gigolo?"

"No. Of course not. I already know you better than that. It's not the money so much as—well—all the people who come with it. They can be very persuasive—sometimes even manipulative. My sisters. Their husbands. Their world. Well, my world—but I've finally broken away from it."

It was the defiant way she said that last bit that gave him pause. It was as though she still needed to fully convince herself of the fact. But if she truly had broken free, then there was no need for them to worry. They would find a way to live outside the Pendleton sphere of influence. On their own terms.

⚜

Michael finally got out of the pickup and scraped the ice off the windshield. The sleet and snow had stopped. Silence filled the snowy fields. Above him, what looked like thousands of tiny flakes sat frozen in the sky. He took a deep breath, fighting back a wave of sadness. He and Brook had worked so hard and so well together to build a life they could be proud of. But now he often got the feeling that she was doubting herself. And them. Second-guessing their choices.

It became clear to him only after they were married, and then more and more as the years went on, that Brook's break from her family was far from complete. In the past, Michael didn't pay much attention to the invisible threads that still bound Brook to Peg and Janice, but lately they seemed as real and painful as barbed wire. Michael kept jabbing up against new differences and problems between them. The town hall meeting. The Boston law firm. The two of them seemed more and more out of sync with each other these days. Pulling different ways. Wanting what the other couldn't seem to give. And Michael hated the feeling. He missed his wife. He needed her help, though he couldn't bring himself to tell her so.

Because he'd begun to dream about Sylvia again. For the first time in years, she slipped into his fitful sleep almost every night now with the same stealth she used to employ when she tagged along behind Troy and Michael. In the past, Michael rarely even registered that she was there. For such a heavy and clumsy girl, she was remarkably quiet. Catlike. Her wide blue eyes watching them from the shadows. No, watching *him*. In his dreams, he could feel her eyes on him again. That adoring and unquestioning gaze. But now her gaze was boring into him. Imploring him. Or was she damning him? Michael, whom she'd loved. Who could do no wrong.

And he'd wake up with his heart slamming against his chest—stifling a scream.

19

"Oh, hey," Julie Dorman said as she opened the door to find Brook on the front porch with her shopping bag full of freshly baked bread. Brook had driven all the way down to Northridge's Bread of Heaven bakery to get the baguettes and peasant loaves. Their yeasty smell filled the Dormans' foyer. "You made it."

"Sorry I'm late," Brook said. It was the first book club meeting she'd been able to get to since the news about the civil suit broke, and she was nervous. The reading group, which Brook's sister-in-law Lynn had founded with a few friends nearly a decade ago, had grown into a nice mix of locals and second-home owners. Smart, fun, and avid readers, these were just the women Brook wanted to be friends with. When she'd hinted as much to Lynn a few years back, her sister-in-law had asked her to join.

At first, Brook felt she made a little headway in terms of acceptance. She was careful not to overstate her opinions. She always brought something special—though not obviously expensive or show-offy—for the potluck dinner. But she was never able to feel entirely comfortable with the group. She was never able to really let her guard down. Because Brook couldn't help but feel that her sister-in-law was always sitting in judgment on her. Lynn, the one woman in the whole town Brook wanted most to be close to.

Older than Michael by five years, Lynn had a wry sense of humor and a no-nonsense attitude that Brook found appealing when they first met. They'd started out on good terms, sharing histories, visiting in each other's homes, slowly building the kind of trust and intimacy that was rare for Brook. But then, when Lynn's husband, Al, lost his job with a local printing company, Brook had stumbled badly.

"Let me know if I can help out," she told Lynn when she heard the news.

"Sorry?"

"I mean, if you guys need any financial help. Just, you know, say the word, okay?"

"I'm not asking for a handout, Brook," Lynn replied.

"Of course not! I know that! I didn't think you were. I'm just saying . . ."

But the awkward conversation had ended poorly. When she told Michael what had happened, he responded with one of the few criticisms he'd ever leveled at her: "I don't think you know how you come across sometimes."

"In what way?"

"Having a lot of money doesn't mean much to you. Because you've always had it. But to most people? It means way too much. Lynn and Al are proud, and they're hurting. So when you act like giving money away is no big deal, they're going to take offense. It's your tone of voice, sweetie—that's all I'm saying."

After that, hurt and confused that her good intentions had backfired so badly, Brook had a hard time acting naturally around Lynn. She knew she was being too upbeat when Lynn was obviously going through a tough time, but she couldn't seem to find the right way of showing how much she really cared and wanted to help. Lynn seemed relieved when Brook finally backed off and stopped trying. They'd drifted apart. There was never any obvious animosity between them. Lynn was never less than polite and accommodating. But it was this very distance that the others in the book group had to have sensed—and it was fairly quickly adopted by them all. Surely, the other women must have thought, something had to be wrong with Brook Bostock if her own sister-in-law treated her so coolly.

As Brook followed Julie down the hall to the living room, where the noise level indicated the dinner was already in full swing, she had to brace herself to face Lynn again. She couldn't let her sister-in-law see—or even sense—how upset she was that Lynn hadn't even bothered to call her when the news about the lawsuit went public. Brook knew that Michael had been in touch with his family directly. But still. Would it have been such an effort for Lynn to pick up the phone when she knew Brook had to be going through hell?

The moment Brook entered the room behind her hostess, a silence fell.

She felt the group staring at her. It took her a split second to realize that, in fact, they'd all just been talking about her. And Troy. Their voices had been raised. Had there been disagreement? Most of the women were mothers and many with teenagers of their own. She realized that Troy had been telling anyone who would listen that the Bostocks had used their money and influence to get the criminal charges against them thrown out of court. That they'd smeared Phoebe's reputation to get Liam off. Of course they'd hold her responsible! Brook's face was burning. What had she been thinking? That this group would know and respect her well enough by now to at least give her and Michael the benefit of the doubt? That her word would mean more than Troy's—someone whom many of them had known all their lives? That Lynn—her own sister-in-law—would have stood up for her? But there was Lynn, looking at her with the same noncommittal expression as everybody else.

She wanted to turn and run.

"Hi, everyone!" she said instead, forcing a smile as she walked over to the side table where the buffet dinner was laid out. "Sorry to be late! But I brought this great sourdough from Bread of Heaven. Have you tried it? It's just incredible. . . ."

She chattered on. She kept her smile in place. She complimented everyone on what they'd brought for the potluck. She put herself in happy-gear cruise control—and did her best not to notice the monosyllabic replies. The turned backs. The sudden need to help Julie in the kitchen or check on the sitter. She followed the discussion just enough to be able to make an observation from time to time. The conversation tended to pause briefly whenever she said anything, then flow on without comment. By the time the evening came to an end, she felt more or less invisible.

As usual, Brook stayed to help clean up. Since joining the group, she'd tried to make herself as useful as possible after the meetings: loading the dishwasher, packing up the leftovers, bagging the trash. She'd hoped her actions would show that she wasn't aloof, that she didn't mind literally getting her hands dirty, that she was just like them. When Julie's kitchen was back in working order, Brook used the powder room in the hallway. She could hear guests leaving, voices in the hall. And then two particular voices, right outside the bathroom door:

"Maybe I should have said something to her," Lynn said.

"Like what?" Julie asked. "Like 'Do you want to talk about what happened?' It was so damned clear she didn't."

"Yeah, she does tend to talk a mile a minute when she's nervous."

"If she *was* nervous," Julie replied. "It seemed to me that she was totally oblivious to the fact that she was the elephant in the room."

"It would have done her good to talk, I think."

"Oh, she talked, all right," Julie said. "About everything under the sun except the one thing on everyone's mind."

Brook leaned her forehead against the door. She closed her eyes. Tight. She couldn't let herself cry. She waited until the women had moved on. She took some deep breaths and opened the door. She retrieved her coat from the hall closet, and then found her hostess in the foyer, where Lynn was taking her leave.

"Thanks so much for a great evening," Brook said, walking up to Julie and her sister-in-law. "It was just super to see everyone again."

"You were right about that bread," Lynn said as she walked beside Brook down the path to the turnaround where they'd parked their cars. "It was very good."

"Yes, I think it's the best . . . ," Brook began to say. She'd gotten through the worst of the evening, so it was ridiculous to lose it now. Childish really. And in front of Lynn of all people.

"Oh!" Lynn said, stopping next to Brook and leaning in toward her. "Are you *crying*?"

"Damn!" Brook said, her shoulders shaking. "And I don't even have a Kleenex."

"I have some in my glove compartment," Lynn said, taking Brook's elbow. "Come on."

Maybe it was Lynn's touch. Or the gentle surprise in her tone. But by the time Brook slid into the passenger seat of her sister-in-law's Prius, she was sobbing. All at once, the growing sense of loneliness and estrangement that had been building in Brook for too many weeks now—gave way.

"Hey . . . ," Lynn said, handing over another wad of tissue. "Are you okay?"

"No, I'm not okay," Brook said between ragged breaths. "Isn't it . . . kind of . . . obvious?"

"It is now. But earlier? No. I'd say you were your usual totally upbeat and cheery self."

"That's just . . . how I cope."

"What? By pretending everything's great when it's really all shit?"

"Yes. That's what I do. That's how . . . I get through."

"Why?"

"Because . . . I always have. I've always tried to . . . put a good face on things."

"Even when you know things are pretty terrible?"

"Especially then," Brook said. "Especially now. How else was I supposed to handle the situation tonight?"

"A little honesty might have helped."

"Honesty? About what? That Michael and I are dealing with the most shaming and terrifying thing imaginable? That I've never been more frightened in my life?"

"Yes, Brook!" Lynn said. "That's exactly what I mean. I kept waiting for you to call me—to ask for my help. Or advice. Or *anything*. Instead, you act like you don't need anyone. Like you have it totally together. Like everything's just super-duper great!"

"You could have called me."

"That's true. I could have, but I have my pride. Too much of it, I know. But I figured it was up to you to make the first move."

"I'm sorry," Brook said. "I'm sorry for what happened between us. I know I've made a lot of mistakes with you. And other people in town. I know I've tried too hard to fit in—to be liked."

"So? Stop trying. Just be—just relax and be who you really are. Be the person who just told me that she's never felt more frightened in her life. There's nothing wrong with letting people see that you're in trouble—with admitting you could use some help."

❧

"The public exposure's bad enough," Brook said a little later. Lynn had turned on the engine and turned up the heat, but Brook remained huddled in her coat. She felt as though she'd cried herself out, but she felt more depleted than relieved. "It's what this whole thing is doing to us personally—that's the really hard thing."

"I don't mean to pry, but you and Michael—you're okay, right?"

"It's been tough. We can't seem to agree on how to handle things. We're meeting with a new law firm next week to talk about the civil suit. I have a feeling we're going to be advised to seek a settlement right away. And I don't know. I feel terrible about what Phoebe went through. A part of me really does understand Troy's anger and resentment. I think maybe we should just give him the money and call it a day. Get the damned thing behind us and try to move on."

"And Michael wants to fight it."

"He keeps saying that Troy's just after a big payout, but I think there's more to it than that. But he keeps so much locked up inside! What do you know about what happened between him and Troy when they were boys?"

"He's never talked to you about it?"

"Not really. Just that they stopped being friends at one point—and Troy really resents him for it."

"They were pretty close the whole time they were growing up," Lynn said. "Michael spent a lot of time over at the Lansings' house. I think he liked it that Troy had so many brothers around. He was so outnumbered by all of us girls!"

"But didn't Troy have a sister, too?" Brook asked. "I think Phoebe once told me that Troy had a younger sister who died pretty young."

"Yes, you're right," Lynn said. "I was so much older I don't really remember her. But I do remember when it happened. I was at SUNY, working in Albany for the summer. No one could figure out what went wrong, but she drowned in a lake up on some mountainside property that the Lansings own. Troy and Michael found her. It really broke the family up."

"It must have been horrible for Troy and Michael."

"Yes, and I think Michael was going through a bad time himself then. My dad was really tough on him, I know. I remember trying to get Michael to talk to me about it when I came home to visit, but he just shrugged it off. He got back on his feet soon enough after that, though. He got through it. Just the way the two of you will get through this."

"Thanks," Brook said, reaching over to touch Lynn's arm. "Thanks for talking to me about all this. Thanks for listening."

"Hey," Lynn said, giving her a hug. "All you have to say is that you need my help. That's all you've ever needed to say."

Brook thanked her again and zipped up her parka. She opened the door and was stepping out when she turned back to her sister-in-law and asked:

"What was her name, by the way? Troy's sister?"

"Sylvia," Lynn said, shaking her head. "So sad, isn't it?"

Part Three

20

❦

"*I*'m convinced Liam's covering up for one of the other boys," Brook said. She and Michael were sitting side by side at a conference room table at Schmidt, Lloyd & Freeman, facing Angela Lloyd and two of her junior male colleagues. The corner office on the thirty-third floor on Boylston Place with its floor-to-ceiling windows offered distant views of Boston Harbor. Airplanes, taking off from or banking for Logan, periodically crisscrossed a pale blue sky. Michael barely noticed any of this. Instead, he kept thinking back on the way Angela Lloyd—smile wide, dark hair pulled back, pin-striped pants suit impeccably tailored—greeted them in the reception area as they arrived: *Mr. and Mrs. Pendleton. So nice to meet you!*

But, of course, as far as this law firm was concerned, that's who they were. That's why they were here. Michael kept telling himself to be reasonable. To be fair. To keep his resentment in check. Nothing had been decided. This wasn't a criticism of how he had handled the situation so far. Or what he thought was right. This wasn't about *him*, okay?

"But it's my understanding that your son says he can't remember what happened," Angela said, frowning as she glanced down at the legal folders in front of her.

"Yes, that's what he claims," Brook said. "But in the beginning Liam flatly denied he'd had anything to do with hurting Phoebe. I was there when he was first accused of it—and I know him so well! I can read his face. He was totally stunned that anyone would believe he could do such a thing. But then, later that night, after he spoke to the other boys on the . . ."

Michael could tell by the noncommittal way Angela and her two colleagues were reacting to Brook's claims that they were probably thinking, *Here's a mom who can't face the truth about her son. Proceed with caution.* The lawyer let Brook talk on for another minute or two, before discreetly interrupting:

"Well, yes, but I'm afraid that regardless of who actually assaulted Ms. Lansing, this case is going to be primarily about your role in what happened that night. The way the Massachusetts courts see it, you and your husband are to be held responsible for the welfare of any minor in your home when underage drinking is involved."

"Yes," Brook said, "I understand that. I just thought it would be helpful for you to know what kind of boy Liam really is—he's not mean or aggressive. He's just young—and overwhelmed. It's been a difficult year. . . ."

Michael saw Angela's two colleagues exchange glances as Brook went on in her usual nervous fashion. Brook was grasping at straws, Michael decided. And she was now convinced that this new law firm was going to be the answer to all their problems. On the drive over on the Mass Turnpike that morning, she'd delivered a running commentary on her thoughts about the meeting ahead with Schmidt, Lloyd & Freeman.

"I spent some time on their Web site," she told him. "And, you know, it's amazing how many lawsuits like this have been brought over the past couple of years. They have a lot of the case studies and press links up on the site. There's a whole section on educating parents about the law, and they've done an incredible amount of public service work to build awareness on the issue."

She went on to tell him that they'd be meeting that day with a woman lawyer, one of the founding partners in the firm.

"I like that idea, don't you?" Brook asked him. "I don't know, I just feel she'll be more sympathetic somehow. That I'll have an easier time talking to her."

"You've been having such a tough time talking to Larry and Martin Freston?" he asked. He knew he was being petty, but he couldn't help himself. He'd agreed to go to Boston to consult with the law firm Staff had lined up because he realized that if he refused, Brook's family would think he was being stubborn and difficult. But he hated the feeling that he was being outnumbered and outmaneuvered by them. And he'd been blindsided when—after the fact—Brook had informed him that she'd asked Larry's and Freston's offices to FedEx copies of their paperwork to the Boston firm. He wasn't surprised when Larry had called him later that day:

"You switching horses?" Larry had asked.

"No, we're just looking over some different livestock. Trying to be prepared if things don't go our way—and Troy goes ahead with a civil suit. Brook's family has taken an interest."

"Ah," Larry said. Then, after a pause: "You know what this firm is going to recommend, don't you?"

"Sure. But I won't do it."

"Think about it hard, Michael. I'd hate to see this thing cause any more collateral damage."

"What do you mean?"

"Your marriage."

❧

"Well, listen, great," Angela cut in quickly when Brook started to wind down. "We appreciate you filling us in on the personal details. That's one of the reasons we wanted to meet with you both face-to-face. There's so much about a situation like this that's hard to gauge from the files. Though we've read everything your local lawyers put together for us." Angela looked down at the folders in front of her.

"We're also very familiar with the firm that's representing the Lansings," Angela went on. "Like us, Cranston has substantial expertise and experience in this area of the law. And we've had the opportunity to sit across the table from them on several occasions."

"I was told they're pretty tough," Brook said.

"Well, so are we," Angela replied. "That's not the problem. Look, I need to tell this to you straight. We've read through the transcripts of the magistrate's hearing and all the supporting documents, and we have to advise you that Cranston has the material to put together a pretty solid case against you."

Angela held up her right hand, fingers spread.

"You knowingly left four teenagers unsupervised overnight in your home where alcohol was available," she said, ticking off the statement with her left index finger.

"You were aware that your son had gotten into trouble drinking before this.

"The prosecution has graphic photos of Ms. Lansing after the attack.

"Ms. Lansing named your son. Liam's claim he has no memory of what happened seems—as you yourself pointed out—less than convincing.

"Plus, your lawyer had the brilliant thought to accuse an innocent virgin of being sexually active. Not a great move."

With each statement, Angela ticked off another finger.

"Which of these things do you intend to deny?" she asked, spreading both hands across the tabletop and leaning forward. "I'm sorry, but I don't see a very good outcome here."

Michael understood that Angela was trying to frighten them—and probably shame them, too. He'd prepared himself for that, but he knew Brook had been expecting something very different from this woman.

"Liam didn't do it," Brook said softly. "*That*'s why I think maybe we should try to fight this. Because if we don't, if he has to live with this thing hanging over his head for the rest of his life . . . I'm afraid it's going to do him real harm."

"I understand that," Angela replied. "But our main concern is the allegations against you as parents. That's why the Social Host law was created—to hold you responsible. The fact that Ms. Lansing was assaulted in *your* home, after drinking with a group of underage boys, where there was absolutely no adult supervision. Though in some cases, the parents not being on the premises might help mitigate the situation, in this instance I'm afraid your absence—knowing what you did about your son's problems—only further complicates the matter."

"So you think we should settle?" Michael asked, although

the answer seemed obvious. As far as Michael was concerned, Brook's brother-in-law had already made it clear to Angela Lloyd what he wanted to have accomplished at this meeting, and she had carried out his orders very effectively.

"I frankly see no other choice," Angela said. "I suggest we start gathering as much information as we can about what Cranston and Cranston is planning—who they've been talking to. What tricks they may have up their sleeve. Our job is to keep the public exposure—and the ultimate payout—to an absolute minimum. And the sooner we start getting our ducks in a row, the better off we'll be when the time comes."

⁓

Brook was silent on the way down in the elevator. She didn't say anything to Michael after he'd retrieved the car from the parking garage and picked her up in front of the building. He glanced over at her as he maneuvered the car through Boston's congested streets. She was staring straight ahead. It wasn't until they'd finally merged onto the turnpike that she spoke.

"You know, it occurred to me in the middle of the meeting that I don't know how you feel about something. Something really important."

"What's that?"

"Do you think Liam did it?"

A part of him had been waiting for this question since the night Troy had first accused his son of assaulting Phoebe. Of course his first response was, *Liam would never hurt her. He's a good kid*. But then Troy had replied: *Yeah? Well, so were you, if I remember right*. And Michael had felt his confidence shatter. As a boy Liam's age, Michael himself had been a different person when he was drunk. Liam had admitted he'd been "totally out of it." Michael knew for a fact that anything was possible in that situation.

"I don't know," Michael said after a pause.

"I don't believe this! You *do* think he did it!"

"I didn't say that. I said I wasn't sure. I think you have to at least keep your mind open to the possibility, Brook."

"No, I don't think I do. He's my *son*, and I know him better than that. He's not perfect. He has his faults. I know he lacks confidence. He tries too hard to fit in. That's why I'm sure he caved in to pressure from Brandon or Carey. But he did *not* attack Phoebe; I'm absolutely certain of that."

"Good," Michael said. "I'm glad you're so positive. He's my son, too, and I know what it's like to be a boy Liam's age. Adolescence is a crazy time, and teenagers can do some crazy things."

"Then I don't get it—if you believe he might have hurt Phoebe, why wouldn't you want to settle the case?"

"And if you think he's innocent, why *would* you want to settle? How is that going to make this any easier for him? And what do you think that tells him about standing up for himself? Besides, as Angela Lloyd kept pointing out, it's not Liam who's on trial here. *We* are. Because Troy sees a way of taking advantage of the situation. It's easy enough for Staff and his lawyer friends to tell us to give in to Troy's demands—and walk away. They don't have to deal with the consequences. They don't have to live in a town that will never think of us in the same way again."

"How do you suppose the town looks at us *now*?" Brook said. "How do you think it's *always* looked at us? Do you know what I took away from that meeting today? I heard Angela Lloyd tell us that we're bad parents. That we made a number of really bad decisions and that we're responsible for what happened. And that's from *our* side of the table! Think what Cranston and Cranston is going to do to us if we go to trial. Do you have any idea how Barnsbury is going to look at us *then*?"

"So, rolling over and giving up is the better option? I don't think so. I'm proud of who we are—and what we've done. I'm proud of Liam and Tilly and the way we've brought them up. Okay, we shouldn't have left them alone that night. We were wrong to think Liam could handle it. But I'm not willing to let that one mistake ruin our life here. I think it's worth fighting for."

"I don't know. I feel like everything—and everyone—is stacked against us."

"Not if we face this together."

"I'm scared. I'm not like you. I'm not self-sufficient. I'm tired of being treated like a pariah. I need people! I need friends! I want to be liked—and to have my children liked! I want to belong somewhere."

"I'm not enough? *We're* not enough?"

"That's not fair."

"And that's not an answer."

Brook didn't reply, and Michael was too disheartened to press her on it. So he'd been right in thinking that she'd been questioning their life in Barnsbury. Which meant she had to be having serious doubts about their marriage. Their love. Everything that mattered to him most in the world. They drove into the darkening afternoon, the silence building between them—like an actual presence. A person. Someone Brook had finally named. They'd just passed the Lee exit and were ten minutes from home when she said: "You know, you keep saying Troy is only in this for the money, but I think something else is at stake. I think a lot of this is really between you and Troy—whatever turned him against you years ago. Maybe that's what you need to settle, Michael. More than any lawsuit."

His heart ached. Brook had no idea how hard he'd worked to put it all behind him. He and Brook were alike in that way: they had both tried, after difficult beginnings, to make themselves over into new and better people. But Brook had always been honest about her struggles, talking frankly throughout their marriage about her family and her girlhood insecurities.

I bet you always had it together, though, she'd told him when they first fell in love. *I bet you were always the strong, silent type. Even as a boy, right?*

I guess so, he'd told her. But he knew otherwise. Silent, perhaps. But strong? Hardly. Though it's what he wanted her to think. It's what he'd told himself that she needed to believe. He'd long ago convinced himself that the facts didn't matter. The truth was dead and buried. Who would know the difference? It had seemed like the right thing to do. Until now.

21

❧

"*I* think Tilly could use a change of scenery," Brook told Michael a few days before Deer Mountain's midwinter break. "I thought I'd take her into the city with me next week. Alice and I have a few meetings lined up and the Ferris Foundation gala's on Thursday night, but there would still be enough time for us to see a show and do a little shopping. I thought we'd stay with my dad. You know how much he dotes on her."

She shouldn't have added that last bit. It was an oversell. And now Michael would suspect what she'd been trying to conceal: it was she who needed to get away. Since their trip to Boston three days before, Michael had been in a total funk. The intensity of his gloom frightened her. He made an effort to be loving around Tilly, he sounded normal enough talking on the phone to his manager and the studio in North Barnsbury, but he'd literally turned a cold shoulder to Brook. They'd been sleeping with their backs to each other.

"Okay," Michael said. It was early in the morning, but he looked exhausted. He didn't glance Brook's way as he poured coffee into his thermos. She realized that he planned to spend the whole day holed up in his studio again.

"You sure?" she asked, watching as he shrugged on his parka. "You don't mind being on your own right now?"

"I said it was okay," he told her as he headed for the kitchen door. It was almost impossible to talk to him right now. Which was why she kept putting off the discussion they needed to have about formally hiring Schmidt, Lloyd & Freeman to represent them. She didn't think she could take another argument like the one they'd had on their way back from the meeting in Boston. They hadn't spoken in any depth since. And, though she was used to Michael's moods, his silences these last few days seemed weighted with painful significance. And Brook, for the first time that she could remember, didn't really want to know what he was thinking.

"Can we go skating at Rockefeller Center?" Tilly asked on the train ride down. "Can we go to the American Girl store? Can we go to the wax museum in Times Square? Lisette was there with her aunt at Christmas and she has all these photos of her with like Michael Jackson and Taylor Swift. They're really awesome."

"Did I just hear the 'A' word?" Brook said. "You know what PeterPop is going to say about that sort of language." It amused Brook that her father was so strict with his grandchildren about their overuse of "like" and "awesome," yet he seemed perfectly happy to have them continue to call him by the silly nickname Liam had first made up for him as a toddler.

"So you think we might be able to visit the wax museum?" Tilly said.

Brook smiled. How long had it been since she'd done that? Days, certainly. Maybe even weeks. She'd been right to take Tilly along with her on this trip. Bright, fun-loving, optimistic— Tilly was naturally what Brook could only work at trying to be. And it seemed to Brook that she'd been born that way: eagerly taking Brook's nipple, sleeping through the night, cheerfully tottering along behind Liam. Though lately Brook sensed a subtle change in her daughter. It was hard to put her finger on exactly, but it often seemed to her now that Tilly was a little *too* sunny. Surprisingly upbeat. Her daughter tended to be so sensitive and perceptive. Could it really be that she wasn't aware of the shadow that hung over her older brother? Or the terrible pressure that her parents were living under?

"Sure," Brook said. "If it makes you happy, I think we could manage to squeeze in Madame Tussauds—and, if I remember correctly, the Hershey's store is right around the corner."

"I wish Liam could be here," Tilly said. "Don't you?"

"Of course," Brook told her, but with a sinking feeling realized that it wasn't true. It was actually a relief not to be thinking about the lawsuit for a day or two. Not to have Liam and his problems dominating every waking moment. And her son's recent behavior was only making matters worse. Because just when Brook longed to feel close to him—just when she wanted more than anything else to reach out and comfort him—he seemed intent on keeping his distance and fending off any genuine emotion. Their weekly phone conversations had become pure torture. Her questions were answered in monosyllables. He was "fine." Everything was "okay." He'd barely responded when she told him they'd been advised to settle the lawsuit. It was clear that he couldn't wait to get her off the phone.

She used to pride herself on how happy they were as a family. They had so much fun together! Who needed more on a snowy winter night than a game of Bananagrams in front of the fire with your husband and kids? What could be better on a hot, lazy summer evening than lingering over supper on the screen porch telling ghost stories? It was everything Brook had ever wanted and never had as a child: the sense of absolute security, of effortlessly sharing, of being surrounded by your favorite people in the world.

But now she felt all that slipping from her grasp. Michael had retreated into himself. Liam had grown more and more detached. Only Tilly seemed unchanged. Unscathed. And Brook? When she allowed herself to think about it, she knew she was probably as lonely and frightened as she'd ever been as a girl.

⤮

"You didn't have to wait up," Brook told her father when she got in Thursday night from the Ferris benefit. It was nearly midnight. She'd spent the morning with Tilly on the ice at Rockefeller Center, then the afternoon and evening on her feet orchestrating the black-tie sit-down gala dinner for 250 guests at the Metropolitan Club. She was exhausted. Though the evening had been considered a great success by her client, Brook was feeling unhappy and on edge. Over the last few nights, after Tilly had gone to bed, Brook had submitted to Peter's probing interrogation about the lawsuit. Tonight, though, she didn't think she could manage another rehashing of the painful subject.

"It's hardly past my bedtime," Peter said, closing his book and putting it down on the side table next to his Eames chair.

For a septuagenarian male who'd lived alone for nearly two decades, the Riverside Drive apartment was remarkably picked-up and welcoming. Tilda Pendleton's expensive classical furniture—overstuffed armchairs and the dainty maple escritoire—had been arranged to contrast artfully with Peter's more modern and eclectic tastes. A small Prendergast watercolor shared a wall with a wildly colorful Rauschenberg lithograph. Built-in floor-to-ceiling shelving that housed Peter's extensive book collection included specially designed cubbies that displayed Tilda's Meissen figurines. An original Eames chair with a timeworn ottoman served as Peter's center of operations.

"How did things go here?" Brook asked, kicking off her heels and sliding onto a low, velour-covered couch. She pulled one of the tasseled silk pillows—a cherished remnant from her mother's collection—into her arms.

"Not well," Peter said. "I had a terrible shock. Your daughter beat me at Scrabble. She managed to score ninety-nine points on the word 'zero' at the very end of the game. It was outrageous. I told her that she needed to start learning some manners."

"I'm sorry," Brook said, yawning.

"She started to cry after I said it."

"What?" Brook sat up.

"You heard me. I was just kidding around, of course! But suddenly I noticed her lower lip quivering and these big tears rolling down her cheeks. When I asked her what the hell was going on, she just shook her head. Refused to say."

"Oh dear. I wonder what's going on."

"I got it out of her finally. I still have a few trace memories left of how to ferret out a story from a reluctant source. I just kept her talking about this and that. School. Her friends. Liam.

This goddamned lawsuit. Do you have any idea how guilty she feels about the whole thing?"

"What? Tilly?"

"Yes, Tilly. It's not unusual for a child to feel responsible when something goes wrong in his or her family. During a divorce, or when a family member dies, whatever the crisis—kids will for some crazy reason become convinced that they caused it. In Tilly's case, she thinks that if she hadn't fallen asleep before Liam got home—if she'd just *been there* for him or some such idiocy—then none of this would have happened. And I take it that the girl involved—this Phoebe person—is a friend of hers?"

"She was Tilly's sitter."

"Well, apparently she's a lot more than that. Tilly clearly adores her. And misses her. And feels guilty, too, that she's no longer welcome at your house."

"I can't believe she didn't tell me any of this," Brook said shakily.

"You can honestly sit there and tell me that you had no idea your daughter was so confused and upset?"

"Daddy, please. We're all going through a hard time right now."

"I know you are," Peter said. "But I don't think that's any excuse. You of all people should remember what it feels like to be young and frightened."

"Of course, I remember—all too well. I think about Mommy every day."

"So what happened? How did you miss the signs with Tilly?"

"I guess she did a good job covering them up. She always puts such a good face on things."

"Brooklet. Sweetheart. That's your *excuse*? Come on! What-ever happened to 'It takes one to know one'? Don't you get it? She's just like you!"

"You're being kind of hard on me here."

"Someone needs to be. Someone needs to tell you that you're so blinded by self-pity right now you can't even see what's going on in front of your face."

"That's not fair!"

"*Screw* fair—it's a fact. All I've been hearing from you these last few days is how everyone else is responsible for what's happened. One of the other boys made Liam take the blame. Troy Lansing is only after your money. Barnsbury has turned against you. Liam is being difficult. Even Michael—because it seems he wants to fight for his good name and your repu-tation."

"Stop it! Why are you—"

"Because your *life* is at stake here, Brook! Your marriage, your family, everything you've worked so hard for all these years. And, if you keep blaming others, if you continue to pass along your own responsibility the way you're doing right now, I'm afraid you're going to lose it all!"

"What are you saying? That it's all my fault?" Brook was stunned by her father's harsh words. He'd never spoken to her this way before. Though she knew him to be fiercely opin-ionated, though she'd heard him lash out against what he saw as political injustices all her life, though she'd read his fiery op-eds denouncing this or that conservative stance or proposal, Peter Hines had always held his famous temper in check when it came to his only child.

"Not all of it. But accidents don't occur because just one thing goes wrong. A series of things usually happens: a rainy road, a tired driver, the oncoming car not dimming the brights . . . and suddenly—*bam!*—a head-on collision. This lawsuit is a major fucking pileup—and, yes, I think you're partially responsible."

"Which part?"

Brook's father took her in over his glasses. He looked sad—and tired, too, she realized.

"Which part, Daddy?" she asked again.

"I don't think that's for me to say," he told her, pushing his glasses up on his forehead and rubbing his eyes. "I've already said more than I should. You know I'm not without my prejudices, Brook. I'm not without my own failings and regrets. I just hate to see you repeating my mistakes."

"What mistakes?"

"Allowing other people's opinions to affect what you know to be right. Your mother would have married me if I'd just pushed her more. I know she was gun-shy after the hell Howard put her through during the divorce. But she was also bowing to pressure from Peg and Janice, who hated us being together. She didn't want to upset them any further. So we let that damned family shame us into putting off making things legal. Even after you were born! What a fool I was. No, what a coward."

"And you think they're doing the same thing to me now?"

"Of course they are! You know perfectly well they are. Who gives a damn what anyone else thinks—whether it's the Pendleton family or the whole town of Barnsbury? If you really believe Liam didn't assault this girl, then you have to ask yourself what a settlement would be saying to him. I think it would be saying that he's guilty. And that it's okay to sweep everything under the rug."

"That's what Michael says, too," Brook replied. "But I'm

really worried about Liam, Daddy. I'm worried about how much he can take. I'm sure he didn't hurt Phoebe, but he was obviously really out of it. And it's hardly the first time. I love him so much—but there's always been a part of him that I can't reach, that's just closed off from everyone—this will make him understand how dangerous it is. I'm sure of it."

"Are you?" Peter said. "I don't think so. You need to do everything in your power to get through to him. You need to make him realize that his actions have serious consequences— alcohol, drugs, letting things get so out of hand that night. This is something you need to face as a family. Whatever else happens, you want Liam to come out of this willing to change. And, maybe even more important, really believing that he can."

22

Phoebe could go to jail for what she'd done. She'd looked it up on the Internet. Though the statute included a lot of confusing legalese, it seemed pretty clear that anyone committing perjury in the state of Massachusetts could be incarcerated for up to twenty years. Troy had laughed when she'd asked him about this on the way back from the meeting at the Cranston & Cranston offices in Boston.

"I wouldn't worry," he told her. "You're still a minor. And besides, who do you think's going to find out?"

"What if Liam changes his story?" Phoebe asked. This possibility had been on her mind a lot lately. "What if he decides to tell the truth?"

"Listen, that's just not going to happen, okay? And who's going to believe Liam if he does try to backpedal now? You don't think Brandon is going to suddenly step up to the plate and say, 'Oh, yeah! Sorry folks, I'm really the guilty party here.' No, it's obvious Brandon has Liam by the balls—and he's not about to let go. You've got nothing to worry about."

But Phoebe had stopped believing everything her father told her. He used to seem so much larger than life. So big and strong and self-confident! Like he could never make a mistake. When she was little, she loved riding around on his broad shoulders, her arms wrapped around his neck, his curly red hair tickling her chin. He was proud of her, too, she knew. He was constantly showing her off to his friends.

"Look at this hair, will you?" he'd say. "Look at those dimples! Isn't she just the cutest thing you've ever seen?"

So it was hard for her to begin to realize that her father wasn't perfect. He wasn't the tough-minded truth-teller he often proclaimed himself to be. In fact, ever since he'd told her to keep the details about what happened that night to herself, she had started to realize that there were things about her father that she didn't much like. He had a way of manipulating Phoebe's mom to get what he wanted—either pressuring her or making her feel guilty. And he was starting to do the same thing to her. When they were alone together—or clearly out of Wanda's earshot—he'd taken to giving her little pep talks.

"You heard what the lawyers said—the media coverage on this is only beginning. The spotlight's going to be on you. So you can never forget that you were the victim in this situation. You're going to have to play that part with real conviction, you know what I mean? It might help if you thought of it as just another acting role—like the great job you did with that Shakespeare thing you were in."

"But this isn't pretend, Daddy."

"You're right. It's absolutely for real! This is your future we're talking about here. Your reputation. Right now, you've got everybody on your side. But if people start to think that you've been having second thoughts—if they hear that you might be waffling about what happened—I don't think I need to tell you that you're going to be damaged goods in this town."

What if Phoebe's mom found out what her dad was up to? A part of her longed to confide in Wanda. At certain moments, when they were alone together, the words were right on the tip of her tongue. But then she hated to consider the consequences of such a confession. It wasn't just her father's wrath that made her hesitate. She was worried that the argument that would inevitably erupt after such a revelation would undo the signs of détente between her divorced parents.

"This is cozy, isn't it?" she overheard Troy ask her mom late one night. Actually, it was almost two o'clock in the morning. Phoebe had slipped out of bed to use the bathroom and had stopped at the top of the stairs when she heard her father's voice. The Netflix movie they'd been watching together had to have ended hours ago. She didn't catch what her mom, who tended to speak softly, said in reply, but she did hear Troy's response:

"Yeah, and I miss the old times. I miss them so badly some days I want to cry. Listen, I know it might take a while, but when this money comes through, things are going to be different for me. I'm going to be able to get back on my feet. I'm going to be able to start taking care of you and Phoebe again." Whatever Wanda had said then, Troy's tone of voice changed:

"Oh, I know that! You've been great on your own. You've been fantastic! I realize you don't need me. I don't pretend to think that you'll ever really need me again. But, come on, admit it: every once in a while—like tonight, for instance—you still want me, don't you? We're still good together, Wanda. We've always been good together."

Phoebe would do just about anything to have her parents

remarry. It was a cherished dream she'd never given up on—not once during the nearly five years that had elapsed since Wanda threw Troy out of the house. She respected the no-nonsense way Wanda had gone about making a living—and a life—for herself and Phoebe. But something was always missing when it was just the two of them. Troy's presence—outsized and demanding—loomed over them even when he wasn't there. Over the last year or so, as Troy slowly started to insinuate himself back into the little clapboarded Cape, Phoebe began to let herself hope that he'd eventually be coming back for good.

Phoebe was pretty sure her parents still loved each other. You could see it in the exasperated smile Wanda would give Troy after he'd said or done something particularly outrageous. Or the hungry, wounded way Troy's gaze followed his ex-wife when he thought no one was looking. The idea of her parents' ruined but still smoldering love appealed to the romantic in Phoebe. *They were good together!* And the last thing Phoebe wanted was to put any new obstacles in the way of a possible reconciliation.

Even if it meant going to jail. Which was something that—when she took a moment to really think about it—appealed to Phoebe's romantic nature, as well. *Yes, she'd lied! She'd lied to hurt the boy she loved. And she'd done it to get revenge—she'd hoped to wound him just as badly as he'd wounded her.* Though in her fantasies she never actually faced a jail cell. Instead, she'd imagine herself being cross-examined during a trial. Liam would be there, too, of course, looking pale and lost. She could see the remorse in his eyes. And then—just as her testimony was about to end—she'd stand up before the court and confess: *Yes, I lied. I lied to hurt the boy I loved.*

Some nights, Phoebe would imagine Liam running to the

front of the courtroom and embracing her. Other nights, over-whelmed with relief, he'd sink his head into his hands. She tinkered with what happened next, as well. Did they walk out of the courthouse together, media swarming the front steps—or escape through some back exit, hand in hand? Once again, Phoebe retreated into her daydreams.

Late one Thursday night in early March, as Phoebe was getting ready to go to sleep, her smart phone jiggled briefly by her pillow.

Hi, Liam had texted.

Hi? She stared at the word. It looked so innocent and straightforward, but she realized immediately that the two letters presented a serious dilemma. For one thing, her dad had made her promise that she would not communicate with Liam in any way. For another, though she'd been longing to hear from him, what she really had been hoping for was an apology. She felt she deserved an *I'm really sorry* at the very least. But *Hi?* It took absolutely no responsibility for what Liam had let Brandon do to her. It did nothing to take back his claim that Phoebe had had sex with him. Or what he'd said about Phoebe's dad only really caring about the money he could get. She was furious all over again just thinking about it.

Sorry. So so sorry.

Phoebe stared down at the second text that followed quickly on the first. It was almost as though he'd been reading her mind. She sat up, cradling the phone in her lap. Her dad would kill her if she responded. The lawyers, too, had made it clear that she shouldn't have any contact whatsoever with "the defendant."

Just say hi back. Pls?

She thought of that brief, thrilling moment when he held her in his arms. She remembered the tender way he'd kissed the top of her head—the warmth of his body against hers.

Hi back, she typed.

✧

In the beginning, his texts were simple enough. Little news blasts.

> Snowed again 2day.
> Warriors 5, Hartford 3.

By then Phoebe had learned that Liam played on the ice hockey team at his prep school. The Warriors' victories clearly meant a lot to him.

Way 2 go, Warriors! she texted back. She never let her phone out of her sight now, and deleted his messages as soon as they came in. He wrote her only at night. Soon it was every night. Sometimes pretty late, but Phoebe always waited up to reply to him. She guessed that it was the last thing he did before he went to bed. They never wrote about anything particularly important. By some unspoken agreement, the subject of the lawsuit and the terrible night that had spawned it was never broached. It was all pretty mundane stuff. But what could be more comforting when you're feeling a little lonely than to share the details of your day with someone you cared about?

> U awake?

It was past midnight, the latest he'd ever contacted her, and in fact, she'd fallen asleep with the phone nestled under the pillow by her ear.

Yep. Where were u?

Down.

Like in sad?

Yeah. Bad day.

Why?

Feel fucked up.

Uh oh.

No—not drinking!

What then?

Can we talk? 4 real?

Give me 15 mins. I'll call u.

Phoebe dressed as warmly as possible and tiptoed down the stairs. Her mom's bedroom door was ajar, but Phoebe wasn't worried. Wanda was a heavy sleeper, and Phoebe had snuck out so many times in the past to meet Liam that she'd developed what seemed to her a foolproof procedure. She knew how to avoid every loose floorboard, each creaky step. How to find her way through the darkened downstairs by the glow of the stove's LED panel in the kitchen. How to ever-so-slowly ease open the back storm door so that the aluminum framing wouldn't squeak. She slipped her winter coat off the peg in the mudroom as she left. She made it to the playground with two minutes to spare.

"Hi," Liam answered on the first ring. His voice sounded as close as a whisper in Phoebe's ear. She was frightened by the reality of it suddenly. She had to adjust her thinking. Replace her imaginary Liam with the boy who was very much alive and breathing on the other end of the line.

"Hey," she said. "Where are you?"

"In my room. Carey's at a piano competition in Hartford."

"So. Wow. Hi."

"Where are you?"

"On our bench," she said. Then, realizing he might not think of it in the same way she did, added, "You know—the one in the playground."

"Sure. Our bench. I can just see you there so clearly! I wish I could be there with you, Phebe."

"Me, too," she said. She was beginning to feel a little better. His voice was becoming familiar again. "So like—what happened today?"

"Nothing really. The Warriors lost a big game, but it's not that."

"You said you were feeling bad."

"Yeah. I don't know. I guess I'm just beginning to realize some stuff. About me. About what happened. I really let you down."

"Yeah," she said. "But it's okay."

"No, it's not!" he said. "After everything I did to you— that I let Brandon do—I can't believe you're still so sweet to me, Phebe. You're so good. I don't deserve it."

"Hey," she said. "What happened? Where's all this coming from?"

"I guess I just finally figured out that I'm nothing but a fuckup." His voice didn't sound right. It wasn't until he took a deep breath and she heard the ragged hitches in the inhalation that she realized he was crying. "And I'm always going to be a fuckup."

"That's not true!"

"Yeah, it is."

"Listen, Liam—I'm sorry but I have to ask you this: *have* you been drinking?"

"No."

"You can tell me! It's okay. You can tell me anything. I just need to know what's going on."

"It's nothing like that," he said. "I'm just—it's just me. I feel like I'm nothing inside. Like I'm never going to *be* anything. I'm just this worthless piece of shit. And then I start thinking about all the ways I've fucked up. With you. With my dad. I just don't see how I'm ever going to be able to make it up to you."

"I don't need you to—"

"I feel like I'm at the bottom of this big hole," he said. "And I'm never going to be able to climb out."

"Hey, there, listen to me," Phoebe said. Her hands were shaking. She knew she needed to say just the right thing now. She had to find the perfect tone. She couldn't get this wrong. "Remember last summer when we made that pact? When you promised me that you'd tell me if you ever thought you might—"

"I remember, Phebe. This isn't that call, okay? I just wanted to hear your voice."

🍃

But still, she was pretty shaken up after they said good-bye. She made her way home through the dark, preoccupied and worried. Even at Liam's most confessional that past summer, Phoebe had never heard him cry. What did it mean? Was he telling her everything? In some ways, his desperate mood was even more upsetting if no outside event had precipitated it. If it arose solely from within—from what he'd told her once felt like an "empty pit" inside him—what could she do to help? Phoebe couldn't imagine feeling that way about herself. Sure, she had her problems, but she never had any doubt about her essential self-worth. It frightened her that Liam could be so down on himself. And that nothing she could say or do seemed to help him. Despite his denial, she sensed that whatever he was going through was far more serious and dangerous than anything she'd ever imagined.

She had so many other things on her mind, she didn't think to erase Liam's recent texts or delete the cell phone number. She didn't notice the glow coming from her own bedroom window. She even failed to keep the kitchen door from closing behind her with a metallic screech. But she did notice, far too late, the figure slumped in the dark at the kitchen table.

"Where've you been?" her father asked.

23

Liam dreaded Sunday afternoons when he was expected to call home. He usually waited until two thirty or so, until after his family had finished their long, leisurely Sunday lunch. He phoned them on his cell. These days, he made the call from the common room to avoid the possibility of Carey listening in. Not that anyone would be able to make very much of the almost entirely one-sided conversations.

"Hi, it's me," he'd say to Tilly, who invariably answered. He could tell from the breathy sound of her voice that she'd run to pick up the phone. This was the only easy part of the call: Tilly filling him in on her school projects and friends, the class visit to Mark Twain's homestead in Hartford, or the trip she and Brook were planning to New York City to stay with PeterPop. As she chattered away into the receiver, he'd let the sweet, familiar flow of her words wash over him—warming him with their innocence. But then, all too soon, he'd hear his mother's voice in the background and Tilly would say:

"Mom wants to talk to you. Bye-bye! Love you forever!"

"Love you, too," he'd tell her as he tried to steel himself for what was coming next.

"Sweetie, how are you?" It was the tone—more than the words—that defeated him. She tried to make herself sound cheerful and unconcerned, but he knew her too well. The anxiety came through as scratchy and disturbing as static on the line. It was the knowledge that he'd done this to her—and was powerless to undo his mistakes—that made it so hard to respond with any warmth. He couldn't even pretend to be the normal, carefree boy she deserved.

"Fine."

"Good! That's great. We're doing fine here, too. We finished up lunch a little while ago—and Tilly was just saying that it was about time you called and . . ."

She never told him what was really going on, though he knew both she and his dad had to be going through hell because of him. She usually went on for another couple of minutes in the same upbeat and innocuous vein. Occasionally she'd mention something about the case—like they were going to Boston to consult with another lawyer—but by her description it almost seemed that they were planning some little spur-of-the-moment adventure.

"So this new firm thinks we should just settle it," his mom told him one Sunday in mid-March. Someone listening in would never guess by the tone of her voice that "it" was a lawsuit accusing her and Liam's dad of being negligent parents. His mom—who was probably the most caring and concerned person in the whole world! And his father—Liam could hardly stand to think about what this was doing to his dad. The whole thing had become such a mess—a rat's nest of cover-ups and lies. And all because of him.

"What do you think of that?" he heard his mom ask gently.

"Of what?"

"A settlement. A trial would mean even more media attention and distractions. Settling things before all that starts would just seem to be the fastest way to put this behind us—behind you."

He wanted to tell her: *No! Don't even think about giving in! Taking the blame! You know perfectly well it's my fault. It's all my fucking fault!* It seemed so damned ironic that the two people he wanted most in the world to please—and have be proud of him—would end up being punished for his failings. Because that's what he was: a failure. And preparing for a settlement confirmed it somehow. What was the point of his parents fighting the lawsuit when it was obvious that their son had screwed everything up once again?

"Sure," he told her. "Whatever."

"Nothing's decided," his mom said. "We're just talking about it."

"Right," Liam said, getting ready for what was always the worst part of the call: the brief, stilted exchange between himself and his dad. When his mom told him that his father was out at a meeting with a client in Harringdale, there was a hesitation in her voice that he didn't pick up on at first. He felt only relief. He was off the hook! Then, almost immediately, he was overcome by the awful certainly of what his mom didn't want him to know: his dad actually *was* there, but just didn't have the stomach to talk to him.

A darkness descended on Liam after that, as crushing as a migraine.

The following Thursday, Brandon, clanking past Liam on his way to the rink, rubbed his knuckles brutally against the younger boy's scalp. It was just a practice game, but the Warriors were gearing up for a major showdown that Saturday with the only other undefeated team in their league.

"Hey!" Liam complained, yanking his head away.

"We need extra luck today, man!" Brandon replied, moving on.

The other players, filing in behind Brandon, obviously picked up on what the captain had done and, each in turn, gave the top of Liam's head a nasty working over. The jabs and knuckle burns hurt like hell. The humiliation added fuel to the bitterness that was already building inside of Liam. He watched the game in a haze of indignation, thinking back on the many insults and put-downs his role as team mascot had cost him. The coach didn't call on him to hit the ice until the final period, but by then he realized that he had come to the end of something. He was through being Brandon's sidekick—and kicking object. Ever since he'd joined the team, he'd been careful not to get in Brandon's way—on or off the ice. But now, joining the opposite side in the intramural matchup as a forward, propelled by weeks of unacknowledged anger, he was able to maneuver the puck past the Warriors' star goalie in the last minute of play, scoring a goal and winning the game.

Nothing was said in the locker room. No one on the team acknowledged the sudden breach between the two players. But before Saturday's tie-breaking face-off, when Liam made a calculated decision to sit in the middle of the bench rather than at his usual position on the end, he heard the mumbled complaints as the first string took the ice.

"What's with Bossy?"

"Can't believe this!"

"What the *fuck* does he think he's doing?"

"Today of all days!"

Brandon moved past the bench without so much as a glance. Who knew if it would have happened anyway? Still, there was something weirdly coincidental—some would later claim jinxed—about how the Warriors lost: in the last minute of play, an opposing forward slipped the puck around Brandon's ankles almost exactly as Liam had done during the practice match. The Warriors still had a perch in the play-offs. There was a good chance they'd take the division again. But their perfect record was ruined. And Liam knew there was very little doubt in anybody's mind who was responsible. Not Brandon, who fumbled the most important defensive play of the afternoon, but Liam, who had refused to offer up his head to the team as a good-luck charm. Well, Brandon would have his head now, Liam knew, but, with a growing sense of elation, he realized that he no longer cared.

For the rest of the day he felt weirdly jubilant. Wired and restless, he skipped dinner and went for a long walk up into the woods behind the main campus. He climbed to the top of the highest ridge. The school had cut a ski run down the mountainside, and Liam—hatless and gloveless—rolled down the snow-covered slope on his side, circling faster and faster. When he finally came to a stop at the bottom of the run, he was so dizzy he could hardly stand. Laughing, he staggered back to his dorm.

It was only then that his actions began to sink in. The building seemed so empty. Unwelcoming. Carey was away for the weekend at a piano competition. He suddenly realized how cold he was—cold and hungry. But the cafeteria had closed hours ago. He climbed under the covers, shivering. But his mind wouldn't stop moving. It felt like his thoughts were rolling over and over—spinning out of control. He realized that he had to find some way to calm down.

Texting Phoebe usually helped him. She had become a lifeline out of the hell that his life at Moorehouse had become. But the decision to talk to her on the phone that night was a mistake. He suddenly broke down and started to cry like some sniveling little kid. God, he was so spineless! Such a loser! He felt worse after they hung up than he could ever remember feeling before. Bad enough to even wish that Carey were there—any other human being besides himself.

He lay on his bed, staring up at the soundproof ceiling. Outside, a full moon lit up the snow-covered landscape and shimmered across the dorm room floor. If only he could de-materialize into that otherworldly glow! If only he could escape from himself. Nothing gave him pleasure anymore. Even the Warriors, his one sure source of pride, had turned against him.

He chose to ignore the persistent knocking on his door. But he couldn't pretend not to hear Brandon when he whispered into the keyhole:

"Hey, Bossy! Get your skanky little ass out here!"

With an effort, he sat up in bed. Why not just get the damned thing over with? he thought. He already felt so bad, it almost didn't matter that Brandon was bound to beat him up. If the older boy was surprised when Liam pulled open the door without argument, he didn't show it. Brandon stood there, swaying a little, his usual posse ranged behind him.

"We're going into town. Girl I know is hosting an open house."

"Have fun," Liam told him. He started to close the door again, but Brandon grabbed the door handle.

"Oh, come on, man. Let it go! I'm sorry if I hurt your tender feelings, okay? But we all deserve a little fun tonight. We need to get that old Warriors spirit back! We need to pull together now. And we need you with us."

∼❦∼

It had been a lovely Victorian once, but it wasn't anymore. Half the railings on the front porch were broken or missing. An upstairs window was covered in plastic. Cars were parked on the front lawn. The boys came in through the back entrance, which led through a butler's pantry into the kitchen. It was empty except for a girl who was washing dishes in the sink. Lady Antebellum's "Need You Now" rose plaintively from a boom box on top of the refrigerator.

"The party's kind of over," the girl said, turning to face them. She was wearing a red checked flannel shirt and a pair of faded jeans. Though her body was already fully developed, she had the gawky stance of someone barely into her teens. Her face was round and wistful.

"Says who?" Brandon replied. "Where's Suze?"

"Upstairs," the girl said. "But it's time for all you guys to go home. You're just going to get her into more trouble."

"Take it easy," Brandon said, opening the refrigerator and crouching down to examine the contents. He stood back up, brandishing two Heinekens in each hand. "Let's rock this place!" he cried, holding the bottles above his head as he strode out of the room. The others followed him, but Liam stayed behind.

"Need any help with that?" he asked, nodding to the sink.

"No, I'm fine," the girl said. She had on yellow rubber gloves that came up to her elbows. Even Liam, who knew next to nothing about housecleaning, could tell that her dishwashing skills left something to be desired. She fished a handful of silverware out of the suds and deposited them—unrinsed—into the grubby-looking rack beside the sink.

"Is Suze your sister?"

"Not legally, no. Not yet."

"Meaning?"

"What's it to you?"

"I don't know," he said. There was something about the girl's proud self-possession that Liam found appealing. "I guess I'm just trying to be polite. I guess I'm just killing time. If you know anything about Brandon Cowley, the party isn't over until he says so."

"Yeah, I know," the girl said, her shoulders drooping. "But if our foster parents find out about this, it's going to be really bad news. We're already on probation after last time. And I bet you anything they told the Linaweavers next door to keep an eye on us. We're probably already fucked."

The word sounded funny coming out of her mouth. Liam guessed she'd picked the phrase up from Suze and was trying it on for size.

"Where are your folks?"

"Foxwoods Casino. They usually get home by two thirty or three—that's why I'm trying to kind of straighten things up around here." She turned back to the sink, her fine blond hair falling over her face and exposing the fragile curve of her neck.

"At least let me help you dry," Liam said.

"You know what you could do to help? Convince your buddies that it's time to go home."

Liam reluctantly left the kitchen and followed the music and jumble of voices down a hallway and up a worn, uncarpeted stairway to the second floor. A number of rooms branched off from a central corridor, each occupied by groups of teenagers, some of whom Liam knew from Moorehouse, others he'd seen around town. Cigarette and marijuana smoke mingled in the air. Liam wandered from room to room, looking for Brandon, torn by his desire to leave—and his impulse to do something to help the girl downstairs. In what looked like a makeshift study at the end of the hall, Liam found teenagers sprawled on a futon and beanbag chairs, watching an old *Star Wars* film. Feeling useless and exhausted, Liam found a place to sit down, his back against the wall. He closed his eyes against the flickering light of the TV screen.

He woke to the sound of someone crying. It was coming from downstairs and was more a kind of keening—like that of a hurt dog or a frightened child. The movie was over now, the room empty except for a couple making out on the futon. The digital clock on the DVD player registered two forty-five a.m. Liam got to his feet and headed back down the hallway. Except for another couple in one of the bedrooms, everyone else seemed to have gone home.

It took Liam a moment or two to orient himself when he reached the bottom of the staircase. The downstairs was dark. He had to feel his way along the wall of the corridor leading back to the kitchen, where, though it had stopped for the moment, he was pretty sure the crying had been coming from. As he pushed open the door to the kitchen—the sudden light blinding him for a split second—the keening started again.

"Oh, come on," Brandon was saying, "just shut up and enjoy it!" The young girl in the flannel shirt was sitting on the counter, shirtfront open to the waist, bra pulled down. Two other boys, both Warriors first string, sat at the kitchen table, watching as Brandon flicked his thumb and forefinger against the nipple of one of the girl's uptilting breasts. Her eyes were red-rimmed, her lips swollen, her gaze widening as Liam moved across the room toward her.

It was only then that he realized who the girl reminded him of. By the time he slammed his right fist into Brandon's side, she'd *become* Phoebe in Liam's mind. An adrenaline-fueled burst of energy surged through him as Brandon spun around. Liam tackled the older, stronger boy and, staggering under his weight, collapsed with him onto the floor. When the back of Liam's head hit the worn tiles, he could feel the impact radiate through his skull and down his spine.

"What the fuck?" Brandon said, rolling on top of Liam and pinning him down. "What's the matter with you?" Liam had a hard time focusing as he gazed up at the flushed face above him.

"Leave her alone," he tried to say, but the sentence didn't come out right.

"Are you telling me what to do?" Brandon said.

"Leave her—" Liam tried again, but once again his mouth was unable to form the words he needed.

"You really think that you can take me on? Just keep this up—and I'll make your life hell. And you can forget about the Warriors. That's over."

24

Brook was asleep, her back curled against Michael's body, her head resting on his upper arm, hair fanned out on the pillow. He listened to the steady rise and fall of her breathing. They'd had a long talk the night before when she and Tilly got back from New York. She'd told him that he was right. If they settled the suit, they might be getting Liam off the hook—but they'd also be letting him down.

"I told my dad something that I realized afterward I really should have told you. There were times I caught Liam drinking and smoking dope over the last couple of years and didn't let you know."

"What?" Michael had asked. "Why?"

"Because you'd get so angry when you heard Liam had done something wrong!"

"But I had a right to know what was going on with him, Brook. He's my son, too!"

"I know. I see that now. But I don't think you have any idea just how badly you'd lose it with him. I thought it only made things worse. I decided it would be better if I just tried to help him on my own. I was wrong. And I'm sorry."

Though still upset, he'd told her that he was sorry, too. Michael hated to think where that anger at Liam came from. He could all too easily imagine whom he sounded like when he "really lost it" with his son. Michael and Brook had made love for the first time in weeks and had slept in each other's arms. He knew it had been hard for her to change her mind. Challenging Troy was going to put her in the public eye in a way she dreaded. And her family was going to be furious. He was proud of her for taking this stand. Now it was time for him to face some difficult things, as well. He owed it to her. And to them.

He waited until the first light of dawn filtered through the bedroom blinds before he gently slipped his arm free and got out of bed. He was usually the first one up in the morning. Brook would probably continue sleeping for another hour or two, long after he'd gone. He left her a note in the kitchen, saying he had an appointment and would try to get back for lunch. He started the pickup and sat in the cab for a few minutes waiting for the engine to warm. From this vantage point on the turnaround, he was able to watch the sun rise above the mountains, a fierce ball of fire that briefly transformed the snow-covered countryside into a dreamscape of pinks and oranges. But by the time he made it to the bottom of the drive, the washed-out March palette had reasserted itself.

He didn't turn right as he usually did when he reached the county highway that led into town, but left along a stretch of slowly rising switchbacks. The road followed the contour of the mountain range that constituted the western border of the county. After nearly ten miles, he made an abrupt right onto an unmarked dirt road, the truck bumping along the uneven surface rutted with frozen-over tire marks and potholes. The surrounding woods were composed of second-growth, mostly deciduous trees, leafless in March. Troy's grandfather had picked up more than a hundred acres of this mountainside for a song at a bankruptcy auction during the Depression, and the Lansing men had been using the area as their personal hunting and fishing ground for three generations.

It was here that Troy and Michael spent a lot of time when they were boys, hanging out in the makeshift cabin that Michael caught sight of ahead through the trees. This was where Troy lived now when he wasn't sponging off his ex-wife or relatives in town. Smoke curled from the aluminum stovepipe, and Michael saw Troy's pickup parked next to a tarpaulin-covered woodpile. A dog rose from his post on the front steps and started to bark. Though nearly twenty-five years had passed since he'd been here last, though the boy he'd been then was a stranger to him now, it seemed to Michael that nothing about the place itself had really changed.

$$\text{\textasciitilde}$$

They both had a certain rough edge to them that caused the other boys to be wary—and the girls intrigued. They were both good-looking, too, though in different ways. Michael—dark, quiet, a little brooding. Troy—redheaded, loquacious, with an in-your-face kind of swagger. What drew them to each other was perhaps more of a mystery, because families in Barnsbury had a way of hiding their problems. But, in fact, what they shared was the carefully concealed pain of unhappy home lives. In Troy's case, a mother who'd walked out on her husband, five sons, and baby girl when Troy was still a toddler. For Michael, the problem was a father whose drinking was escalating out of control.

The boys didn't talk to each other about any of this. They didn't need to. They spent a lot of time in each other's households, and they couldn't help but overhear things, including the seemingly endless arguments between Michael and his dad.

"No, I'm not driving you," Troy might hear Michael tell his dad, who, having lost his license after a DUI, ordered his son to take him up to a bar in Harringdale.

"Yes, you will, you little prick. You think you're so holy and pure? Let me tell you something—I know who you really are. I know what you're really made of. You're going to find out soon enough what life has in store for you."

Michael never responded to any of his father's diatribes. In fact, he tried to pretend that he didn't hear them—that the words simply could not penetrate the thick skin he'd grown to protect himself. But they did penetrate, of course. Slowly, inevitably, the ugliness seeped in and found its way to his heart.

Maybe things would have turned out differently if Troy's older brothers hadn't given him a quart of Canadian Club for his sixteenth birthday. By then, Troy and Michael were driving regularly up to the cabin to smoke and hang out. Often, they were forced to bring Troy's sister, Sylvia, with them. Just a year younger than Troy and without a mother to care for her, Sylvia had increasingly become Troy's responsibility as the two of them grew up. Michael didn't mind her tagging along, and he sensed Troy appreciated this. Not everybody felt that way about Sylvia.

"Try this," Troy said, handing the bottle to Michael. It was early summer, school just out. They were sitting on the steps in front of the cabin. Sylvia, who'd come along, was inside reading. Troy, leaning back against the top step, seemed relaxed and happy. But Michael was dreading the long, unstructured weeks to come.

The whiskey burned in his throat. He started to cough, but swallowed hard instead. It was the first time he'd ever tasted alcohol. His dad's problems had made him wary. But it was the weight of those very problems that prompted him to reach for the bottle now. What had his self-restraint gotten him but more abuse? He took another swig and felt his face start to flush. He passed the whiskey back to Troy, who sat with it resting on his knee as he shared with Michael his plans to pitch a tent up by the large, spring-fed lake on the Lansings' land near the top of the mountain.

"I want to really rough it for a couple days. We can hike up there from here with all the supplies and get the hell away from everything for a while. What do you say?"

"Sounds good," Michael replied, but his mind was on the whiskey. He felt warm and loose and wonderful. He wanted more. He reached over and took the bottle from his friend. As he was tipping his head back to take another swallow, he heard Sylvia's voice behind them on the porch.

"Can I have some, too?"

"No, you cannot!" Troy said, turning around to face his sister. "This is for me and Michael. You go back into the cabin and get yourself a Coke or something—and stay there until we're ready to go home."

Michael managed to kill off the rest of the bottle before the afternoon was out. He didn't remember exactly how it happened. He woke up around five o'clock, sprawled on the steps, the hot June sun full on his face, his throat parched and his head throbbing. Sylvia sat beside him on the step, her leg pressing heavily against his. Though only fourteen, she was already obese.

"You were snoring," she said. "I like to watch you sleep."

"Oh, Syl," Michael said, closing his eyes again with a sigh. He often caught her staring at him these days. He sensed she had some kind of a thing for him. He never gave it much thought, or let on to her or Troy that he knew. It was just funny and kind of sad. Nothing to be taken very seriously.

That was the first of many such afternoons for Michael. Sometimes it was Michael who siphoned off an inch or two from various bottles among his father's stash in the basement. Other times, it was Troy who paid one of his older brothers to get the booze. But it was always Michael who ended up draining the bottle, long after Troy had said he'd had enough. After that first harsh swallow, the heat coursing through his veins, Michael just didn't know how to stop. All he wanted was to get back to the feeling that nothing mattered and no one could touch him.

The couple of times the two boys camped up beside the lake that summer, Michael had a buzz on the whole time. If Troy was annoyed by his friend's behavior, he didn't say anything. It became clear that the main purpose of these trips for Troy was to get away from his home—and let someone else in his family take care of Sylvia for a while.

On Labor Day weekend the boys decided to have a final campout by the lake. They were heading back to school the following week, and they were both looking forward to one last taste of freedom. But when Troy came to pick up Michael that Friday afternoon, Sylvia was in the backseat with the camping gear.

"Sorry about this," Troy said as Michael climbed in. "It was either bring her along or not go at all. She's promised to stay out of our way."

Sylvia kept her word, and was in many ways a useful addition to the party. She eagerly collected kindling, helped with the cooking, and washed the dishes after every meal. She'd packed a stash of comic books and would pore over these for hours while the boys swam and fished.

Michael, who brought along some whiskey he'd stolen from his dad, kept himself well lubricated but functional through Saturday. By bedtime, though, he was reeling. They each had their own pup tent, and Michael stumbled into his that night and passed out cold.

On Sunday afternoon, Michael let Troy go fishing across the lake without him. He was feeling hungover and sad. The weather had turned cooler, and Michael noticed red flares in the maples on the mountainside. He dreaded summer's end. What was he going to do? He grabbed the bottle of whiskey, walked down to the lake, and, sitting against a limestone boulder, began to drink.

The next thing he knew, some fly or gnat had landed on his cheek. He swatted it away. But it came back. He tried to brush it off again. It giggled.

"Hey, there," Sylvia said.

Michael turned his head to see her crouched beside him, holding a feather in her hand.

"What?"

"I've been tickling you!" she said, rocking back on her heels. "For about an hour."

"What time is it?" Michael asked, trying to stand, but the trees spun overhead. It was almost dark. He'd emptied the bottle.

"I have a secret," she said. "Something I want to tell you."

"Oh, for chrissakes," Michael said, furious that he couldn't even sit up straight.

"It's nothing bad," Sylvia said. "It's good. I love you."

Michael dropped his head into his hands.

"I love you," Sylvia said, stroking the top of his head with the soft little pats one might give a kitten.

"Don't!" he said, jerking away. "Cut it out."

"No," she told him. Before he knew what was happening, she had her arms around him and was squeezing him to her. He could feel her big belly and loose breasts pressing against him. She smelled of sweat and some deeper, ranker odor.

"Jesus!" he cried, trying to push her away. "Get off me!"

"What's going on?" Troy called from the lake. He was paddling quickly toward them.

"Your stupid sister is—," Michael began to say when Sylvia suddenly released him. She gave out a moan.

"I'm not stupid," she said, scrambling to her feet.

"What's going on?" Troy asked again as he reached the shore and started to climb out of the boat.

"I'm not stupid," Sylvia said. Through his alcoholic fog, Michael watched her run clumsily toward the lake.

"What the hell are you doing?" Troy cried, as she passed him and entered the water. "You can't swim!"

"I can, too!" she said, splashing water back at him.

"Hey!" Troy called after her. "Be careful—it drops off quickly."

But Sylvia continued to wade out, the water rising around her.

"Don't go out any further, Syl!" Troy called. He started to follow her. "I'm telling you—it drops off!"

"No!" she shouted. "I'm not—" Suddenly, she seemed to slip, her arms flailing backward.

"Troy!" Michael heard her terrified cry.

Michael watched in confusion as Troy dove in and began

to swim out to where his sister was thrashing. He heard her choking as she swallowed water.

Michael tried to get to his feet. He fell over. He tried again and this time he made it upright, but he staggered badly as he tried to move forward. The water's edge seemed so far away! He had a hard time focusing, and even when he could, it was difficult to make out what was happening. Where was Sylvia? All Michael could see was Troy diving repeatedly under the water. Each time Troy resurfaced, he gulped in air—and then screamed for Michael's help.

Help that, by the time Michael finally reached his friend, turned out to be shockingly little and just minutes too late.

ॐ

Michael parked the pickup next to Troy's and looked up into the woods, his heart pounding. As he stepped down from the cab, he heard the door to the cabin open. Troy stood in the doorway, arms crossed on his chest.

"What are you doing here?" Troy called down.

"I just want to talk," Michael said, walking across the rutted clearing in front of the house.

"I've got nothing to say to you. You want to talk, give my lawyers a call. I'm sure they'd be happy to hear from you."

"I'm not here to talk about the case."

"I don't care—get the hell off my property."

"I'm here to tell you that I'm sorry, Troy. I'm sorry about how I acted when we were kids. For what happened."

"You've got to be kidding!" Troy said. He began to laugh. "You have got to be fucking kidding me! You actually think I'm going to forget about the lawsuit because you finally got around to telling me that?"

"No," Michael told him. "I know you're not. I just needed to say it. I needed to clear the air. I was really screwed up back then. Just the way Liam is now. And I didn't have anyone to help me."

"Yeah. Well, I'll tell you what. I know the feeling."

"Troy—listen. I'm here to say I'm sorry. I'm sorry about Sylvia. Not a day goes by when I don't—"

"You're breaking my heart," Troy said, turning to go back inside. He slammed the door behind him.

25

*L*iam knew he wasn't thinking straight, but he didn't know exactly what was wrong. As he made his way back to campus after his fight with Brandon, he felt as though he were watching himself from above. Or on some kind of weird monitor inside his head. A boy trudging alone through the cold, empty streets of a small town in the middle of the night. Then—*whoosh!*—he'd be somewhere else entirely. His thoughts kept jump-cutting across space and time, starting with the day early last summer when everything really began to fall apart.

"What would you expect? His dad's a carpenter, isn't he? I doubt he ever even went to college. Mom said that it sure wasn't his raging intellect that attracted Aunt Brook to him."

Liam didn't mean to listen in on the conversation between his two older cousins, but they were right ahead of him in the buffet line at the reception and were making no attempt to lower their voices. The girl who was talking was the younger sister of the bride. She and the other cousin, both bridesmaids, were wearing pink, floor-length silk princess-style sheaths that accentuated their thin arms. Liam's mom had been so happy when Aunt Peg had asked if they could hold the June wedding in Barnsbury—and if R.S.V.P. might want to cater the affair. Brook had been working for months to make sure every last detail of this day—including the hors d'oeuvres that his cousins were busily piling on their plates—was absolutely perfect.

"I know, but he's just so weird. I mean, he's like something out of *Lost*. Like he's been living up here in the wilderness and raised by wolves."

By now, of course, Liam realized that his two cousins had to be talking about him. Which, frankly, he could handle. It was almost funny, how their criticisms were the opposite of the kind of shit he got at Deer Mountain—like "one percenter" and "Trump." But it infuriated him to hear them talking about his dad this way—right here in the home he'd helped build. Like they knew anything about him! *Carpenter?* They had no idea what kind of amazingly beautiful things he created! Expensive, one-of-a-kind pieces that were collected all over the world. And what the fuck difference did it make if his dad hadn't gone to college? Hadn't he taught himself everything he needed to know to become a success? And didn't that take more guts, more intelligence, more of *everything*, than getting free passes to Moorehouse, Princeton, and Harvard Law the way his Pendleton uncles had? Liam itched to share his outrage with the twits in front of him, but in one instance they were right: he *had* been feeling like something out of *Lost* all afternoon.

While Brook and Michael had their hands full as hosts, and easygoing Tilly was quickly taken up by a coterie of younger girls, Liam was forced to hang out with his older cousins, with whom he'd always felt tongue-tied and out of place. There were three of them—these two girls and a boy, the last of his aunts' large broods. They called each other by nicknames that Liam had a hard time keeping straight: Diffy, Mix, and Embo. A long sit-down dinner at their table, followed by a night of dancing with a live band imported from Manhattan, loomed ahead for Liam.

Four other family friends—all in their twenties—were at the older cousins' table. Everyone but Liam was either in grad school or launched on some career path in the city. They seemed to have gone to all the same schools together and knew the same people. None of them appeared to notice how amazing the sunset looked outside the tent, the way it lit up the cloud banks above the mountains in shades of red and purple. They seemed to exist only in their insular and entitled world.

"... No, just totally forget the LIE. You take Sunrise Highway out to . . ."

". . . I ran into her at the Bobbi Brown counter at Bendel's and I swear to God I didn't . . ."

". . . The Tabata instructor at the Columbus Circle Equinox is definitely the most . . ."

Liam just sat there, a stupid smile pasted on his face, turning his head from time to time, pretending to be part of the conversation. When the waiter circled the table, pouring wine, nobody registered the fact that he filled Liam's goblet as well. As the four-course meal progressed, Liam's quickly emptied glass was routinely topped off. Liam knew his parents would be furious with him if they realized what he was doing, but they were at a table well out of view. Besides, it was his mom's stupid fault that the wedding was here and he was miserable and alone in his own backyard. And who would ever know?

At first, the wine just helped to dull the anger he felt toward his cousins for what they'd said about his dad. Then it started to numb his sense of estrangement. This was what Liam liked best about getting high: all the things that usually worried him melted away. He was still ignored, but it no longer mattered. He felt himself floating above it all. By the time slices of wedding cake were being distributed and the groom was leading the bride to the dance floor, Liam was stumbling from the table, desperate to find a bathroom that was free. He wasn't sure how he ended up passed out on the front lawn a few hours later, reeking of wine and having peed in his dress pants.

Even now, as Liam cut through a field that bordered the campus, he could feel the ache of shame and humiliation that had overwhelmed him then—and which, in so many ways, had been building ever since.

"We think you're going to be happier there," his mom had told him when his parents broke the news that they were sending him to Moorehouse. That he was heading to the prestigious prep school his Pendleton cousins had attended didn't really register with Liam. What he heard was that he was being sent away. What he felt was that they didn't know how to handle him. That maybe he was beyond help. This was always his biggest fear: that there was something inside him that made him different. That made him unworthy and unlovable.

"Do *you* want me to go?" he'd asked his dad. He'd overheard enough over the weeks leading up to this discussion to know that his Pendleton aunts were pressuring his mom to enroll him at Moorehouse. But he'd been holding out hope that his father would stand up for him. That, no matter what, his dad still believed in him. Now, as he saw the look of pain in Michael's eyes, he knew that he was lost. His father had given up on him, too.

As he approached the security kiosk, he tried to focus his mind on how he was going to explain to the night watchman what he was doing out this long past curfew. When he left the dorm with Brandon and the others, they'd been able to slip out through an unalarmed emergency exit. This entrance was the only way back into his dorm at night.

But as Liam came up to the kiosk, he realized the security guard was asleep. He could hear the snores as he approached. Liam looked down at the slack face, the body sprawled uncomfortably in the cramped space. It was Russell, an older, heavyset man who seemed for whatever reason to have taken a liking to Liam. The guard made a point of wishing Liam luck when the Warriors were playing and was always ready with a smile and kind word. He knew Russell would be disappointed when he heard that Liam had been dumped from the team. The thought of facing him—and everyone else—suddenly seemed unbearable.

And then it occurred to him he didn't *have* to go back to his dorm room. He didn't need to face Carey or Brandon or any of them. He could just keep walking.

It helped that it was Sunday. Everyone would be sleeping late. The cafeteria served breakfast until noontime with students drifting in and out all morning. Nobody would miss him. Nobody would even notice that he'd disappeared until Carey got home late that night from his competition in Hartford.

Even then, as the two boys were no longer communicating, Carey might very well assume Liam had gone home for the weekend or spent the night elsewhere.

He followed the moonlight through the trees, down the wooded hills and sloping pastureland that slowly leveled off to the next large town north of Moorehouse. It was an eight-mile hike. By the time he made it to the outskirts of town, the moon was setting and the early-morning sky had taken on the heavy, pewterlike cast of snow. Everything seemed unreal to Liam as he trudged along. The houses, the cars, the gas station with its brightly lit automatic pumps—they all looked dreamlike and changeable. The one thing that seemed to attach him to the world—that made him believe he was actually awake and alive—was his hunger. He stopped at a diner, the only place open at that early hour, and ordered a breakfast of bacon and pancakes. When it came, though, he looked down at it in disgust, remembering that it was what Tilly and Carey had made for him the morning after the disaster.

"You okay, hon?" the waitress asked when she came to clear his almost untouched plate.

"I'm fine," Liam said. "Just not as hungry as I thought. There's a bus that comes through here, right?"

"Where're you heading?" she asked, smiling at him. It was an innocent enough question, but Liam felt instantly suspicious and on guard.

"North," he told her, not meeting her gaze.

"It stops right over there in front of the tourist office. But it's Sunday, so you may have quite a wait. You're welcome to keep your eye out for it from here. Let me top off your coffee for you."

"That's okay," Liam said, grabbing the check and sliding past her out of the booth. He couldn't stand the kindness and concern in her voice. Besides, he guessed she'd figured out that something was wrong with him. He'd probably just gotten to the point where everybody could tell that something was wrong with him.

He stopped at the drugstore across from the diner and picked up things he was beginning to realize he'd need. A plan of sorts was forming in his brain. He used the Visa card his mom had given him to buy trail mix, canned soup, safety matches, a flashlight, Kleenex packets, and a couple of pairs of cheap heavy socks. He waited for the bus across the street from the tourist office, out of view of the diner. The ticket to Northridge ate up the rest of his cash. It started to snow when they were on the highway. As Liam watched it begin to accumulate on the fields and farms outside the window, his confidence began to fade. He hadn't prepared for bad weather. He hadn't really thought any of this through very well. The bus's oversized windshield wipers worked at top speed as they headed into the unexpected late winter storm.

~

He got off at the second stop in Northridge, the one by the shopping mall and across from the acres of flat marshland that bordered the state park. The snow was coming down hard now, accumulating quickly on the ground. The bus lumbered off again, taillights bleeding briefly into white, then gone. There were very few cars on the road. With his hood up and scarf wrapped around his nose and mouth, Liam knew there was little chance that he could be spotted in the near-blizzard conditions. He crossed the highway and walked onto the snow-covered marsh, his boots sinking into the frozen-over surface of matted grass and mud.

It was like walking across a soft mattress. The sense of unreality returned as he headed toward the mountains in the distance. Though now the feeling was mixed with a giddy surge of relief. He'd cut himself off from all the bad things that had been torturing him. No one knew where he was. No one could get to him now. Finally, he'd taken matters into his own hands. He'd done it. He was free!

He decided to wait until he set up camp before calling Phoebe. But he misjudged the distance to the state forest, and he was forced to stop and rest on the far edge of the marshland, stamping out a little shelter among some frozen brambles. He ate a bag of trail mix and a couple of handfuls of snow. He only meant to nap for an hour or two, but when he woke again, it was nearly dark. Another couple of inches of snow had fallen while he was asleep, and it was still coming down.

He pulled out his cell phone and saw that his mom had called him three times since late afternoon. His fingers were so cold he had to blow on them before he could delete her messages. There was no way that he could stand to listen to them now. Instead, he scrolled down to Phoebe's number. He decided to call her, rather than text. He needed to hear her voice.

It rang only once before it was picked up.

"Who's this?" the man asked.

"Sorry. I think I must've—"

"That you, Liam?"

Liam just sat there, phone pressed to his ear, wishing he could start all over again. Not just with the phone call, but with every single stupid fucking thing he'd ever done. But he knew that was just wishful thinking. And that, along with any hope he had of connecting with the one person who could comfort him, was behind him now.

"Don't you ever contact my daughter again. Don't call her. Don't text her. Don't even *think* about her, do you understand me?"

Ahead was the snow-shrouded night—and loneliness. And, after he swiped the "end" icon on his cell phone, silence.

26

It was impossible for Brook to concentrate on the updated income and expense estimates that Alice had e-mailed her for the Huntsford Foundation gala. Rental fee, invitation printing, per-person dinner cost, photographer—the columns blurred together on Brook's computer screen. Alice was projecting a shortfall of nearly eight thousand dollars and was looking for ideas from Brook about where they could save on the expense end.

Should I call the caterer and see if we can renegotiate the price? Alice had e-mailed her. *Maybe they can help us come up with some less expensive menu options. Take a look, and let me know what you think.*

Outside the snow was still falling. It was ten in the morning, and eight inches had accumulated since the late March storm blew in the day before. The latest weather report predicted as many as fifteen inches by evening, when it was supposed to begin to taper off. With all that heavy snow weighing down tree branches, the whole area faced power outages.

Tilly's school had been called off. Brook watched her

daughter making snowballs in the kitchen garden and throwing them for Puff Daddy—who was barking and chasing his tail in excitement—to catch and retrieve. The poor dog would race to the spot where the snowball had landed and sniff around confusedly for a while, before bounding back to Tilly to try again. If Brook hadn't been so worried, she probably would have laughed at these antics. But there was really only one thing on her mind.

Where was Liam?

When he didn't make his regular Sunday afternoon call the day before, Brook had asked Michael if he thought they should phone him.

"I think we agreed that he shouldn't feel that he *has* to call us, right? And we don't want him thinking that we're monitoring his every move. Probably best to give him some more time."

Though Brook tried her son surreptitiously on her cell a few times over the course of the afternoon, it wasn't until six that evening that Michael finally said, "Okay, you're right. It's unlike him not to call."

Brook knew it was silly of her to hold out hope that Michael would somehow be able to reach Liam when she couldn't. When he hung up the receiver in the kitchen after leaving a message on Liam's cell, Brook's anxiety level really began to spike.

"Should we call his dorm prefect?" she asked.

"No, I don't think so," Michael said, not meeting her worried gaze.

"All right," Brook said. "But if we don't hear back from him by nine tonight—we're calling. I don't care what happens."

When they phoned the dorm prefect later that evening, however, he seemed calm and unconcerned.

"I know the Warriors had a special practice session this evening and most of the team went out for pizza in town afterward. That's probably where he is, but I'll check around. One of us will get back to you."

But the call from the housemaster a half hour later was far less reassuring. Liam had not been at the special practice or out for pizza.

"Any chance he went to Hartford with Carey at the last minute?" the housemaster asked.

"Shouldn't you have that information there?" Brook replied, her voice rising with concern. "Don't they need to get passes from you? Aren't you supposed to be keeping track of what these boys are doing?"

"Yes, of course we are, Mrs. Bostock. So if he did go, it was without official permission. Carey's due back within the hour, and we'll see what he might know."

But Carey knew nothing about Liam's whereabouts. It was the headmaster himself who called them with this information just past midnight.

"We've searched all the dorms," Foster Norwood told them, "and we're talking to the students. The last time anyone remembers seeing him was Saturday afternoon at the Warriors' home game. He was apparently pretty upset when they lost. We all were."

Michael, who was on the upstairs extension, said, "Don't you have room checks at night? Can it really be that you have no idea where Liam's been from Saturday afternoon until now? And if we hadn't called, how long would he have gone missing?"

"Yes, of course we check. I'm looking into where and how our system might have failed here. In the meantime we have campus security combing the buildings and grounds. And the town police are doing a street-by-street search. The snow isn't helping matters, but we're on this. If he's still at Moorehouse, we'll find him. Don't worry. We'll call you the moment we have anything to report."

The question that remained unanswered—and that haunted Brook and Michael throughout their sleepless night—was, what if Liam was no longer at Moorehouse? What if he'd left for some reason in the middle of the snowstorm? But why would he have done so? And where in the world would he have gone? They kept trying his cell phone every hour or so, but the calls clicked over into his mailbox, which soon filled with their increasingly alarmed messages.

For Tilly's sake, Brook tried to appear calm that morning. She made a show of being pleased and excited about her daughter's snow day, promising to let her help make brownies later. But Michael, after pacing around for an hour or so, finally went outside to chop wood and stack it in the woodpile under the kitchen overhang—an activity he claimed calmed his nerves. The loud report of axhead hitting hard wood, however, followed by the sound of the log splintering apart, had the opposite effect on Brook. Both of them were waiting so intently for the phone call from Moorehouse that when it finally came around ten thirty, Brook grabbed the receiver in the middle of the first ring—and Michael was back in the kitchen a second or two later. After a glance at Brook, he quickly climbed the stairs to get on their bedroom phone.

"Norwood here. Moorehouse security and town police have worked together through the night. The search has been systematic and thorough. But I'm very sorry to have to tell you that there's still no sign of your son. In the meantime, the administration has been talking to everyone who knows Liam—

the Warriors, Carey, all the boys in his dorm, his classmates. We've been able to ferret out some information about what happened and where he was, at least up until Saturday night. I'm afraid none of this news is good."

"Go ahead," Michael said when Brook found herself unable to respond.

"Liam did something at the Warriors game that upset a lot of the players. It turns out that the team has this little ritual of rubbing Liam's head—for good luck apparently—before hitting the ice. For whatever reason, your son wouldn't let any of them touch him on Saturday. I know it sounds unreasonable, but a lot of the boys blame him for the team's loss."

"Am I right in remembering that Brandon Cowley's on that team?" Michael asked.

"Yes, he's co-captain, as a matter of fact. He was the one who filled us in on a lot of this. He's very upset about what happened. Apparently, he tried his best to cheer Liam up after the game. He went around to your son's room and asked him to join a group of the boys at a get-together in town. We encourage the students to make friends with the local teenagers, so I was pleased to learn that Brandon had taken the initiative to do just that. Unfortunately, though, after the boys got to the house, it became clear that the party was unsupervised. And there was alcohol on the premises. Brandon tried to get everyone to leave, but Liam refused to go. Though Brandon wouldn't admit it, I have to say that I got the definite impression from him that Liam had been drinking. He became unruly. Brandon tried to subdue him, but Liam fought him off. Both boys fell at one point—and Liam hit his head."

"How? How badly?" Brook demanded.

"Just on the floor. Not seriously as far as Brandon could tell, but Liam refused to let Brandon help him get back to the campus. That's the last time anyone saw him."

"Have you gone to the house where this party was held?" Michael asked.

"Yes," Norwood replied. "I've just come back from talking to the parents. They weren't there when all this happened. They had no knowledge of the party—and were very upset to hear that there'd been drinking."

"We need to alert the state police," Michael said. "I'll do that right now. And then I'm coming down there and I'll want to talk to everyone—"

"There's no point in you coming down," Norwood said. "The roads are a mess. We've already—"

"I'll be there as soon as I can," Michael replied, hanging up before the headmaster could say another word.

꧁

Brook usually looked forward to a good snowstorm. It was one of the things that drew her to the idea of moving up to Barnsbury after 9/11. She and Michael visited Michael's widowed mom every year between Christmas and New Year's, and Brook came to love the peaceful majesty of the snow-covered mountains and rolling fields. It seemed that there was nothing more calming than watching the rough edges of winter subdued and softened by a fresh blanket of white. But this late March blizzard terrified her. It had come on so fast and force-fully. And there was something ominous about it coinciding with Liam's disappearance. Even now, though the wind had died down, the snow continued to pile up.

After Michael called 911 and talked to Chief Henderson about contacting the state police immediately, he got ready to leave for Moorehouse. Brook begged him not to go.

"You heard what Norwood said," she told him. "The roads are terrible, and it's still coming down hard. Why don't you let—"

"I don't trust that man," Michael said, zipping up his coat. "I'm not saying he's lying, but there's too much about what he said happened—or what Brandon told him—that just doesn't ring true. This business of Brandon trying to 'cheer him up'? If the Warriors really thought Liam was to blame for their loss, the last thing they'd want to do was make him feel better."

"I'm worried about this fight he had with Brandon," Brook said. "What if he's really hurt? What if he has a concussion and—"

"Hey, don't do this to yourself," Michael said. "He's fine. He'll be fine."

"It's weird, isn't it, that the parents weren't there and didn't know their kids had been drinking? Just like us."

"Yeah," Michael said. "And you know what my first thought was? 'How the hell could they have let that happen?'"

"I thought the same thing," Brook said, looking up at him with tears in her eyes.

"Listen," Michael said, pulling Brook to him. She wrapped her arms around him. "I have to go down there. If I can talk to Brandon and maybe Carey, I just think I'll have a much better chance of getting to the bottom of this."

"Okay, but please, please be careful," Brook told him. "Go slow. Stick to the main roads. And call me. Let me know you're okay."

Brook forced herself to keep moving after Michael left, but

she knew she was operating on autopilot. She responded to Alice's e-mail, endorsing her ideas but also suggesting they ask the Huntsford Foundation board members to make personal calls to major donors who'd yet to RSVP. She made Tilly's favorite grilled cheese and tomato sandwiches for lunch and then made good on her promise of baking brownies. They worked quietly side by side in the spacious, warmly lit kitchen as the snow continued to fall outside.

And then it occurred to Brook that the room was *too* quiet. That her usually talkative daughter hadn't said more than a word or two all morning. In fact, Tilly had been going through the paces—measuring out the baking soda, buttering the baking pan—as mechanically as Brook. Of course, Brook realized, Tilly had just been playing along for her mother's sake. She must have known since the day before—when the eagerly awaited call from her older brother never came—that Liam was in some sort of trouble again. After they put the brownies in the oven, Brook turned to Tilly and said:

"Listen, sweetie, I think you should know that we called Liam's school when we didn't hear from him yesterday—and he seems to be missing. Daddy's gone down there to try to find him."

"You think he left Moorehouse?"

"We're not sure, but it looks that way."

"Good! I told him to. I told him to at Christmas. I told him to come home. He never should have gone to that place."

"But it's a really good school. All your male Pendleton cousins have gone there. It kind of gives you a leg up in the world."

"Maybe for them, but not Liam. He needs to be here with us."

It was a moment of painful clarity for Brook. As the afternoon settled into evening, Brook moved restlessly around the downstairs waiting for Michael to call. She stood at the French windows in the great room as the snow *tick-tick-tick*ed against the glass. Liam was out there somewhere, frightened and alone. *Please let him be okay,* she pleaded with the darkening world, *just let him come home safely!*

How was it that she needed her ten-year-old daughter to tell her something every mother should instinctively know? You don't send a troubled teenager away—you do whatever possible to bring him closer. Out of fear and insecurity, she'd put everything she truly cared about in jeopardy. A terrible lack of judgment on her part had brought her family to this precipice. But she knew now that she would never make a mistake like that again. Something had shifted inside of her. Something fundamental had changed. Whatever happened, Brook understood that she was standing on her own two feet at last. She only hoped it wasn't too late.

27

🌿

The visitors' parking area near the Moorehouse administration building seemed to be the only lot that had been plowed,
so Michael pulled in there and called Brook to let her know he'd
arrived safely. He wasn't about to tell her how treacherous the
trip had actually been. Even on the highway, the snowplows had
been unable to keep up with the steady accumulation. There'd
been spinouts and accidents the whole way down. But he would
have made the trip no matter what the conditions. And now that
he'd arrived, he felt the knot between his shoulders start to ease
a little. He was determined to get the answers he needed.

The pathways through the campus grounds had disappeared under the snow, and Michael found himself slogging
through knee-high drifts on his way to Foster Norwood's home
down the hill from the dormitories and faculty housing. The
lighted windows of the stately white clapboarded colonial
beckoned to Michael across the snow-covered yard. He had to
knock several times before the front door was opened by a
young girl.

"Who is it, Stephanie?" Michael could hear Norwood's voice call down the hall.

"A man," the girl said, looking Michael over solemnly.

"I'm sorry, but we're about to sit down—," Norwood was saying as he came up to the door. When he saw who it was, he patted his daughter on the head and said: "Tell Mommy I'll be there shortly. Now scoot."

Norwood showed Michael into his office and closed the door.

"Listen," he said as he crossed the room to his desk. "I told you there was no point in you coming down here. We've already done everything we possibly could."

"I know," Michael said, working to control his temper. His son was missing and this man was about to sit down to dinner. "I just want to talk to Brandon and the other boys who saw Liam last."

"You've contacted the state police?"

"Yes, right after we spoke. But at this point Liam could be anywhere. I know we could find him a lot faster if we knew why he left—and where he might be headed. So, please, could I just talk to Brandon?"

"Sorry, but no."

"What?"

"It's school policy. I can't let you interrogate Brandon or any of the others. Parents' access to the student body is limited to their own children. Period. These boys are under my protection."

"Is that so?" Michael said, trying hard to keep his voice steady. He forced himself to unclench his fists. "Then what about my son? What sort of protection did you offer *him*?"

"Listen, we do our best to keep an eye on the students, but

we can't prevent them from leaving the school if they decide to. All we can do is try to instill in them a sense of responsibility and an understanding that their actions result in consequences. It appears that Liam left the campus of his own free will. Though, frankly, if what I heard turns out to be true, he would have been expelled from Moorehouse anyway."

"So you're washing your hands of him?"

"We spent the past eighteen hours turning this place upside down trying to find him. I'd hardly say that was shirking our duties. I'm sorry. I know you're upset, but there's really not a great deal more I can do for you. I've already told you everything we learned from talking with the boys. I tried to tell you on the phone that coming down here was a waste of your time. As far as I'm concerned, this is a police matter now."

"Right," Michael said, his mind working furiously to come up with a way to get around Norwood—and at the truth. "I understand, and I'm sorry, too, but I'm sure you must realize how frantic we are. My wife is beside herself. She asked me to check Liam's dorm room to see if he might have left a note or any sort of clue about his state of mind. That's allowed, I assume?"

"Yes, of course," Norwood said, though Michael sensed the headmaster's ambivalence. On the one hand, Michael's mention of Brook hopefully reminded Norwood that he was dealing with the Pendleton family. On the other, his dinner was getting cold. "Though I'll have to escort you. Wait in the hall a minute while I talk to my wife—and grab a coat."

Liam's room was in the new dormitory complex, completed a few years earlier, that was composed of a dozen or so large clapboard cape-style houses linked together by brick paths and covered walkways. The buildings, nestled among plantings of hemlocks and white pines, their many-paned windows aglow, looked like a small, carefully maintained New England town. The quaint effect was offset somewhat by the tall wrought-iron fence that enclosed the area and the guard who sat sentry by the gate.

Norwood and Michael entered through the main building, which housed the dorm master and boasted a spacious common room with beamed ceilings, several bookcases, and a fireplace.

"Wait here, please," Norwood said, showing Michael over to a chair by the fire. A half dozen boys were sprawled on couches and chairs around the room, bent over books and laptops. In a low voice, Norwood added, "I trust you not to talk to anyone."

"Of course," Michael said, but as soon as Norwood left the room, Michael glanced surreptitiously around the room. Only one boy looked up, but it was no one Michael recognized and he looked down again just as quickly.

Ten minutes later Norwood returned and led Michael down a corridor, up a flight of stairs, and down another long hall to Liam's room. Michael remembered the hallway with its tasteful prints of rural New England scenes from when they'd dropped Liam off at Moorehouse in September. Norwood opened the door and stepped aside so that Michael could enter the dorm room before him.

"I asked Carey to step out for a minute," Norwood told him. "I'm sure you'd prefer to have some privacy."

"Great," Michael said, though he felt just the opposite. It was Carey whom Michael had been hoping to find there—and talk to—a possibility that Norwood had obviously anticipated. The room was small, but well planned, with two raised bunk beds and built-in desks. With the headmaster standing in the middle of the room—seemingly protecting Carey's side—Michael silently sorted through Liam's books and papers. He disconnected his son's laptop from the wall, and tucked it under his arm.

"I'm taking this with me," he said, turning to face Norwood again. "And the notebooks."

"Fine," the headmaster said, opening the door for Michael to leave. They didn't say anything further until they were outside again, retracing their steps through the snow.

"I'll let you know immediately if I hear anything that might help," Norwood said as they reached the drive that would take Michael back up to the parking lot. Michael knew that his anger toward the headmaster was conflated with his own regrets and growing despair, but he still couldn't bring himself to say "thanks."

"Right," he said instead, as the two men parted ways.

As Michael walked back up the hill, he was concentrating so hard on what might have happened to Liam Saturday night that he didn't register at first the fact that he was being followed. Though he had a vague sense that he wasn't alone in the hushed darkness that had descended as the snow slackened off, he attributed it to the intensity of his feelings—a longing to find his son that was so powerful it seemed to have taken on its own shadowy reality. It wasn't until he started to cross the parking lot and heard the ice crunching behind him that he realized he wasn't alone. He turned around warily.

"Hey," the tall boy said, raising an arm in salute. "It's me."

"Carey?" Michael said, taking a step toward him.

"Yeah—would it be okay if we talked?"

"I'm sorry," Carey told him after they had climbed into the cab of the pickup. Michael turned on the ignition and cranked up the heat, but the teenager remained hunched over in the passenger seat shivering. "I don't have any idea where Liam might be. We haven't been talking much since Christmas. No, scratch that—we haven't been talking at all."

"What happened?" Michael asked gently. Carey's tension and misery were palpable.

"The truth is? I got jealous. And he didn't like it when I accused him of sucking up to my brother."

"What made you think he was he doing that?"

"Why else was he protecting him? What else did he think he was going to gain by taking the heat for what happened?"

"You're saying Brandon assaulted Phoebe?"

"Yeah."

"You saw him? You were there?"

"I went to bed before it happened, but I saw enough to be sure. Brandon was all over her—I even warned him to leave her alone."

"Where was Liam?"

"Pretty out of it. He and Brandon had been drinking Johnnie Walker and snorting OxyContin on the drive up."

"Jesus," Michael said under his breath.

"Yeah, I know. But if it helps any, it was mostly Brandon's doing. His idea. I'm not trying to get Liam off the hook for doing what he did, but my brother can be pretty damned persuasive. He sweet-talked Liam into it. Just the way he talked Phoebe into drinking and letting him put the moves on her."

"And you? Where were you in all this?"

"Me? I don't do that kind of stuff. I told Brandon to leave Phoebe alone. But I should have done more. I just threw up my hands and went to bed. Even though I pretty much knew what was going to happen. It's happened before."

"You know that for sure?"

"It's one of the reasons my folks sent him to Moorehouse. An all-boys school sounded like the perfect solution to them. Anything but dealing with the problem. They think they're being loving and supportive—but they're not. They're only encouraging him. They're cowards just like me. Because Brandon knows how to get his way. He knows how to manipulate people like nobody I've ever seen. And it's too bad. Because, in the long run, I know it's going to catch up with him."

"This must be hard on you, too," Michael said.

"I worry what's going to happen to him. He's been getting his way for so long now, I think he's come to believe he's infallible. He doesn't understand about limits and rules—except how to bend them to what he wants. And he's always been that way, even when we were really little. But is it his fault nobody's ever tried to stop him? People have just given him a free pass to do whatever he wants."

"You're a good brother," Michael asked.

"No, not really. If I was, I'd have tried to stop him myself. Like Liam did the other night."

"What do you mean?"

"I guess Norwood told you what happened in town, right?" Carey said, glancing over at Michael, who nodded. "Well, that's just Brandon's bullshit version. Brandon and Liam did get into a fight, but it wasn't because Liam was drinking and Brandon tried to get him to leave. Who but Norwood would believe that kind of crap? I overheard some of the guys who were there talking about it. Brandon got blasted and was doing his usual number on a girl at the party when Liam tried to pull him off. He was really laying into him, too. I think Liam had just finally had enough."

"I see," Michael said.

"And apparently Brandon got really pissed off. He pinned Liam to the floor and told him he was going to get him kicked off the Warriors. I think Liam must have felt like he'd burnt all his bridges. I mean, he really did look up to my brother for a while there. It's not that hard to do if you haven't lived with him all your life. And I know that the Warriors meant everything to Liam."

"I think you're right. Liam must have finally had enough. But you really don't have any idea where he might have gone? Does he have any other friends here who might be willing to talk to me?"

"They're all Brandon's crowd," Carey said, shaking his head. "It wouldn't do you any good. But I do know he's been texting Phoebe. We have the same kind of iPhone and I picked his up by mistake about a week ago. It was open to his messages—and they were all pretty much to and from her."

"Thanks, Carey," Michael said. "I can't tell you how—"

"I feel like I let him down, you know?" Carey said. "I should have tried to warn him about Brandon. I should have been a better friend."

"You could be now. You can tell the truth in court. I know it's a lot to ask—Brandon is your brother."

"I should have called him on his bullshit a long time ago. But, yeah, I'm willing to do it. If you need me to."

28

Phoebe had spent the afternoon of the snow day at the Barnsbury town library, supposedly working on a history paper. She'd occupied most of her time, though, on the public computer terminal, checking to see whether Liam had e-mailed her. But there was still nothing from him at five o'clock, when the library closed for the day. She hadn't been able to talk to him since early Sunday morning, when her dad had caught her sneaking in from the playground and had confiscated her cell phone. She walked home, hoping maybe her mom wouldn't be around and that she could use the Lansings' landline to reach Liam, but she heard Wanda's voice in the kitchen as she came through the front door.

"... I wouldn't wish that on anyone, not even the Bostocks," her mom was saying as Phoebe walked into the room. Wanda was on the phone. When she saw her daughter in the doorway, she quickly added, "Listen, Phoebe just got in. Okay. Right. Thanks for calling. Of course, I'll let you know."

"What about the Bostocks?" Phoebe asked, alarmed. She

hadn't stopped worrying about Liam for a single minute. She couldn't manage to shake the feeling that something was wrong. Something had happened and—at the worst possible moment—Liam hadn't been able to reach her.

"That was Aunt Vera," Wanda told her. "Liam's missing. Uncle Fred got a 911 from Liam's dad this morning. They think he ran away from school."

"Ran away?" Phoebe said, dropping her backpack on the floor. She stared at her mom, though she was thinking about Liam—and the despair in his voice on Saturday night. "When? Where did he go?"

"I don't know. I don't think anybody does at this point. What's the matter, sweetie?"

"Oh, Mommy," Phoebe said, covering her mouth with her hands. She didn't want to face what this might mean. She didn't want to say what she was thinking. But she knew she couldn't keep it bottled up inside any longer—and the last remnants of trust and faith she'd felt for her dad had disintegrated after he took her phone away. It was his fault that Liam hadn't been able to reach her.

"What's going on?" Wanda said, crossing the room to her daughter. As she put her arms around her, she could feel Phoebe's shoulders begin to shake. She let her cry for a moment; then she led her to the kitchen table and made her sit down.

"Talk to me," Wanda said, sitting in the chair beside her. She tucked a loose spiral of hair behind Phoebe's left ear before taking both her daughter's hands in her own. "You know you can tell me anything, right?"

"I've been lying," Phoebe said, looking down. "I lied about Liam hurting me. It wasn't him—it was his friend Brandon—but I was so mad at Liam, and then Daddy just assumed, and I said yeah, it was him, but it really wasn't! And then I felt bad, but Daddy said it was all right and not to say anything."

"Daddy said *what*?"

"When I told Daddy what really happened? He said I should stick to my original story. He said no one would believe me if I changed what I said. He said that people in this town would—"

"He knew all this when he made you go see the lawyers in Boston?"

"Yeah," Phoebe said, bowing her head.

"It's okay, honey," Wanda told her, smoothing down her daughter's hair. "I understand." Phoebe continued to pour out her story. That she and Liam had become close last summer after he first got into trouble. That she loved him and wanted to help him, but that she'd ended up making everything a hundred times worse.

"We've been texting for the past couple of weeks. I snuck out of the house to talk to him Saturday night because he sounded so sad. So down on himself. It really scared me. Daddy was staying here, remember? He was waiting for me downstairs when I got in—and he took my cell away. He said my talking to Liam could screw up the lawsuit. But I bet Liam's been trying to call! I know he wouldn't have left that school without telling me! What are we going to do?"

Wanda just sat there, staring out across the room. Then, she turned back to her daughter, squeezed her hand, and said:

"We're going to do what we can to make this right."

❧

Wanda told Phoebe to wait upstairs while she called Troy, but Phoebe was still able to hear snatches of the conversation, because her mom's voice was so loud and shrill:

"How dare you manipulate her like that? . . . Knew perfectly well what you were doing . . . Don't even begin to try to justify any of this. . . . Yes, I'm going to tell them. . . . That boy's life could be at stake, here. . . . All you can think about is yourself. . . . Willing to sacrifice everything that matters . . . Want that cell phone in my hands in ten minutes or I'm calling Fred . . ."

Phoebe remained in her room when her father came to the house. She couldn't make out what her parents were saying, but she did hear the door slam behind Troy as he left. From her bedroom window, Phoebe watched her dad march back to his idling pickup. He opened the car door, but turned around before he got in, his face flushed an angry red. He stood there, scanning the house, his gaze resting on Phoebe's window for a moment before she stepped back into the room and out of his sight.

❧

It seemed to Phoebe like years had gone by since she'd last seen the Bostocks' house. It rose into view as she and Wanda came up the drive, its many windows aglow against the snowy night. But as they pulled into the turnaround where two patrol cars and three state cruisers were already parked, it became clear to Phoebe that a crisis of her own making was waiting for her behind the lovely facade. She hesitated after her mom parked and opened the door to get out.

"I don't think I can do this," Phoebe said. "Would it be okay if you just went in and explained—"

"No," Wanda said. "It wouldn't. You say you really care about Liam? Well, this is how you prove it."

Phoebe had so been dreading seeing Mrs. Bostock again

that sometimes her fear and guilt would emerge in dreams where Phoebe's former employer would berate her for what she'd done, publicly accusing her of being a liar. She was afraid of seeing Tilly again, too. She knew how much the younger girl had looked up to her, and Phoebe had let her down so terribly that she couldn't imagine how she was ever going to redeem herself. She followed her mother down the flagstone path to the Bostocks' front portico, longing to run the other direction. After ringing the bell, they waited for what seemed to Phoebe an eternity. It was Tilly who finally came to the door, peeking out timidly at first, but then, after seeing who was standing there, pulling the door wide.

"It's you!" Tilly cried, hugging Phoebe to her.

"Hi," Phoebe said, her eyes filling with tears as Mrs. Bostock came toward them down the hall. Liam's mom looked pale and exhausted, but her expression brightened when she saw Phoebe and Wanda.

"You've heard something?" she asked Phoebe eagerly. "Liam's called you?"

"No," Phoebe told her. "I'm sorry, but—"

"We have a lot to tell you," Wanda said, propelling her daughter in front of her through the door. "I take it that Fred's here, too? I think he needs to hear what Phoebe has to say."

❧

It wasn't as bad as Phoebe feared, once she started talking. It was a relief, actually, after all these weeks, to tell her side of the story. The truth, finally. Phoebe's uncle Fred made her stop several times to repeat herself. He sat beside her on the couch in the great room, while his deputy took notes. Mrs. Bostock and Phoebe's mom pulled up chairs. Liam's aunt Lynn herded

Tilly off to the kitchen for supper. Police officers kept coming and going from the room, walkie-talkies crackling. When Michael had called Fred from Moorehouse to fill him in on what Carey had revealed, they'd both agreed that they thought Liam could be heading back to Barnsbury. And, at Michael's suggestion, the local and state police forces decided to make the Bostocks' home their base of operations.

"And he didn't say anything more than that? Just that he was feeling bad about letting everybody down?" Fred asked when they finally reached the part about Liam's call to her that past weekend.

"No, but he was crying. He said that he felt like he was at the bottom of this big hole and didn't think he'd ever be able to climb out."

"Did he say anything to you about wanting to leave school?"

"No."

"Anything else that stands out in your mind?"

Phoebe hesitated, thinking about Liam's final words to her.

"Last summer? When we'd meet in the park?" Phoebe said as her uncle nodded in encouragement. "He'd talk about how down on himself he could get. Kind of the way he was talking last weekend. He said once that he sometimes thought about—"

Phoebe glanced over at Mrs. Bostock, who was sitting upright in her chair, arms crossed tightly on her chest. Phoebe had managed to suppress just how kind Liam's mother could actually be, how she had a way of always making Phoebe feel special and appreciated. Phoebe hated adding to the pain she'd already caused her.

"Go on, Phoebe," Mrs. Bostock told her. "It's okay."

"He said he sometimes thought about ending it all. I made him promise me—I actually made him hold up his hand and swear to me—that he wouldn't hurt himself, that he wouldn't even *think* about doing anything like that before calling me first. So I asked him—at that end of our last talk—if that's why he was calling. If this was maybe *that* call. And he said no. He said he just needed to hear my voice."

The room was silent as the significance of what Phoebe had said sank in. If Liam had felt desperate yesterday—and hadn't been able to reach Phoebe—what actions might he have already taken?

"It's going to be okay, honey," Fred said, patting her shoulder as he stood up. "We're going to find him." He'd been holding the cell phone that Wanda had given him when they first arrived. Now he flipped it open and handed it back to Phoebe.

"Check your messages," he said.

There was only one. It was sent Sunday night at 7:03, almost exactly twenty-four hours before Phoebe was finally able to read it.

Tried to call u. Hope u get this. So, so sorry. Love u Phebe.

"Call him for us now, okay?" he told her. "Keep it simple. Just—where are you? Don't let him know that we're all here or that anyone's upset."

With everyone standing around watching, Phoebe tried Liam's number. It rang five times before the automated message clicked on, announcing that the voice mailbox was full. Phoebe shook her head as she looked up at her uncle.

"Text him, then," Fred said. "Nobody here needs to see what you say. But make it clear you really want to talk to him."

She sat alone on the couch, her fingers trembling as she thumbed her message:

Love u too! Where are u? Miss u—CALL me!

Phoebe knew Liam usually kept his phone on vibrate, and that he would usually respond to her right away. But when there was no reply after several minutes, Phoebe's uncle said gently, "That's okay. He probably has it turned off to save on the battery. He's bound to check later. Let me keep the cell for now. If he calls, I'll give it right back to you, okay?"

She nodded and handed over the phone. Phoebe's mom came and sat beside her as Fred and the other police officers discussed the situation. Phoebe tried to follow the conversation:

"Cell phone tower data wouldn't be able to pinpoint his location like GPS data does," said the state police detective who seemed to be in charge, "but it could tell us which side of the tower the signal is coming from and, based on the pings, how strong it is. Enough to get a general idea of where he is."

"Phone has to be on, though, right?" Fred asked.

"Yes, but I assume your son relies a lot on his cell?" the officer asked, turning to Mrs. Bostock. When she nodded, he said, "So I'm guessing it's what the chief here said before—he has it off right now to conserve power. He'll turn it back on at some point, and when he does, I want us to be ready to move. So we need to get in touch with his wireless carrier now and get them on board."

It was Fred who, with the information Mrs. Bostock supplied, contacted the phone company. It took him several calls to get through to someone who could help, but even then there was some back-and-forth about privacy rights and a waiver that the company claimed had to be signed before they'd release the data. Finally, Phoebe's uncle lost his temper.

"Look, I don't think you understand. This is an emergency situation. A teenage boy has been missing for nearly forty-eight hours. We don't have time to get you a goddamn warrant! I want to talk to someone who can help me save this boy's life *right now*!"

After a moment of silence, Fred started nodding. "Good," he said, "great. I appreciate that."

The night wore on. Liam's dad arrived back from Moorehouse and huddled in the kitchen with Fred and the state police. Neighbors began to stop by with offers to help. Phoebe lost track of time. At one point, Wanda said to her: "If you want to take a nap, sweetie, that's fine. I promise to wake you the minute he calls."

"That's okay," Phoebe replied. "I'm not going to sleep."

But after what seemed like only minutes, Phoebe woke to light in her eyes, the smell of coffee, and the sound of her uncle's voice.

"We finally got a location!" he was shouting to someone. "But I don't know. . . ."

Phoebe jumped up and ran into the kitchen. From the look on her uncle's face she knew that something was wrong.

"Did he call me?" she asked, looking around the room. Liam's mom was holding the cell phone. There were tears in her eyes as she handed it to Phoebe. The text message read:

Sorry—nothing left to talk about.

29

ᜪ

Michael and Brook followed the caravan of police cars through Barnsbury. The road hadn't been plowed in a couple of hours, and between the drifts and the frigid early-morning temperatures, the driving was treacherous. Phoebe was somewhere up ahead, riding with her mom in the back of her uncle's cruiser. A half dozen cars full of volunteers followed behind Michael's truck in carefully spaced intervals.

Though they'd since lost contact, the initial signal that the wireless tower had picked up from Liam's cell was coming from somewhere inside the state forest that spanned nearly one hundred square miles southwest of Barnsbury. Trying to locate Liam in the heavily wooded, rocky terrain wasn't going to be easy, but no one had hesitated when Chief Henderson suggested that the family and friends who'd gathered at the Bostocks' form a search party. They'd agreed to park at the base of Deer Mountain, across from the high school, and access the park from the trail that led up to one of the summits.

Liam's last text message had filled Michael with an awful sense of foreboding, but Lynn had taken him and Brook aside as the group was getting ready to leave.

"I know you two must be worried sick, but don't forget that teenagers can be incredibly dramatic, okay? I wouldn't be a bit surprised if Liam walked through the door any minute. I could stay here with Tilly if you like, and keep an eye on things."

"Thanks," Michael said, hugging his sister. When it really mattered, Lynn had come through. He'd watched the way she had stood by Brook through the bleak early-morning hours, keeping the coffee supply going, making phone calls, stepping in whenever his wife needed a hand. The misunderstandings and resentments that had divided them seemed unimportant now.

"Look around," Lynn said, nodding at the volunteers who crowded the kitchen. "Word travels fast in a small town— which can be a blessing at times, don't you think? A lot of people have come out for you guys this morning."

But even this unexpected show of support could do little to ease Michael's fears. And the news that they'd been able to trace Liam to the state forest had done nothing to lift his spirits. He knew the dangers of the area probably better than anyone. He could think of dozens of frightening possibilities including Liam's cell phone signal coming from the bottom of one of the park's many steep ravines.

⁓

"I need to tell you something," Brook said as Michael eased the pickup onto Route 31. The cruiser in front of them was going a little more than twenty miles an hour, so Michael was forced to do the same, though he would have given anything to be able to floor the gas. He'd been so much in his own private hell that he hadn't really noticed that Brook had been nearly silent until now. He glanced over at her. She was looking straight ahead.

"Okay."

"I made a terrible mistake forcing Liam to go to Moorehouse."

"We made that decision together."

"No, not really. You didn't want him to go. I talked you into it. Even though I wasn't sure how I felt, I convinced myself Janice and Peg would know the right thing to do. I let them decide for me—and I'm sorry. I've never been more sorry about anything in my life."

He reached over and squeezed her hand. He'd been waiting for the right moment to tell her the truth about himself. But he realized now that it was never going to come. Even if it meant destroying her faith in him, he knew he had no choice. He couldn't let her go on blaming herself for what had happened. At this frustrating speed at which they were crawling along, it would likely take them at least another twenty minutes to reach the turnoff for Deer Mountain—more than enough time to explain to her why their lives had veered so far from the course they had hoped to travel.

"Listen, Brook—you were right about Troy," he began. "The lawsuit is payback time for him. I'm sure he'd deny it. He may not even realize it himself. But he's hated me for so long that I just know he was waiting for an opportunity to get even. And the thing is—he has every reason to hate me."

"Oh, Michael, I don't believe that. We all know he's—"

"No, he has every reason to hate me," Michael said. He

was gripping the wheel so hard his knuckles were white. "I want you to know what happened. . . ."

❧

As simply as he could, he told her about his dad. Not the happy-go-lucky man that his mom liked to recall and that he'd let Brook believe in, but the angry drunk he'd grown into by the time Michael was a teenager.

"I understand him better now. Looking back, I can accept that it wasn't him but the booze talking. But, when he drank, he turned into another person. No, he turned into a monster. And I despised him for it."

He told her that Troy had been his best friend then. That they used to go up to the cabin in the woods, where the two boys could be alone, smoke cigarettes, and hang out.

"In a lot of ways, we were still just kids, really. But the summer I was fifteen, I started drinking—and I couldn't stop. It's hard to explain how wonderful that first gulp of whiskey tasted. How totally great it made me feel. Almost immediately, it seemed like the perfect solution to all my problems."

"Michael?"

"No, please, let me finish," he said. "I need you to hear me out." He refused to look over at her. He had to keep going. She deserved to know everything.

"That summer we went camping a couple of times up by this isolated lake on the Lansings' land. It felt great to get away—do whatever we wanted. We both really needed to let off steam. Troy had a younger sister. Her name was Sylvia."

"Yes, I know," Brook said. "Lynn told me about her."

"What did she say?" Michael asked, glancing over at his wife.

"Just that she—she drowned," Brook said softly. "And that you and Troy found her. It must have been—"

"It was the worst thing that ever happened to me," Michael said. "It changed everything. And Lynn was wrong about us 'finding' Sylvia after she drowned. We were right there."

He told her everything. How they had to take Sylvia with them that weekend. How he started drinking when Troy left to go fishing. How Sylvia had told him that she loved him—and that he'd pushed her away.

"So she had a crush on you," Brook said. "It's not your fault if you didn't feel the same."

"No, but I was cruel," Michael said. "Sylvia wasn't a regular kid. She was slow. Something went wrong during her birth. I don't know what exactly, but she was never mentally older than maybe a seven-year-old. That's why Troy's mom left, I think. She just couldn't handle it. So Sylvia ended up being Troy's responsibility a lot of the time. I know he felt saddled with her, but he tried to be kind. People made fun of her. They called her 'Silly.' She hated that. She hated any mention of her not being normal. And then I had to go and call her 'stupid.' That's why she ran into the lake. That's why she died."

Not knowing how to swim, weighed down by her wet clothes, increasingly panicked, Sylvia had drowned within a few feet of her brother, while Michael stumbled through the water, too drunk to help.

"He blamed me. He screamed and screamed at me. Told me I was a fucking no-good alcoholic just like my dad. But after we finally pulled Sylvia's body out of the water, he never said another word about it. To me—or to anyone else about what really happened. I think he must have blamed himself, too."

They were less than a mile from the turnoff, but Michael knew that there would never be enough time to explain to his wife why he'd kept this from her until now. How he'd had to use every ounce of willpower he possessed to change his life after Sylvia died. To stop drinking. Remake himself from the ground up. He'd walked away from his fifteen-year-old self, and he'd never looked back. No, he'd been afraid to look back. He knew that a part of him always hoped that if he just kept walking, kept moving, he'd finally be able to leave that boy behind him forever.

"I should have told you this before," Michael said as they pulled off the road behind the police cars. Brook's silence frightened him. Was it possible for her to understand what it had been like for him? Would she be able to see that he'd believed then it was the only way he could turn his life around? Or would she just see what he realized now: that what he'd done wasn't just futile—but wrong? By refusing to acknowledge his past, he'd made it possible for their son to repeat his mistakes.

He shut off the engine—and turned to her.

"I'm sorry," he said.

"I am, too," she said, looking up at the mountain. Cars were pulling in around them, doors slamming as people emerged into the cold morning. There was such a sadness in her voice that he couldn't help but believe it was all over. Their marriage—his life. Something inside him began to collapse and he could feel himself plunging downward. Then Brook said:

"I can't bear the thought of you having to carry this inside you all this time."

Snow had transformed the heavily wooded mountainside, bowing the branches of the evergreens, softening the contours of rock and fallen tree limbs, muffling sound.

"Liam!"

"Liam!"

The voices that floated down from the trail ahead of Michael didn't carry far. He followed behind Brook, reaching out to steady her from time to time as she stumbled up the steep incline. Blazed trees marked the route, but the path itself was sometimes knee-deep in drifts. They'd been climbing for almost an hour and were just now reaching the first summit. Michael and Brook approached the group gathered by a lean-to that gave out on a panoramic view of the snow-shrouded wilderness. One of the officers was scanning the area with high-powered binoculars. Fred and a state police detective were studying a contour map, comparing it with the glassed-in trail map posted inside the lean-to.

"Okay, we're going to divide up here," Fred said when everyone in the party had assembled. "Try to stick to the trail as marked. If you think you see Liam—or anything that might lead us to him—send one of your party back here where we have radio contact and we'll send a rescue team. We're working on getting helicopter support, but that's going to take another hour or two. Whatever you do, be careful and stay together. We don't need anyone getting hurt on top of everything else."

Michael and Brook joined the group that took the trail leading north into the highest elevations. The path wound for over fifteen miles through stands of maples and birches and limestone outcroppings with views in places that took in three different states. Michael had often come up here as a boy. When the Bostocks had first moved back to Barnsbury, Michael took Liam camping somewhere along this ridge. It had been at the height of summer then, the world a lush, hazy green. Now the snow cover and leafless trees made the mountaintop seem barren and forbidding.

Once again bringing up the rear, Michael found himself thinking back on those early camping trips with his son, especially the summer they'd first moved into the house—when Liam had still been so excited about his new life in his father's hometown. He recalled sitting by the campfire one night and telling Liam the story of the Indian maiden who, rumor had it, jumped to her death from the very ridge on which they were camping. As he watched Liam's rapt expression across the fire, his heart had ached at his innocence and the thought of what life had in store for him. How little he could do really to help his inward, solitary son find his place in the world.

The sky had cleared to a glacial blue and sunlight dazzled across the snow. Michael hadn't slept and exhaustion weighed on him. And something else. Something that made him slow his pace. He began to fall behind.

He stopped and turned around. Several hundred yards back along the trail he saw a stand of towering spruces, forming a kind of gateway to a long wooded landmass that jutted out over the valley. He recognized it now as the turnoff to the area where he and Liam had spent that memorable summer night.

He stared out across the promontory, wondering.

"Brook!" he called to his wife, who was now several dozen yards ahead of him. "Brook, hold on!"

She turned, waiting for him.

"I think I know where he is," Michael said, breathing hard as he approached. "Back there—you see that ridge? Liam and I used to hike up here—and I just have this feeling—"

With growing excitement, he grabbed her arm and said:

"Run on ahead, and tell the others to wait. If I'm wrong, this won't take more than ten minutes. If I'm right—you'll hear me call you. From the end of that ledge—an echo carries across the valley for miles."

❧

He was sure of it now. Liam had come back to a place that had once made him happy. What Michael didn't know—and filled him with dread—was in what kind of shape he would find him. Michael didn't want to think what three days of exposure and loneliness, on top of Liam's other problems, might have done to his son, or forced him to do to himself.

The path out to the end of the ridge wasn't marked and had become overgrown. Michael kept having to backtrack around fallen trees and densely matted brambles. But he reached the clearing at last—and what he saw before him on the ground made his heart beat with excitement. A backpack, food wrappings, and empty soup cans were scattered around the burned-out remains of a small fire. He squatted down and touched the ashes. They were still warm. Footprints dotted the area—leading back and forth into the woods, around the fire, and, finally, out to the end of the promontory, where, Michael remembered, the drop was sheer and straight down. Following the prints, he came to the very edge of the outlook. Dizzy with fear, he forced himself to lean over and look.

Liam sat huddled on a little ledge below him, hood up, arms

wrapped around his knees. Motionless. Michael couldn't tell if he was awake or asleep. He was close enough to touch him.

"Hey," he said.

Liam jerked around, his eyes red-rimmed, his skin ashen.

"Be careful," Michael told him gently. "That's a long fall."

"Yeah, I know," Liam said, turning back around. "I've been trying to get my nerve up. But I'm a coward."

"No, you're not."

Liam didn't respond. He just hugged himself tighter, and Michael could see that he was trying to control his shivering. Michael edged toward him, hoping to get close enough to be able to grab hold of him if he had to. But he knew how much better it would be if Liam crawled to safety on his own. Faintly, from somewhere to the north, Michael heard the sound of a helicopter. His time alone with Liam was running out.

"Phoebe told everyone what really happened," Michael said. "And Carey told me what you did to Brandon. I'm proud of you."

"But I lied for him—and messed everything up for you and Mom."

"I think I know why you did it, Liam. I didn't stand up for you the way I should have. I let you down. And I'm sorry."

It wasn't until Liam started to cry that Michael could let himself believe it was going to be okay.

"Hey," he said to his son. "Hey, give me your hand. Time to go home."

30

"I found him!"

Michael's cry still echoed joyfully in Brook's memory, though nearly a month had passed since his voice first reached her that morning across the mountaintop. They'd been able to medevac Liam by helicopter to the hospital in Harringdale, where he was treated for hypothermia and exhaustion. Brook and Michael were at Liam's bedside when he woke from a long, restless sleep.

"Hi there," Brook said, taking his hand.

"Where am I?"

"Harringdale Medical Center," Michael told him. "Do you remember how you got here?"

"Not really," Liam said, closing his eyes again. He drifted in and out of consciousness for several more hours. But when Michael and Brook worriedly consulted the doctors, they were assured that a certain amount of mental confusion was to be expected and that all of Liam's vital signs were returning to normal. As the aides came through with the dinner carts, Liam woke again.

"I'm totally starving!" Liam said, and Brook knew her son was going to be okay. His fatigue and disoriented state of mind hung on for several days, though, after they brought him home. Even when Liam seemed able to finally piece together the jumble of events that had led to his hospitalization, Brook felt something wasn't right. He was still holding something in—or back—and it worried her.

Two weeks after Liam's return, the Bostocks learned that Troy's lawsuit against them had been dropped. Phoebe's decision to tell the truth about Brandon, supported by Carey's statement, had caused the whole house of cards to collapse. Brook began to hope that their lives—especially her son's—could now start to return to normal. Phoebe came by to visit Liam, and Brook was relieved to hear them talking and listening to music in Liam's bedroom. The Bostocks invited Carey up for a weekend visit, and he told them about his decision to transfer from Moorehouse to a prep school in Boston.

"It has a great music department," Carey explained over a low-key supper around the kitchen table the night he arrived. "And I really want to start to concentrate on what I'm good at."

"And your brother?" Michael asked Carey. "What's he planning to do?" Brandon's expulsion from Moorehouse for drinking, lying, and sexual assault—facts that came out after further investigation at the prep school—had permanently derailed Brandon's hopes for Brown.

"My parents have decided he should repeat his senior year at a private school in Syracuse," Carey said. "That way they'll be able to keep an eye on him. Brandon hates the idea, of course."

Liam's future, on the other hand, was still an open question. Brook and Michael had agreed that he should decide for himself.

"There are a couple of great prep schools right around

here," Brook had mentioned to Liam a few days after Carey's visit. "You could go as a day student—or board if you like. Whatever you want to do is fine with us."

But what Liam wanted—or even what he was thinking—continued to puzzle Brook. He'd responded to her comment with a shrug. The good news was that he was no longer sullen or withdrawn. And he seemed to be enjoying his unscheduled vacation, playing endless rounds of Ping-Pong with Tilly in the basement, and hanging out with Phoebe after school. He'd even gotten in touch with some of his old, oddball friends from Deer Mountain. But, though a cloud had definitely lifted from her son, Brook had yet to feel the warmth he used to generate. She missed his sly sense of humor, and the way he used to tease her. She longed to hear his laugh. It occurred to her that he'd simply outgrown that side of himself. That what he'd gone through at Moorehouse and with Brandon had fundamentally changed him. But her uneasiness persisted. Finally one night when she and Michael were lying together in bed reading, she said, "I think we need to tell Liam about your dad."

"You mean we need to tell him about me."

"That, too, yes. And Troy and Sylvia. I feel like he's been walking around with only half the story. Knowing the truth would help him deal with his own problems, don't you think?"

"I was planning to talk to him," Michael said, sitting up. "But I was waiting for him to feel better. I was waiting for the right moment. But that's bullshit, isn't it?" Michael threw back the sheets and started to climb out of bed.

"You're going to tell him *now*?"

"I can hear him practicing guitar in his room," Michael said. "And you're right—I just have to get this done."

Brook could only imagine how tough the conversation was going to be for Michael. She now understood why her husband had such a hard time opening up about his feelings. In fact, since he'd finally told her about Sylvia, so much about Michael's reserve made sense to her. If anything, she loved and admired him even more because of it. Her heart went out to the confused and terrified boy he'd once been. It pained her to think of the battles he'd had to fight. But Michael's strength and discipline had been formed and tested by that experience. And it was those very qualities, after all, that had first drawn her to him.

The guitar playing stopped. She heard Michael and Liam in the hall, then their footsteps on the stairs. The lights came on in the kitchen. Her husband had a slow and deliberate way of speaking, and she could faintly make out those cadences coming from below.

She must have dozed off. The next thing she knew, Michael was closing the book she'd had on her lap and pulling it free.

"How did it go?" she asked.

"Fine," he said, leaning over to turn out her bedside light.

"I need a little more information than that," she said, sitting up her elbow. "What did he say?"

"He thanked me," Michael told her, as he got under the covers.

"That's all? You two were down there a while."

"He's been talking to Phoebe and some of his friends at Deer Mountain. He thinks he might want to go back there next year."

"Wow. He's not worried about being ostracized again?"

"He says he thinks he can handle it. Apparently Phoebe's

been busy on Facebook, and word's gotten out about how he beat up Brandon. I believe she made it sound a lot more like a TKO than it actually was."

"Good for her."

"You okay with this, then?"

"Of course."

"Because you mentioned those other prep schools. And he's worried that you might be disappointed if he doesn't go that route."

"No, I think it's great he wants to go back. It takes some guts, don't you think?"

"Yes, I told him I was really proud of him," Michael said, pulling the sheets up around her shoulders. "It's something I realize now that I never used to say to him."

"That's only because nobody said it to you," Brook replied, moving into her husband's arms.

❦

The idea occurred to Brook gradually, though Liam's decision to go back to Deer Mountain certainly played into it. Julie Dorman's call also helped shape her thinking.

"I'd like to talk to you about helping me put together a really special and different sweet sixteen party for my girls," Julie said. The Dorman twins were a year ahead of Liam at Deer Mountain. "Now that I'm working full-time again, I know it will be more than I can handle on my own."

"I'd love to help," Brook said. The party, which included thirty teenagers from the Barnsbury area and several parents, was what really solidified Brook's decision. It was themed "Night of the Living Dead," and Brook had all the guests come dressed as zombies. She'd gotten three leads from the event and was in the process of planning two other birthday parties and an anniversary dinner. She was also talking to the *Barnsbury Banner* about an ad promoting R.V.S.P.'s services in their June issue.

"Someone mentioned to me what a great job you did for the Dormans," the editor told her when Brook called about advertising costs and deadlines. "I'd love to do an article on you as a local business, but I take it you're really based in Manhattan?"

"Actually, I'm trying to get more work up here," Brook said. "And an article on R.S.V.P. would be wonderful. Would you like to drop by for coffee sometime and talk?"

The day after the editor visited—and came away with a legal pad scribbled with information, a number of digital photos of Brook in her "office kitchen," and an R.S.V.P. gift basket overflowing with goodies—Brook finally took the plunge and called Alice.

⸙

"What's all this?" Michael asked the following evening when he came down from his studio after work. He found Brook in the dining room, laying the table for two. She'd set out the hand-blown Venetian glasses and her favorite French linen napkins.

"Oh, I'm just in a festive mood," Brook said, turning around. She was wearing the blue silk dress she knew he liked.

"Did I forget something?" he asked, frowning, taking in the candles and the arrangement of early tulips. "I mean . . . our anniversary's not—"

"No, don't worry," Brook said. "I thought it would be fun to do something special for the two of us. Wanda took the kids out to the movies and pizza."

"Wanda?" Michael asked.

"Yes," Brook said, "I think she's trying to make amends—though I've tried to tell her that we don't blame her for anything." But Phoebe's mom clearly felt responsible for what had happened and was doing her best to set the record straight. Wanda's very vocal denunciation around town of Troy's underhanded dealings had firmly swung public opinion around in the Bostocks' favor. Brook could feel it everywhere she turned these days. It was one of the good things that had come out of the long, bad months she and Michael had suffered through together. The other was what she told him that night over dessert.

"I'm thinking of selling the business to Alice."

"What? But why? It's going so well. Aren't you busier now than you've ever been?"

"Exactly," Brook said. "Which means there's enough steady income at this point for Alice to get a loan to start to buy me out—and hire someone new to help her manage things in the city. I'll keep rights to the R.S.V.P. name to use up here."

"But . . . I guess I don't understand. You built the company up from nothing. And you're so proud of it."

"I can still be proud—selling a business at its peak is a pretty great feeling. But I'm tired of trying to deal long-distance with all the problems. And having to run down to the city every couple of weeks to help with events. These last few months I've felt torn every time I had to leave Barnsbury. Torn and, frankly, less and less interested in the big-deal benefits we have to put on in the city. I still love what I do. But I know I'm going to be a lot happier building a different kind of R.S.V.P.—more creative and informal—one that fits better with the way we live up here."

Michael just sat there looking at her across the table.

"You're sure about this?" he asked finally.

"Yes."

"And Alice is on board?"

"I think she's thrilled—and relieved," Brook said. "I had no idea how much slack she's been picking up for me this year. But she said a few things when we talked this through that made me see that she's been shouldering a lot more of the workload than I realized."

"She's a good friend."

"And a good business partner," Brook said. "But I'm more than ready to let that side of things go. I plan to hold on tight to the friendship, though."

"I'm all for that," Michael said, reaching across the table to take Brook's hand. "We owe her a lot."

"How do you mean?"

Michael tilted his head and smiled at her.

"Do you think you're ready for another deep, dark secret of mine?"

Her heart skipped a beat as she remembered—though it seemed like years ago now—what Alice had told her at Christmas. So much had happened since then that she'd almost managed to forget her husband's deception. But not quite.

"It depends on what it is," she said, pulling her hand free and crossing her arms on her chest.

"What's that look for?" he said with a laugh. "It's nothing terrible, I promise. Just a little heads-up that Alice gave me a long time ago. It seemed like nothing at the time, but I think in many ways it's really responsible for our being together."

"Well? What is it?" Brook said, trying not to listen to all the alarm bells that were going off inside her head.

"She took me aside at the benefit auction where we met, and told me you were 'one of the *Pendleton* Pendletons.' She said she could tell I was really interested in you—and that I shouldn't let your name get in my way."

"Really?" Brook said, trying hard to act surprised. In fact, she was stunned by the calm, lighthearted way he was telling her all of this. "So why did you pretend not to know for so long?"

"To give us a chance," he said, searching her face.

"I don't understand."

"I'm sorry," Michael said, his tone changing. "I can tell this is upsetting to you. I thought you'd find it kind of amusing after all this time. I mean, honestly, do you really think I'd have had the nerve to pursue you if I knew who you really were?"

"But apparently you did know—and you did pursue me."

"Only because you didn't know that I knew."

"This is getting complicated."

"Well, it was a pretty complicated situation. And I realized that my only hope was to keep it simple. I fell in love with you the moment I saw you."

"And me you."

"So do we have a problem here?"

She looked in his eyes. She took in his smile. She realized now that she'd never really doubted him. It was herself she always had such a hard time believing in. But that was changing.

"No, we don't," she told him.

"Good," he said, rising from his chair and reclaiming her hand. "So, how long do you think we have until the kids get home?"

Liza Gyllenhaal spent many years in advertising and publishing. She lives with her husband in New York City and western Massachusetts. She is the author of the novels *Local Knowledge* and *So Near*, both published by NAL.

A Place for Us

LIZA GYLLENHAAL

This Conversation Guide is intended to enrich
the individual reading experience, as well as encourage us
to explore these topics together—because books,
and life, are meant for sharing.

A CONVERSATION WITH
LIZA GYLLENHAAL

Q. Where did you get the idea for this novel?

A. A few years ago I heard a news story on our local public radio station in Massachusetts about a married couple who were being arraigned under the Social Host Liability law. Two teenagers had been seriously injured in a car crash after drinking with the couple's son at a party in the family's basement. Though the parents had been asleep upstairs and unaware of the underage drinking, one of the injured teenager's family was bringing a lawsuit against the couple. Understandably, the rural community where the accident occurred was upset about the incident— but also divided about where the responsibility rested. As someone who loves writing about families and small towns, the story couldn't help but capture my imagination.

I began to think about how I might turn this basic premise into a convincing work of fiction. I let the idea simmer while I finished my novel *So Near*, but then started to outline a plot and flesh out the characters.

Coincidentally, as I began writing the novel, a very

similar incident took place in a town not far from us in the Berkshires. In this case, tragically, one of the teenagers involved was killed. This senseless death brought home to me how serious and pertinent the problem of underage drinking remains.

Q. The story is told from the different points of view of four main characters. Did you find that difficult to pull off?

A. Both of my previous novels, *Local Knowledge* and *So Near*, were written in the first person, though in *So Near* it was a husband and wife who alternately told their stories. I thought it would be interesting to try more points of view with this novel, but I also realized that using four different first-person voices would probably drive me—and readers—crazy. So I decided to write the novel in what is sometimes called the close third person, which means that the story is being told by "he" or "she" rather than "I" but, hopefully, from pretty deep inside the head of the character in question.

In the first person, you can write "I did this" or "I felt that," which gives the story an automatic believability. For me, the third person—which puts readers a little more at a distance—is more of a challenge. I think that to write convincing fiction you have to be able to empathize with your characters. You need to know them deep down. You have to believe in them. But you also need to step back and give them breathing room to be themselves and make their own choices. It's very tempting when you're writing in the third person to manipulate your characters and force them to do what the story line dictates. But I think readers can always tell when a character is acting and talking . . . well . . . out of character. The most important thing I learned from writing this novel in the third person is that if something doesn't seem to be working, it probably isn't the fault of the character—instead, there's something wrong with the plot.

Q. Two of your main characters are teenagers. How did you manage to empathize with them?

A. Though I don't have children myself, I am lucky to have a number of wonderful teenage nieces and nephews in my life. I listen hard to what they say—and, perhaps more important, wonder about what they keep to themselves. But, as I started to write the first chapter from Phoebe's point of view, I remembered a relationship I had when I was about her age. It was with a boy who, like Liam, was going through a very hard time. He also happened to be the most popular boy in our class and, when it became obvious to everyone that we were spending a lot of time together after school, it was assumed that I was his new girlfriend. So I suddenly became very popular, too! But, in truth, all we were doing together was talking. Actually, he was talking and I was listening. More than anything else, I think I drew from that memory to create the strong bond that Phoebe and Liam share.

Q. Is there an underlying theme in A Place for Us?

A. Yes—and it's right there in the title. It's the age-old yearning to fit in and be accepted. In my novel *Local Knowledge*, I wrote about a woman raised in a small town who is befriended—and ultimately betrayed—by a wealthy female weekender whom she tries to emulate. My character Maddie wanted to be accepted by this glamorous new friend so much that, as a result, she ended up sacrificing everything truly important in her life.

The natural human desire for acceptance has always interested me as a writer. We've all felt that longing at some point, and very often the power of it has made us act in ways that we later regret. In *A Place for Us*, I decided to turn the tables on the social situation I'd set up in *Local Knowledge* and have my character Brook be a very wealthy transplant from New York City who longs to fit into the small town where her husband was raised and to which her family relocates after 9/11. Brook's struggle to fit in, as well as her son Liam's yearning for acceptance, propels the story along and acts as the novel's thematic underpinning.

Q. What sort of research did you do in writing the novel?

A. I spent a lot of time on the Internet reading up on the Social Host Liability law and the many cases in Massachusetts that have resulted from the law's passage. The more time I spent researching different stories and exploring various sites, the more the name Richard P. Campbell kept cropping up. Digging a little deeper, I discovered that Mr. Campbell is the founder of a prestigious law firm in Boston, president of the Massachusetts Bar Association, and a driving force behind Social Host Liability legislation. He created a multimedia program, *Be A Parent, Not A Pal*, to educate students, parents, teachers, and members of the community about the Social Host Liability law. It's a first-rate tutorial on the subject. For more information, please see: http://www.socialhostliability.org/programs/beaparent.php.

I was very lucky to have the opportunity to interview Mr. Campbell by phone one afternoon. He had agreed to a one-hour session, but we ended up talking for much longer than that. He was outspoken and full of great anecdotes.

And he was tremendously helpful, clarifying many complicated legal issues for me. He was also a passionate spokesperson for a cause he obviously believes in very deeply. At the end of the conversation, he said, "Whatever else your novel does, please have it make a case for how deadly underage drinking can be." I hope I've done that!

Q. What authors do you like—and would you like to recommend?

A. I read a lot—poetry, fiction, history, memoir. I spent last winter in eighteenth-century Russia, with Robert Massie's fascinating biography of Catherine the Great. This spring, I relived the Kennedy assassination and Lyndon Johnson's remarkable early achievements as President via Robert Caro's latest installment on Johnson's life. I loved Ann Patchett's most recent novel, *State of Wonder*, and Edith Pearlman's collection of short stories *Binocular Vision*. I'm thinking about trying my hand at writing something that revolves around a mystery, so I recently reread all my favorite P. D. James novels, and I'm currently working my way through Agatha Christie. After Nora Ephron's death, I read everything she wrote in book form—and laughed out loud for a couple of days.

Q. Do you have a set writing routine?

A. I usually wake up early and reread whatever I've been working on. I revise constantly on the computer. (It continues to amaze me how Tolstoy could have written *War and Peace* in longhand!) Then I let the demands of daily life intervene for several hours and pick up again in the afternoon. Most days, I don't hit my stride until three o'clock or so, and then, if I'm lucky, get two or three good, productive hours in. I think a lot about what I'm working on when I'm not actually writing. When I'm running, for instance, or driving the car back and forth between the city and our weekend place in Massachusetts. I try to work out problems—a scene I can't get off the ground, a character who refuses to behave—during that two-and-a-half-hour stretch.

Q. Where do you write?

A. In the city, I usually write in a beautiful old Eames chair that I commandeered from my husband. But sixteen years ago, we bought a place in the beautiful Berkshire hills of western Massachusetts. It included a small farmhouse and an old horse stable that became my "writing studio." It still has the old iron stall feeders and leather harnesses on the walls. It remains permeated by a wonderful smell of animal and old hay.

When we're in the country, I wake up early and reread and rewrite on my laptop in the house, but in the afternoon I go out to the studio, bolt the door, and start the hard work of writing the next new word, sentence, paragraph, chapter. In the winter, I have a fire going in the Jøtul stove; in the summer, I have all the windows open and can hear the brook and birdsong. This summer, I watched a family of wild turkeys—seventeen in all—parading up and down in the old paddock. Other sightings: woodchuck, coyote, fox, and, early last spring, when the trees were just greening out, a big black bear.

Q. Are you working on anything new?

A. As I mentioned earlier, I'm interested in trying to write something with a mystery at its heart. I don't think it will be a traditional police procedural, though someone will be murdered and the story will explore the reasons why—and probably end with the discovery of who did it. But I'm hoping the novel will be more about the characters and the small New England community where they live. I'm an avid amateur gardener and I loved writing about gardening in *So Near* and talking about my garden on my blog, so I'm pretty sure I want my main character to be a landscape architect or professional gardener. I also know who gets killed—and when. But that's all I really have figured out so far. A lot of the joy of writing—just as it is in reading—is discovering what's going to happen next.

QUESTIONS
FOR DISCUSSION

1. Do you think that a state law—such as the Social Host Liability statute—should be able to dictate what you can and cannot do in your own home?

2. Do you think it's ever right to withhold something about your children from your spouse?

3. Michael's mother turned his father into a "plaster saint" after his death. Do you believe that "you should never speak ill of the dead"?

4. To what degree do you think Brook and Michael were responsible for what went on under their roof when they weren't there to supervise?

5. Do you think Troy responded appropriately to what happened to Phoebe?

6. Brook says her marriage works because she's rich and Michael is good-looking. Does your relationship rest on the same kind of implicit principle?

7. Michael refused to share his own boyhood problems with Liam. Do you think children have a right to know about their parents' pasts?

8. Troy tries to convince Phoebe that it's okay to lie about who assaulted her by saying, "Don't forget that the Bostocks' lawyer felt it was perfectly okay to claim you had sex with Liam. . . . You sticking to your story is nothing compared to that." Do you agree with Troy?

9. Phoebe spent a lot of time fantasizing about Liam—before and after they became close. Do you think that's normal behavior for a fifteen-year-old girl?

10. Who do you think is the best parent in the novel—and why?

11. Brook tends to handle bad situations by putting on a "happy face" and "pretending everything's great." Do you have similar coping mechanisms?

Praise for the Novels
of Liza Gyllenhaal

So Near

"Intriguing . . . a real page-turner!"   *—Publishers Weekly*

"Where is the truth in the midst of a family tragedy? Liza Gyllenhaal plumbs the complexity of human emotions in this wonderful novel. With sensitivity and compassion, she creates characters that will pull at your heart on their journey through grief. I loved reading *So Near*, a truly believable and compelling story."

                    —Katharine Davis, author of *A Slender Thread*

Local Knowledge

"A bighearted debut."   *—The Miami Herald*

"This is a book to savor. . . . Selling real estate is the surface story, but as you peel back the layers throughout the chapters you realize it is about family relationships, old friends, and new friends."

                              —Publishers Weekly

"A damn fine novel. . . . Gyllenhaal truly makes the Berkshire setting jump to life. And she is terrific with character—I particularly admired the way she wove personality into action—so that the behavior of her characters in her setting seems natural, unforced, and often really compelling. In a way, this is what really makes a novel like *Local Knowledge* exciting—I constantly felt as if I knew the people on the page, so I was captivated by their story. . . . I really look forward to her next novel."

                    —John Katzenbach, bestselling author of *What Comes Next*

continued . . .

Written by today's freshest new talents and selected by New American Library, NAL Accent novels touch on subjects close to a woman's heart, from friendship to family to finding our place in the world. The Conversation Guides included in each book are intended to enrich the individual reading experience, as well as encourage us to explore these topics together—because books, and life, are meant for sharing.

Visit us online at www.penguin.com.

"Gripping and deeply perceptive, this powerful debut novel reveals the pleasures and struggles of true friendship and the painful decisions we often make for acceptance and love. Small-town life and work are rendered in vivid detail, as are the memorable characters, who come alive in the hands of a gifted new writer."
—Ben Sherwood, author of *Charlie St. Cloud*

"A powerful and deeply moving novel about the lies we tell ourselves, the moral corners we cut, and the loved ones we betray to get what we want. Gyllenhaal has X-ray vision into the human heart and a sharp eye for contemporary mores and social maneuvering. She knows women and men and children, and pins them to the page with some of the most dazzling prose I've read in a long time."
—Ellen Feldman, author of *Next to Love*

"Liza Gyllenhaal's new novel invites instant immersion. . . . With insight and sensitivity, Liza Gyllenhaal deftly draws the reader of *Local Knowledge* down through the layers and layers of intimate entanglements her characters have with each other, the land, and the new and old ways of life. I highly recommend *Local Knowledge* to anyone who loves good writing, a good story, and hopes to come away from a book with a deeper understanding of others' lives and choices." —Tina Welling, author of *Cowboys Never Cry*

"Enjoyable and intriguing. . . . Gyllenhaal has a magnificent grasp of small-town dynamics. . . . Gyllenhaal breaks the mold of expectation by weaving in complex interactions over years of shared economic and emotional struggles. That weaving is both figurative and literal. The alternating story line is far more effective than [the] typical flashback passages of many novels. The background chapters flow beautifully with the present and explain the long-standing tensions among Maddie, Paul, and Luke. . . . [T]hrough Gyllenhaal's superb skill there is an almost poetic quality to how the events of the past tie into the fragile relationships of the present."
—Jody Kordana, *Berkshire Eagle*

"How accomplished this first novel is. . . . A rich, authentic read . . . with a tightly focused cast of characters once again proving the old adage that less is more . . . a timely enough message if ever there was one." —*Berkshire Living*